Advance Praise for *Fatal Option*

"A sharp, intelligent thriller...there's no easy way out, and fate isn't always kind. Really top notch."

–NEELY TUCKER, author of *Only the Hunted Run*

"A wintry tale of violence and redemption, artfully balanced by a touching portrayal of a family in crisis."

–PETER SWANSON, author of *The Kind Worth Killing*

"A story about the devastating moral consequences of a dangerous choice. Relentlessly suspenseful, with brisk pacing and intrigue on every page."

–NORB VONNEGUT, bestselling author of *Top Producer* and *The Trust*

"Emotionally visceral. The violence and action sequences really gripped me and I loved the strength of the teenage girl, Sara. I loved the ending too. What subtlety! There's a sense of the world restored but not quite. Not sugar-coated and not expected either. Completely real."

–JORDAN DANE, bestselling author and recipient of *Publishers Weekly* Best Book and Readers Choice Awards

"*Fatal Option* grabs you from the first page as a complex tale about a family in crisis and murder. Plan to stay up late."

–KATHLEEN ANTRIM, Co-President, International Thriller Writers and author of *Capital Offense*

Praise for *Double Abduction*

"With a child in jeopardy, a suspect with secrets, and a killer watching every move, *Double Abduction*, by new author Chris Beakey, has it all in a fast-paced thriller."

–ROBERT K. TANENBAUM, *New York Times* bestselling author

"A living nightmare that will be hard for readers to shake off."

–PETER BLAUNER, Edgar Award winner

"If you're looking for a fast, smart thriller, with an intricate plot and an interesting cas of troubled, all-too-human characters, you can't go wrong with Chris Beakey's clever debut novel, *Double Abduction*. It's a tense, emotionally charged book, with strong visual imagery and a lot of imagination, and the surprises just keep on coming."

–BART YATES, Alex Award winner and autho *The Brothers Bishop* and *Leave Myself Bel*

FATAL OPTION

CHRIS BEAKEY

A POST HILL PRESS BOOK

Fatal Option

ISBN: 978-1-68261-154-8
ISBN (eBook): 978-1-68261-155-5

Cover Design by Christian Bentulan
Interior Design and Composition by Greg Johnson/Textbook Perfect

Post Hill Press
Posthillpress.com

Published in the United States of America

FOREWORD

A few years ago I drove down a winding road through a dense forest on a cold winter night. The darkness had come unexpectedly early, and with it a sudden drop in temperatures and a patch of black ice that sent me into a skid when I took a curve just a bit too fast. For an instant—as the back end of my Jeep went into a terrifying sideways slide—I was certain that my life was going to end in a violent smashup of glass and metal and old-growth trees.

Thanks to the absence of oncoming traffic and just enough roadway I spun around and stopped without hitting anything. Yet it only took a moment to imagine something worse than my own death, coupled with circumstances that would have turned me into a pariah for the rest of my life.

That's where this began, as a story about a man who does a very bad thing for very good reasons. It took many, many more drives down that dark and winding road to get the story right. Fortunately, I was blessed with good friends and guidance at every turn; first from Deb Rohmann, my first fan, who reads hundreds of thrillers a year, and always with a keen eye that's yielded plenty of lessons for me. Second, through bestselling writers who offered advice and praise. Third, with support from Michael Weider and the rest of my family, who expected me to hold the knife to my own jugular every time I sat down to write.

Now that the journey's over I welcome conversation with readers who want to share their feelings, observations, and perhaps even a moral slap on the hand if the notion strikes them. That's what I'm expecting, because of the choices I've made in telling this story as it is.

You can find me online in all of the usual places, where I'll welcome comments and conversation about what's happened here.

PROLOGUE

The blizzard winds hit the bedroom windows with brute-force, the *wump* sounds registering in the recesses of Stephen Porter's mind as he hugged the extra pillow and yearned for a blackout sleep to take the sad night away. His arms and legs were heavy, his sinuses swollen from the emotions that had struck the moment he had climbed into bed. From downstairs he heard the chimes of the grandfather clock—a lonely sound resonating through the sparsely furnished rooms of his sprawling suburban house.

Wump

The windows shuddered again as he slipped into a deeper doze. He sensed a vague threat in the sound—a notion the glass might break as it persisted—

WumpWUMP

—louder now, nudging its way into the dream-space between wakefulness and sleep, still a part of the physical world of his bedroom and his house...but with a reverberation of the past.

No, he thought.

Not again—

Not tonight—

He tightened his hold on the pillow, as if it would slow the back-sliding feeling; tried to move against the solid weight on his chest as the sound and the memories took him back to another kind of storm, with gusting winds and thunder and lightning shattering the heat of an August day. Back to the rapid-fire deluge of rain on the roof. And the sight of it overflowing the gutters and pooling in the streets. And the conversation at the front door, riddled with assurances that did not ring true.

"It's 8 o'clock."

"But I have to go—"

"It's not safe—"

The voices had a tinny, ethereal tone, and gave way to images triggered by both certainties and imaginings of what must have been:

The Lexus, silver-gray in the steely downpour, backing up and driving away.

The rain obscuring visibility as it traveled from the neighborhood streets to the highway and then toward the mountain to the north.

The Lexus moving too quickly for the weather or the narrow road as it climbed, up and up toward the mountain's highest perch.

The Bluetooth ringing, the calls ignored as the speedometer needle swept higher, and higher—

50

60

70

"STOP!"

He felt a jolt in his neck as his eyes flew open, the sound of his voice—either imagined or spoken—still echoing through his mind as he sat up—

And heard the ringing phone, a dislocated sound amid the nightmare images still flickering through his mind as he looked at the clock:

12:13

He rubbed his eyes as the room began a slow turn around him, and listened as the next ring was interrupted by the *click* of the answering machine kicking in with his own recorded voice:

"*You've reached the Porters. We're not here right now—*"

His temples throbbed as he reached for the receiver, and knocked it to the floor.

He groaned as he picked it up.

"Hello?"

He heard nothing in response. The connection had broken. He thought of his son, Kenneth, soundly asleep in his room down the hall, and his daughter, Sara, at her friend Madison's house, just four blocks away.

Nothing to worry about. He sucked in a deep breath, willing his mind to calm. *Everybody's okay.*

He gazed at the empty space beside him as the phone rang again. There was a mild tremor in his hand as he answered.

"Hello."

"Daddy…"

The line filled with static as the windows shuddered from another gust of wind.

"Sara?" He pressed the phone against his ear and spoke louder. "I can barely hear you."

"Something happened—"

There were several seconds of silence before her voice came through again.

"—scared. I don't know how—"

He heard a dial tone. His heartbeat quickened as he turned on the bedside lamp. His cell phone was on the dresser, plugged into the charger. He scrolled to Sara's number, and went straight into her voice mail.

The landline rang again. He snatched it up.

"Sara, what's wrong?"

He heard more static. "The Jeep won't start—I'm stranded. Can you come pick me up?"

Stranded? The word hit him wrong. He remembered she had driven to Madison Reidy's house; remembered cautioning her about the icy roads. But if she had had car trouble it would have taken no more than five minutes to walk back home.

"Is Madison with you?"

Sara sniffled. "No."

"What do you mean, *no*?"

"I'm somewhere else. I *really* need to get out of here."

"Where's Madison? Where's her mom?"

"I don't know. I'm not with them." She paused, and took a deep, audible breath, as if mustering her composure. "I'm really sorry daddy—"

And then she started crying—with hard sobs that made it sound as if she was struggling to catch her breath.

Stephen pressed the phone harder against his ear as he opened the bedside table drawer and scrambled for a pen.

"Sara, tell me where you are. What's the address?"

"I'm…at a house, with a boy from school. It's 4334 Rolling Road. Off 15 North. Up on the mountain. Can you *please hurry*?"

And then they were cut off again.

He sat on the edge of the bed and tried to process what he had just heard. Sara was not with her friend Madison. She had lied to him about where she was going. And now she was stranded, *at a house on the mountain.*

On Rolling Road

Images from the nightmare rushed back—with memories of that same narrow, two-lane roadway, hemmed in on both sides by towering trees, undoubtedly coated with snow and ice—

"Hell," he whispered, his heart racing as he reached for his jeans and pulled on a heavy corduroy shirt. On the table next to the bed was an empty glass, a reminder of the last shot of straight bourbon; one on top of way too many before. He remembered sitting alone and sipping it slowly, doing his best to blot out the sadness that had followed him up to his room.

It had been less than an hour since that last drink and he knew it was still coursing through his system as he went into the adjoining den where he kept his computer. He turned on the overhead light—a bright white flash that sharpened the pain at his temples—went to Google, and typed in the address.

A map came up. He recognized the arc of Route 70 and the bisecting line of Route 15, and then the turnoff to Rolling Road, a zigzagging thoroughfare that led up to the top of the mountain.

The address Sara had given him—4334—was marked by a green arrow on the screen. He stared at it for a long moment, wondering how tonight—of all nights—she had found her way there.

And then he got moving, returning to the bedroom, where he pulled a pair of woolen socks from the drawer and took a wintergreen Life Saver from the bedside table, the taste reminding him of the antacids that he had been downing almost every day. A wave of nausea made him gag as he moved out to the hall and down the curved stairway. Into the foyer with its green marble floor. Through the kitchen of granite and steel. Into the two-story family room, where the air had grown chilly in the deepening night.

He scribbled a note—GONE TO RESCUE YOUR SISTER IN THE SNOW—on the family message board on the extremely unlikely chance that Kenneth would wake up and come downstairs before they got back, then grabbed his barn coat from the mudroom and stepped into the garage.

Harsh overhead lights flickered on as he pushed the button for the automatic door. It rose a few feet and came to a squealing stop halfway up. He cursed and hit the button again. Like every other upgrade in the new house, the mechanized door had been installed by the builder. It had been on Stephen's mental list of things that needed to be fixed for over a month but he still hadn't found the time.

A gust of wind blew a spray of snow into the garage as the door finally rose all the way. He took the shovel from its hook on the wall and moaned, "Good God Sara, you're gonna kill me," and stepped out into the brutally cold air to clear a path from the driveway to the street.

He was panting and sweating when he finished, his vision vibrating as he reached for the handle of the driver's side door.

You drank too much, he thought. *Shouldn't drive.*

He swung the door open anyway, dropped heavily into the seat of the Ford Explorer and turned on the ignition, then backed slowly down the sloped driveway and tapped the brake, which sent the car into a sideways skid before stopping at an angle just before the sidewalk.

It's a blizzard.

Nausea crept up the back of his throat.

Probably even worse, at the top of that mountain.

He sat for several seconds before another option came to mind, then reached into the back pocket of his jeans for his wallet, wincing at the dull twinge of pain that the shoveling had brought to his lower back. He turned on the Explorer's overhead light and sifted through the unorganized jumble of credit and business cards until he found the worn membership certificate for AAA. The print was small, blurry in his vision, readable only when he squinted.

He tapped the number into his phone and cleared his throat as he looked out at the snowbound night. There were five other houses on the street, all equally grand and new, and all lived in, Stephen expected, by middle management executives who had migrated to the outermost suburbs in the quest for bigger houses, better schools, and safe distance from urban problems. After five months he still knew his neighbors solely by sight since most, like himself, left by 7 a.m. and returned after dark as a result of monstrous commutes to work.

He felt a twinge of loneliness as his gaze came back to his own house, and as he thought of the all the empty rooms inside.

The operator from AAA sounded harried when she finally answered and he had the feeling she was only half-listening as he told her about the disabled Jeep and gave her the address Sara had called from. There wasn't a trace of give in her voice when she told him there was absolutely no chance of getting it towed any time soon.

His offer to pay a premium was answered with a weary sigh.

"I'm sorry, there's nothing we can do. We have three tow truck operators in your area and all are backed up with calls because of the storm."

Stephen cleared his throat, conscious of the tightness of his grip on the phone.

"Look, I'm really worried. My daughter's only seventeen. She was very upset when she called me. She was crying—scared. I think she's in trouble."

"Then maybe you need to call the police."

He shook his head. The idea of cops going to Sara's rescue made him even more uneasy. He wanted to believe her crying was an over-reaction, perhaps to the heavy snow and the lateness of the hour and the fear that she was going to be in trouble for lying to him.

"You have to help her," he said.

The dispatcher hung up.

"Shit!" He punched his fist against the seat as a hard gust of wind hit the Explorer, blowing the snow sideways and nearly obscuring the sight of the house at the top of the long driveway. He narrowed his eyes, saw a double image of the gauges on the dashboard, and swallowed back the sickly-sweet blend of wintergreen and the lingering taste of alcohol in his mouth; the sensations hitting him like a warning, urging him to heed the dispatcher's advice.

He dialed 911 and nervously tapped his fingers against the wheel.

"911. What is your emergency?"

Stephen told her about Sara's call.

And realized his voice was slurring.

The pause that followed worried him; made him wonder if she had figured out what kind of condition he was in. As the silence lengthened he heard the voices of other dispatchers in the background, an undertone of tension among them.

"Hello—you still there?"

"Sir you need to call the non-emergency line at 445—"

"This *is* an emergency! She's stuck by the side of the road in a goddamn blizzard!"

There was another pause; the sound of typing on a keyboard.

"I'll notify the Frederick County Sheriff's Office, sir." The woman's voice was a monotone. "We'll ask a deputy to respond."

"You have to...*please*."

The call ended.

He leaned forward and pressed his forehead against the wheel as he replayed the conversation. He considered the possibility of doing what he had been told and simply waiting until someone from the Sheriff's office reached her, and then realized that the dispatcher had not even asked for a number where he could be contacted.

He sat back, gripping the wheel with both hands as he thought about the panic in her voice, and about Rolling Road with its blind rises and sharp descents; the hairpin curves that led to Brighton Gorge—

You can't just sit here.

Can't leave her up there.

"God help me," he mumbled, and backed out of the driveway and into the street, the Explorer's back-end sliding sideways over the icy pavement as he righted the wheel, a torrent of snowflakes blowing into the windshield as he drove into the night.

PART ONE

THE DAY BEFORE

1

The day began in the pre-dawn darkness as Stephen stared at the LED numbers on the alarm clock and counted the minutes until the verdict would be delivered.

I'll send you a text when the decision comes in, the insurance agent had told him, *but we'll need to talk it through on the* phone.

The agent had told him not to expect the text before 7:30 a.m. but he checked his cell the moment he got out of bed any way, and checked it again after he stepped out of the shower. He thought about making the call himself—catching the agent on her way into the office, but decided to focus instead on getting Kenneth and Sara off to school.

They were at the breakfast bar when he stepped into the kitchen, arguing about some kind of special shampoo, purchased by Sara, appropriated by Kenneth, and now at the center of an argument that made him wonder if his two children were about to come to blows.

"It cost me six dollars *Kenneth*."

Kenneth gave his sister a cool sideways look under the shaggy honey-brown hair that swept down to his eyebrows.

"I told you I'd pay for some of it," he said as he reached for the box of cereal.

"Even though you used more than *half* the whole bottle. Which you took from *my* closet."

"The closet's in the hall. It's not all yours."

"Well you have your own closet, with your own stuff. Which is twice the size of mine."

"God, are you *really* fighting over closet space?" Stephen wrinkled his brow in mock anguish as he poured a cup of coffee and sat down between them. "If so I wish you'd stop."

Sara crossed her arms over her chest. "You're going to take his side?"

"No." He kept his eyes on hers, but reached across the countertop, his palm up. "Kenneth, give me a dollar."

With a slight, knowing smile, his son reached into the pocket of his jeans and put a buck in his hand.

Stephen squinted down at the money, and shrugged. "Well, maybe."

"Dad!" Sara's eyes widened with indignation.

He laughed. "What can I say? Money talks."

"And bullshit walks."

"Whoa…" Stephen sat back and frowned at the harsh language and the sour expression on his daughter's face. "When did you start talking like that?"

"What does it matter?"

"It matters. I'm your father, and I don't like it."

She said nothing. Her insolent look spoke for itself.

"You're going to apologize, right?"

Her eyes turned glassy.

"Sara?"

"I'm sorry I said that to you. But sometimes I just *hate* him."

Kenneth, appearing unfazed, poured the cereal into his bowl.

"You don't hate your brother," Stephen said.

"Sometimes. He acts like such a queer."

Kenneth looked at her. "Which is better than being a bitch."

"*Jesus*, would you two stop?"

His children went silent, but continued to radiate a smoldering anger at each other. Stephen was once again amazed at how the bumpy rhythms of stress and hormones could flip their moods in an instant. Even so he knew it was only a matter of time—minutes or even seconds—before they slipped back into the natural rapport that had bound them together from the earliest moments of childhood. They had been born one year and one day apart and he often found himself thinking of them as if they were twins, linked on some kind of emotional see-saw, their moods interdependent, with the happiness of one always balanced on that of the other.

Sara picked up the milk carton, read the label, and set it back down.

"What's wrong with the milk, Sara?"

"It's whole milk. Which means it's loaded with fat."

"You don't need to worry about fat."

"Right, tell that to my butt."

Stephen smiled at her self-deprecating humor, then reached over and brushed her hair away from her cheek. Sara had her mother's gray-green eyes and clear, pale skin, and a lovely, heart-shaped face that still projected a pensive innocence even under the heavy makeup she had been favoring.

He glanced at his watch, knowing he needed to get a jump on the traffic, but decided he wanted to sit with his kids for a few minutes longer.

"So, what kind of day are we going to have today?"

"Terrible," Kenneth said.

"Horrific," Sara added.

"Well all righty." He clasped his hands together, grinning as if all was well. For a fleeting moment the gesture made both of his kids smile. "Really, what's happening?"

Sara poured a dash of milk into her cereal bowl. "A test in physics and a stupid role-playing thing in Spanish, followed by various *grossities* in the cafeteria." She picked up her spoon and tamped down the cereal. "Drama club this afternoon. I won't be home till late."

"What about you, Kenny boy?"

"Just the usual stuff. Classes. Studio art—"

"Getting clobbered," Sara interrupted.

"Shut up!"

"Well you *know* it's going to happen."

Kenneth was glowering at his sister, his strawberry blond complexion blotchy with embarrassment.

Stephen treaded carefully. "*What's* going to happen?"

Kenneth stared down at the table without responding.

"Yo, Ken." Stephen used his *buck up* voice. "Somebody giving you a hard time about something?"

Kenneth pushed his cereal bowl aside and avoided Stephen's eyes. "I don't want to talk about it."

But you have to, Stephen thought. He wanted to get up and hug his son, but at fifteen, that was the last thing Kenneth would tolerate.

So talk around it. But let him know you understand.

"You know, high school basically sucks," he said.

"Now who's cursing?" Sara countered.

"It *does*!" Stephen laughed, and turned to Kenneth. "Tell her I'm right."

Kenneth gave him a grudging smile. "Yeah, you're right."

"So, what the heck. Before you know it, it'll be over. Then you'll go to college, graduate and get a job. Get a big mortgage. Add a few lumps to the waistline. End up like your old man."

Kenneth met his eyes. "Oh. Great."

"I can't believe you said it *sucks*," Sara said. "Especially after giving me a hard time about my BS comment."

"Well, you know my approach to the whole parenting thing. Do as I say, not as I do. Besides, I'm the dad. I have special rules."

Sara sighed. "Whatever."

"Yeah, whatever," Stephen replied. "Who loves you?"

Sara gave him a weary look. "You do."

"Kenny?"

"You."

"God it's so easy living with teenagers. I should write a book about how great I am at it."

Kenneth and Sara both managed a brief smile across the table, a moment of solidarity in acknowledging the absolute lameness of anyone over thirty. Stephen saw it and relaxed, hoping that enough had been said. His daughter was troubled but undoubtedly tough enough to withstand the pressures of boys and body image that her mother had always predicted. His son was a sensitive kid who was being forced to deal with bullies, but Stephen was almost certain that the smart-ass Porter attitude would carry him through.

His cell phone chirped. He glanced over to the kitchen counter where he had set it down, and anxiously looked at the screen.

It was an incoming call from his office, not the insurance agent.

He put the phone back down.

"Are you going to get that?" Sara asked.

He shook his head, and tried to smile, feeling desperate to maintain the happy feeling the moment of humor had given him, like catching a ray of sunlight breaking through gray clouds.

Focus on something to look forward to, he thought. *Something to keep this connection going.*

He thought of his brother and his wife and their twin teenage daughters, who were lifelong friends of Kenny and Sara.

"We should talk about this summer. Instead of going to the beach, I've been thinking about Uncle Frankie's place in the Finger Lakes."

Another cell phone rang. Kenneth reached into his pocket. Sara gave him a *don't bother* look, said "It's mine," and grabbed the purse slung across the back of her chair.

"Can you answer it later?" Stephen asked.

She retrieved her phone, and frowned at whatever she saw on the screen.

"Sara, *please*?"

She stared at the screen for a moment longer, and put the phone face-down on the table.

Her posture was suddenly stiff. She looked past him, toward the window that offered a view of the backyards of the neighboring houses.

Stephen sighed. "Frankie emailed me yesterday. He's got a new boat—"

The cell phone on the counter rang again.

"Damn it!" Stephen snapped.

The spell was broken. Sara and Kenneth both stood up and rinsed their bowls and put them in the dishwasher, and then trudged up the house's second stairway, which led from the family room and kitchen to their bedrooms. Stephen stayed at the table, determined to finish the mug of coffee without interruption. A brief chime from the phone told him that a message was waiting. He glanced at the clock, thinking of another ten-hour day at the struggling public relations firm where he'd worked for more than a decade. Lately every block of time he had with his kids could be measured in minutes, and almost always with an underlying sense of fear they were slipping away from him completely.

"Damn it," he muttered as he stood up and then dumped the coffee into the sink and headed into the foyer and up the front stairway into his own wing of the house. He took the last few steps of the morning ritual: brushing and gargling, then tightening his tie and checking the slight jowl under his chin and the exhaustion and sadness that now seemed permanently ingrained in his face.

"Okay, wheels up!" he called out.

He went to Sara's room and realized she had already gone downstairs as he stood at the threshold to what had recently become an "off-limits" space. For as long as he could remember his daughter had been fascinated by costume drama movies and historical fiction, and had decorated her walls with movie posters and artistic photography. He recognized the images that he had glimpsed on the rare occasions when her door had been left open, but noticed they were now interspersed with dark and disturbing images that didn't seem to belong: Gargoyles, robed figures, strange shadows under arched doorways.

Goth

He felt a sense of unease. He was still trying to get used to the dark clothes she had come to favor, and to worry less about the great stretches of solitude that she seemed to crave behind her bedroom door. He wanted to believe that he was witnessing nothing more than a harmless phase of adjustment to the new realities of his family's life.

Yet the anxiety lingered as he stepped back and moved down the hall to Kenneth's room, an airy haven built over the garage. He started to call out, but through the half-open door he caught a glimpse of his son in front of the mirror over the bathroom sink. Kenneth was tilting his head and gazing at the way the light struck his hair as he combed it. There were highlights that Stephen was fairly sure hadn't been there a few days earlier, which explained the special shampoo, another one of his son's experiments…

He remembered the recent, nasty bruise that Kenneth had claimed to be from a fall. Thought of him being *clobbered* amid taunts as the high school mob mentality gained its inevitable momentum.

Jesus

He took another few steps back so Kenneth would not know what he had seen, his voice unsteady as he called out "Time's a wastin', Kenny boy."

There was another moment of silence, long enough to make him wonder what else his son was up to as he waited outside his bedroom door.

"Kenny?"

"Ready." Kenneth stepped into the hall and shut the door behind him, as if sealing off his personal territory.

Stephen followed him down to the foyer and opened the door to a blast of Arctic air under a light gray sky. He turned on the radio as he warmed up the Explorer. The weathercaster was going on and on about the incoming "weather situation" and its likely impact on traffic later in the day as he headed out of the subdivision, then heard the *beep* of an incoming text.

Violating his rule to never text and drive, he looked down and saw the message from Denise Wong had finally come.

He tapped it open.

Stephen, the investigative committee has reached a decision. Please call me to discuss this.

He set the phone down on the console and gripped the wheel with both hands. Denise Wong had been his insurance agent for more than twenty years and he knew that she too had anxiously awaited the "decision" that would be part of his family's history for the rest of their lives.

He was still thinking through the best and worst scenarios when the sharp blast of sirens filled the air.

He froze, his arms and shoulders rigid as he looked in the rear-view mirror and tried to see past the column of SUVs and trucks behind him. Three Frederick County Sheriff's cars and an unmarked sedan streaked by on the shoulder and made sharp right turns into the garden apartment complex ahead.

An ambulance came next, but it was moving slowly, the driver making only a marginal effort to get through the heavy traffic. Stephen pulled over to the shoulder, and waited for it to pass. Its ambling pace felt like an omen for the news that Denise Wong had to share. Ambulances raced to accidents to save lives, but they were also called to carry away the dead, when nothing else could be done.

The thought was like an undertow, pulling him toward the darkness. He took a succession of deep breaths, and swiped the moisture from his eyes as he prepared for the day ahead.

2

Madison Reidy pulled her Range Rover diagonally across two spots at the inner edge of the Langford Secondary parking lot—a fairly bitchy thing to do since spaces were limited, but totally necessary given the probability of dents and scratches from juniors in crappy cars who were still learning how to drive. She was glad to be there fifteen minutes early, which gave her ample time to re-do her eyes and figure out the best way to get even with Sara Porter.

She turned off the ignition and checked her phone. Sara had ignored her text message from twenty minutes before, which only made her angrier as she dialed Marco Niles.

He answered after the first ring. "What?"

The sharpness of his tone startled her. Her mind raced with worry that she might have done something to annoy him. "Are you okay?"

"What the fuck's that supposed to mean?"

"You sound mad."

"I lost my wallet."

She exhaled, feeling relieved. His anger had nothing to do with her. "Oh no. Where?'

"I don't know. Somewhere." He sounded short of breath, as if he had been running. But then she heard a rumble of an engine, and guessed that he was behind the wheel of one of his father's Hummers, on his way to school. "Any way, what do you want Madison?"

She paused, and brought a wounded sadness to her voice. "Sara Porter is *such* a bitch."

"What—*why*?"

He sounded surprisingly anxious. She knew she had his full attention.

She made a vague sniffling sound, as if she had been crying.

"She called me a *whore*."

Silence on the other end. She had an uncomfortable sensation—a sense that he might be smirking, given the lengths she had gone to over the weekend to try and keep him happy.

"Marco?"

"Why did she do that?"

"I don't *know*!"

"What are you gonna' do about it?"

The question set her back. In her mind, Marco would be the one *doing something* about it, not her. She tilted the rearview mirror down to look at her face. Her eyes were what her mother called Indigo Blue and they looked absolutely gorgeous in contrast to the dusty rose blush on her cheeks and the fresh, sunny highlights in her thick dark blonde hair. She would need more lip gloss before she saw Marco at lunchtime.

She squinted slightly, and found just the right words. "I think her brother wants to give you a blow job."

"*What?*"

"I'm serious. You should have heard him working on that display outside the Art League yesterday, talking to one of the other freaks about the *aesthetic symmetry* or some shit. But of course he got distracted when you walked by."

"What's that supposed to mean?"

"He said you had a nice *ass* Marco."

She heard him gasp.

"And I wasn't the only one who caught it," she said. "Tyrone Nichols and Jerome what's-his-name were walking by and I could tell by the way they glanced at each other they heard it too."

She waited a moment, for effect.

"I hope they don't jump you in the locker room or whatever. You know, once word gets around—"

"Holy shit."

His voice was breathless, as if he'd been punched in the stomach.

"You really shouldn't be surprised Marco. You already knew Kenneth Porter is *that way*."

She heard the squeal of brakes, and imagined him pulling off of the road and overcome with anger. A flighty sensation coincided with the quickening of her heart as she saw Sara Porter's beat-up Jeep heading toward her, with Kenneth in the passenger seat. Kenneth met her eyes with a shy smile and a tentative wave. She felt a fleeting moment of guilt over the lies she had just told, but decided that *in essence* they were pretty much true.

"Marco, are you okay?"

"No, *Madison*, I'm not okay."

She thought of her mother and the soothing voice she sometimes used after a couple of hours with her "life-coach;" the post-orgasm moodiness that usually precipitated a night of boozy psychobabble.

"It's really bad for your *karma* to be angry, Marco."

She gave Kenneth Porter an exaggeratedly sweet smile as the Jeep rolled by, and then glanced at a group of fellow cheerleaders who had gathered on the sidewalk; all of them waiting for her to step out and accompany them so they could proceed, as a group, into the school.

"But you need to find a way to deal with it if you are."

❄ ❄ ❄

Sara had a bad feeling in the brief moment of eye contact with Madison in the parking lot and tried to ignore it as she dropped

Kenneth off and watched him head into school. He hadn't said a word to her in the car, and had been noticeably nervous, gripping his black leather portfolio as if he was terrified someone was going to suddenly rip it away. She felt badly about the way she had talked to him at breakfast, knowing that she had only added to the anxiety of another day at a new school without a single friend to count on.

The sense of doom stayed with her all the way into the afternoon, and spiked with the text message from Madison that arrived during the last class of the day.

fuck u

It was a clear escalation from the one-word text—FREAK—from the morning. The message had stunned her when she had read it in the kitchen, in front of her father and Kenneth. It was cruel, even for Madison, and she could only hope that eventually her former friend would get bored and find someone else to torture.

She glanced at the clock over the door and was relieved to see the hour ending. She closed her laptop and slipped it into her shoulder bag just as the bell began to ring. On the way to the door she had to walk past a girl who was part of the clique that followed Madison's every move. She made a feeble effort to offer the girl a distant smile. Over the past few days she had attempted to adapt an attitude—or at least an appearance—of indifference to her lack of friends, but she knew that her emotions were betraying her. She was almost certain that Madison and her crew knew she spent much of every day on the very edge of tears.

Just get past her, she told herself. *Don't give her another thought.*

Langford Secondary combined grades seven-through-twelve and sprawled over acres and acres of what had once been a big farm. Sometimes it took a full five minutes to get from one class to the next. Fortunately, her next period was in the immediately adjacent wing, and designated as her tutoring time for Aidan O'Shea, a sweet, sensitive, autistic eighth grader who probably wouldn't have even been at Langford without the guidance of Kieran, his beloved older brother.

As always her mood lifted with the certainty that Kieran would come by the tutoring center at the end of the session. After so many weeks of "friendship" she still felt as if she was under some kind of spell every time she looked into his beautiful pale blue eyes or ran her fingers through his wavy, black hair, or simply gazed at him as he walked the hallways, a teacher who somehow got away with wearing jeans and steel-toed boots and silver studs in his ear, projecting an almost forbidding sense of authority and a mysterious, irresistible vibe.

The happy feeling stayed with her as she passed the Art Wall, a large cinder block space at the interior of the building that had skylights instead of windows and a long wall that had been turned into a display space for the most creative and least popular oddballs in the entire school.

As expected, Kenneth was there, sitting on the tile floor, his attention focused on the sketchpad on his knees. Last week he had told her that his art teacher had given him his first "commission"—a large collage for the wall that would combine photography, graffiti art, and picture frames placed in what Kenneth had called "a deliberately random way along the whole piece." She had rolled her eyes and called him "pretentious" but had actually been interested in what he came up with. So far the wall was blank but there were two large leather satchels leaning up against it, most likely containing some of the photographs Kenneth had either taken or gathered from the innumerable places in the cyberspace where he spent most of his time.

Even from a distance she could tell he was completely absorbed in whatever he was drawing. She glanced at her watch, told herself *don't worry, he's fine*, and turned around to head to her class.

Everything that happened next occurred very quickly. At the far end of the hall, amid the dense crowd of students in motion, she caught sight of Kieran, standing with his arms folded across his chest, playing the role of hall monitor but somehow finding her, *focusing* on her across the vast space. The connection between them felt like an electric current, a hum that vibrated through her whole body as she gazed back. She stood completely still but she felt him touching her from a distance; felt a tingle in her breasts and the feather-light brush of his lips, his hands stroking her neck and running through her hair…

She wanted to walk toward him but found that she couldn't move. Even so her knees were vibrating as if an electrical current bad become trapped within her. She stayed that way for an infinite moment before a loud *smack* made her turn around. She saw Kenneth standing, and then walking backwards, his eyes wide with terror at the sight of Marco Niles advancing. There was a forward hunch in Marco's broad shoulders and his fists were balled at his sides. She had a brief view of the tile floor as the crowd parted around them, saw the scattered photos and realized that the smacking sound had come from the leather portfolio, upended by Marco and then tossed back down.

Marco shouted "Faggot!" the word cutting like a firecracker through the air.

Panic flooded her thoughts but she remembered what she had told herself she would do when this finally happened.

A witness; a teacher; you need a teacher to witness—

She spun around; searched frantically for Kieran; saw nothing but the blur of teenagers; turned back toward Kenneth, hidden now, hemmed in by a tight circle of football players—Marco's friends—blocking the view. But then Kenneth's head rose briefly above the crowd. She realized then that he was being lifted off his feet by Marco Niles and heard a sickening *umph* as he was slammed backward against the wall; heard it again as she rushed toward her brother and screamed "GET AWAY FROM HIM" just as a fist flew backward, hitting her hard in the stomach and knocking her to her knees.

Bright white light flashed in her vision as Marco stepped aside and gave her a full-on view of Kenneth, his eyes half-open and dazed, the blood streaming from his nose as he slid down the pale yellow cinder block wall.

❄ ❄ ❄

"They're ruling it as a suicide, Stephen. I'm really, *really* sorry."

Denise Wong's voice sounded as if it was coming from the end of a long tunnel, her tone as surreal as the message she was conveying. Unable to respond, Stephen pinched the space between his eyebrows and shut his eyes. In quick, flickering images he saw his wife coming briskly down the stairs and pulling her jacket and umbrella out of the hall closet; recalled her drawn, anxious expression during the mysteriously awkward conversation in the foyer; his mind capturing in freeze-frame the downward tilt of her head as she stepped out the door and into the rain.

Her last-minute appointment with the decorator they had hired for the new house had been scheduled for 9 p.m. At 8:45, according to the official police report, a driver had rounded a bend and seen her Lexus at the bottom of Brighton Gorge, filling with water from a flooded stream. The man had called 911 and then climbed down the embankment, and had nearly been swept away by the fast-moving current as he tried to reach her.

"The investigators are wrong," he said. "Lori would never..."

He looked at the closed door of his office and fought to hold back the tears.

"I honestly don't believe it either," Denise told him. "Unfortunately the lead investigator said he can only look at the physical evidence."

The evidence. No seat belt despite the fact that Lori always buckled up. No sign that she ever touched the brakes. No way to challenge the investigator's estimates that his wife had hit a speed of 70 mph as the car struck the guard rail, then flipped and tumbled down the gorge.

"They're only seeing what they want to see," he said.

Denise was silent. In the weeks leading up to this moment she had advised him of his right to contest the decision that would be made by the insurance company's claims department if it wasn't what he wanted to hear. She had assured him there would be "due recourse," but not without expensive lawyer fees, and depositions, and arguments that would dredge up the details of Lori's death again and again.

He had also endured numerous conversations with the Frederick Sheriff's Department Detective, which had been repetitive and draining.

Something's not right, Mr. Porter.

Call me Stephen.

All right, Stephen. I think we need to go over this again.

He turned his attention back to Denise. "Did the committee look at Detective Caruso's statement?"

He heard the click of her fingers on a keyboard and a sense of resignation in her voice as she responded.

"They looked at everything, including the report that came in last week."

Stephen sat up straighter. "Last week?"

"There was an addendum from Detective Caruso. Basically just saying that the investigation would be ongoing, which means, I think, that he also still has questions. But he reiterated the medical examiner's determination of the cause of death."

Stephen pressed his fist against his lips and thought once again about the circumstances that had been in the initial report:

The malfunctioning airbag.

Her head hitting the windshield.

The water rushing in.

"He also conveyed his concerns about the note," Denise said.

The note had been addressed to "My Wonderful Family." Stephen had found it underneath the hand mirror on Lori's chest of drawers the day after she died. It was typewritten, and printed out on plain white paper, and unsigned. Just a simple short letter describing her "deep sadness" and desire to end her life. It had been dated the day of her death, but Stephen had found no trace of it on the computer he and Lori shared, nor on those used by Sara and Kenneth.

"I told Detective Caruso, Lori did *not* write that note."

"Well I'm here for you if you have any other questions," Denise told him. Her voice sounded more grounded now, more in tune with her professional persona as a representative of the insurance company that went by the slogan, "Agents for Life." Stephen remembered her office walls were covered with Asian art conveying various symbols of luck and fortune.

The thought of those images only made him feel more worn-out as he whispered the question that had been at the front of his mind for five months.

"What am I gonna tell my kids?"

Your mother loved you, he thought. *She would never leave you.*

"Stephen, I'm so sorry. If you need to talk to someone—"

He set the receiver down on the desk, disconnected the line, and felt a hollow, scraping sensation at the back of his throat as the receptionist buzzed him.

He hit the speaker button. "I'm not taking any calls, Carole. I need to be left alone."

"It's Sara calling. From school. She said it's urgent, Stephen. I think she's crying."

3

Sara made the call to her father in the hallway outside the school clinic where Kenneth sat in a chair while the nurse tried to stop the bleeding from his nose. He had cried for a couple of minutes after the fight, his face bright red with rage and humiliation. She had tried to hug him; he had abruptly pushed her away. By the time the nurse came in she was shaking uncontrollably and feeling her brother's embarrassment as if it was her own.

Her stomach was still tender from the blow that had knocked her down. She tilted her head away from anyone who might have been walking by, and told her father just a few details about what had happened. She regretted making the call as soon as she started talking—knowing it would have been better to say nothing and just hope the incident went unreported. So she did her best to minimize it by telling him *you'll only make it worse for us* by getting involved and hoping he didn't march out to the school and demand that someone do something. Because in truth there was nothing that could be done. Langford Secondary had strict rules about fighting and every incident that she knew of had resulted in *both* students being suspended.

She also knew that any punishment directed toward Marco Niles would only make him angrier, and more determined to hurt her brother again.

"It was just an argument, dad. Kenneth has a bloody nose and a bump on his head. The nurse wants him to rest awhile and then I'll drive him home."

Her father demanded more information but she begged off, claiming that she had to get to class. She headed toward the school's back wing as she hung up, feeling lightheaded and disconnected from reality as she moved down two flights of stairs in a hallway filled with the sharp smell of industrial cleaner. She went through two sets of heavy double doors and stepped into another hallway where she heard the squeal of mechanized saws and the pounding of hammers and competing tracks of country and rap music as she moved past the various workshops where the vo-tech kids spent their time.

It was 2:15, the beginning of Kieran O'Shea's forty-five-minute break; a special benefit, he had told her, granted because of the unique demands of his day. Her knees were still shaking from nerves and she felt as if she might actually faint as she stepped into his office. He caught her with one arm behind the small of her back and quickly shut the door. She heard the faint *click* of the lock sliding into place. Then he had her in his arms, in the corner of the room, carefully out of sight from anyone who might have looked through the frosted glass window.

She rested her head on his chest and let the tears roll down her face. Kieran said nothing. He didn't need to. He just let her cry, in his office, behind the safety of the locked door. She felt his fingers gently kneading the back of her neck and the firmness of his muscles as he held her—

And realized something was wrong.

His eyes were bloodshot, and there were dark circles underneath them. She felt a slight quiver in his upper body as he held her.

"Kieran, are you all right?"

He still looked distracted, and she wasn't even sure he heard her, until he nodded slightly. When he licked his lips she thought he might kiss her. Instead he used his fingertips to wipe away her tears, and then slowly released her.

She looked at the computer screen on his desk. He was logged onto one of the local TV stations. The words BREAKING NEWS flashed in bright red letters across the screen. She remembered how the same TV station had covered her mother's death, with stories that showed the smiling photo they had taken from her Facebook page and descriptions of the winding mountain roads and references to "unanswered questions" that swirled around the mechanics of what had happened.

Kieran took her hands in his own, drawing her back to him.

"What's wrong, Sara?"

"Didn't you see?" Her mind flashed on the instant before the attack, the connection that had drawn her to him across the crowd. "Kenneth—by the Art Wall?"

He frowned, and slowly shook his head.

"It was just a second after I saw you in the hallway, during the class change. My brother got beat up. Marco Niles threw him against the wall and knocked him out. I tried to help him but one of Marco's friends elbowed me in the stomach before I could reach him."

"That's really terrible." He gave her a cautious look, as if he knew she was about to cry again. "You think that *slut* girlfriend of his put him up to it?"

She flinched, surprised by the intensity of his reaction. She had talked with him at length about Madison Reidy and the problems between them, which seemed inextricably linked to the problems of her life in general. Kieran had never offered much of a response; nothing more than a few words of acknowledgment or a question here and there.

Yet the hard look in his eyes made it obvious that he hated Madison too. She felt her tension easing, because she knew that she could talk with him about absolutely anything.

"I wouldn't be surprised," she said. "She *is* an evil little bitch. But she's also a popular mean-girl-I-rule-the-school kind of—"

"*Slut* bitch?" Kieran was smiling now, with a gleam in his eyes that was somehow both hateful and comforting.

She managed a smile back, and squeezed his hands a little tighter. "Yeah, a slutty, *skanky…*"

His smile broadened. "Whorish…?"

"BITCH!" they both shouted, a feeling of absolute wonder sweeping through her as he held her eyes. She could barely imagine what would have happened to him if anyone outside the tiny office ever heard him—a teacher—talking this way. But he knew he could be completely candid with her.

"Maybe you'll get lucky," he said. "Maybe she'll just die."

She rolled her eyes, but felt an uncomfortable prickling of the skin on her forearms. "Like that would ever happen."

Kieran shrugged, and frowned slightly. "Yeah well, you never know. Girls like that always get what's coming to them, sooner or later."

She nodded, remembering her first impression of Madison. "She's an only child, and not really a happy person. She hates her mom. Her dad left when she was a little girl. I think she's really needy and maybe that's why she's so anxious to control other people."

"Who the fuck cares Sara?"

She flinched again—Kieran was now glaring at her as if she had said something terrible.

"I'm just saying I think I know why—"

"It doesn't matter *why*."

He looked toward his computer screen, then back at her.

"You know, you really disappoint me sometimes."

She felt a sense of vertigo, as if she had been knocked down, then been lifted up, and then knocked down again. She still could not determine what she had said to make him so angry. "What do you mean?"

"It doesn't matter *why* Madison or any of these other little bitches at this school are the way they are Sara. They don't give a fuck about you and you shouldn't give a fuck about them."

"I *know*. I'm sorry."

He crossed his arms over his chest as his expression suddenly softened. "You're *different* Sara. I've told you that so many times."

She gazed back at him, feeling dizzy and depleted, hating herself for making him mad and even more for the *disappointment* she had caused. "I know you've said that."

"So are you saying you *want* to be like the rest of these people?" He was frowning again, challenging her.

"*No*." She sat up a little straighter, gave him a resolute look. "I mean I don't really care that I don't fit in anymore. I like the way I am."

"Well you *should*. You never would have gotten hurt today if you hadn't tried to protect your brother. You rushed to help him without thinking of yourself."

She nodded, remembering…he was right about the *not thinking* part; right about the sudden impulse to rescue Kenneth from something that she had known was going to happen. Even if he hadn't been there, it felt as if Kieran had somehow experienced it all. From the first moment she had actually *talked* with him, she had had an inkling that he could see things; that he *knew* things.

Especially about her.

"It's like we discussed this morning, in our email exchange," he said. "You're there for him, because you feel *responsible* for him, like you have to protect him from what's out there. The meanness. The stupidity. The waste. You carry the burden without completely understanding it. I mean, really…"

He smiled, an inkling of cheer coming back to his eyes.

"Don't *most* sisters and brothers *hate* each other?"

He nodded toward the photo on the desk. It showed his autistic brother Aidan at age nine or maybe ten, dressed in a race car driver costume, with a small flag in one hand and a helmet in the other.

"That's *why* you're different, Sara. You're a caretaker. It's one of the things that gives you your maturity, and your ability to be completely disconnected to all of this."

Now his expression captivated her with its kindness as he absently ran his fingertips over the narrow braided bracelet he wore on his right wrist. Aidan had a matching version, "so he always knows I'm thinking about him," Kieran had told her.

Another sign of what a good, kind person he is, she thought.

"Oh, *Kieran.*" She whispered his name as if she were calling out to him in a dream. She loved saying it; loved being hidden away with him in this basement room, sequestered from the rest of the school. Her eyes had locked onto him the first few times she had seen him in the hallways between classes, but on recent days she had started looking at the crowds *around* him, noticing the way his presence registered on the faces of other girls, as if the air itself became super-charged with a feeling of dark magic whenever he was nearby. He was a teacher but he was also one of the most beautiful men they could imagine, and she knew that many must have fantasized about his life away from school.

But he was with *her* in this secret moment, right *now*.

He slid his hand gently up her forearm, and softly kneaded the base of her throat with his thumb. The gentle touch lulled her against the quickening beat of her heart. She closed her eyes and leaned her head back for the kiss that she knew was coming.

He touched her mouth with his fingertips instead, his work-toughened skin brusque against her soft lips.

"Are you feeling better now?"

She opened her eyes. He laughed slightly, and she laughed in response, a simple acknowledgment of how good it felt to be touched.

And loved.

"We've been talking about extra help for Aidan," Kieran said. "*Home*work. He's got a lot of it this weekend, so if you want to come over tonight. . ."

For a moment he looked just a bit shy, uncertain. She felt a surprising rush of power, and control. She gave him a toying smile, showing him that she knew what was involved here, what was at stake.

"Yeah I guess Friday night's as good a time to do homework as any," she said.

He smiled, and pressed his fingertips to the base of her throat again, a gentle touch that instantly made her envision the two of them. Making love.

When it became too much she glanced at his computer again. Underneath the BREAKING NEWS banner on the TV station Web page that filled the screen was a photo of an ambulance in front of a familiar looking apartment building.

Kieran reached over and touched her face, drawing her away from the screen, so she was looking into his eyes once more.

"Aidan will be really glad to see you, Sara."

He leaned close, and whispered into her ear.

"I can't wait to see his face when you walk through the door."

4

Frederick County Sheriff's Detective John Caruso cursed under his breath at the sight of the WTLA TV news truck emblazoned with its "Channel 9 for Breaking News!" banner and its thirty-foot antenna reaching up into the sky. The truck had appeared at the murder scene roughly ten minutes after deputies had been dispatched by the 911 call from a neighbor, and was already broadcasting by the time he and Detective Joseph Niles arrived.

Caruso walked quickly past the reporter, who was in the middle of her stand-up beside the truck, with the low-slung buildings of the apartment complex as a backdrop. Yesterday's conversation with Stephen Porter's insurance company came to his mind the moment he stepped into the first floor unit, giving him the uncanny feeling that there had to be a connection, one step removed, to what he saw in the bedroom.

The woman, identified as Cherilynn Jenkins by the 911 call, was face-up on the tangled sheets, a heavy cloth protruding from her open mouth. Her lifeless eyes were half-open. Her neck had an off-kilter angle and was covered with blue-black bruises that indicated a prolonged struggle before death. Her nightgown had been ripped open, exposing bright red marks at the top of her breasts.

Taser burns.

The realization factored into the way Caruso viewed other elements of the room: the gray dirt tracked into the beige carpet.

The open window, which explained the cold air. The view beyond the window, of old-growth forest beyond the apartment complex's small back lot.

He took a moment to envision how it might have happened. The woman could have been in a deep sleep as the intruder raised the window and stepped inside. The heavy cloth had probably been wadded into a tight ball, then shoved down her throat an instant before she awakened, her airway clogged as the attacker shot her with the stun gun, then hit her in the face, then yanked the blankets and bedspread down; her head whipping back and forth as he wrapped both hands around her long, white neck—

"Yo, Caruso, you okay?"

He felt a heavy hand on his shoulder, steadying him from the dizziness brought on by the rush of blood from his face, then turned and gave Detective Joseph Niles a short nod.

"Yeah, I'm fine."

But still the vision lingered as he continued gazing at the blue-black bruises on the woman's neck, the cloth that held her mouth open, and the tousled spread and sheets at the foot of the bed.

"Okay then." Niles dropped his hand and took a step back. Niles was six-foot-three and built like a heavyweight boxer. At six inches shorter, Caruso felt uncomfortably dwarfed in the tight space of the room.

The air was cold enough to reveal the faint vapor of his breath as he pointed toward the window.

"Looks like a logical exit point," Caruso said. "You should take a look at the ground outside."

"Sure thing *boss*."

Caruso tensed. Niles had been on the job for less than a year but had come to it after a decade of experience in Washington, D.C., and had suggested more than once that he would have been happy to work cases on his own. Despite his crushing workload, Caruso had rebuffed him, and had made it clear that he wanted to stay in charge.

"I appreciate it, Joseph." He responded with a carefully moderated tone of voice, as if he was oblivious to the tension between them, and turned to watch as the crime scene technicians shot photos of the room, which was small and crowded with heavy antiques that were too big for the space, most notably the bed, which was queen-sized and anchored by a large, intricately designed brass headboard.

The computer appeared to be untouched. The CPU was tucked underneath a large oak desk, the flat screen monitor on top.

He moved toward the window, which was surrounded by heavy, burgundy-colored velvet drapes, and watched as Niles inspected the frozen ground for footprints. Niles moved slowly, carefully, as he walked away from the building and toward the edge of the woods in back of it. The woods were thick even in the dead of winter with the absence of underbrush and canopy, and it was easy to imagine the killer disappearing into them, and making his way to a vehicle that might have been parked on the rural road that Caruso guessed was about two hundred yards beyond. A dark and easy cover for a getaway.

He stayed at the window as he thought through the obvious similarities to the murder of another young woman five months before. Danica Morris had also been beaten and strangled, her body left at the edge of the woods, not far from her car, which had been disabled at the side of Rolling Road. The time of death had been between 7 and 8 p.m., according to the autopsy, occurring shortly before Lori Porter drove her car into Brighton Gorge less than a mile away.

A low cough from Paul Ralston, the medical examiner, took Caruso's attention away from the memory.

"What's up Paul?"

Ralston had on his latex gloves and was lightly touching the victim's shoulders and upper arms. The half-open velvet drapes darkened the room somewhat, but Caruso was reluctant to open them any further until he was sure the photographer had gotten enough shots of the scene as they had found it. Ralston used his pen-sized flashlight like a pointer, directing Caruso's attention to the undersides of the victim's upper arms.

"There's bruising here—*older* bruising," Ralston said. "You can see the yellowish tone, where they've partially healed."

Ralston pointed to her wrists. About half an inch above them were narrow red indentations ringing her lower forearms.

"And here, these marks...you can guess what they mean."

Caruso nodded and looked at the brass headboard. The finish was cheap and marked with indentations, right at the spots that Caruso expected.

"You want to take a look in her closet?" Ralston asked him.

Caruso pulled his own pair of latex gloves from his pocket as he approached the walk-in closet, which was a surprisingly large, then gently sifted through the clothes that were hung on the rod that spanned the closet's left side—sun dresses, cotton blouses, a skirted suit of conservative brown tweed. On the opposite rod there was a whole different set of clothing. At least a dozen pairs of faded and frayed jeans that would have hugged the woman's tight frame. Small knit tops with spaghetti straps that would have been worn without a bra. Racy lingerie on padded hangers.

He remembered the shelves of the living room next to the gas fireplace held photographs of the victim with her parents and friends. She had lively green eyes and a smile that radiated kindness. *Wholesome*, Caruso thought. The images seemed well-suited to the clothes on the left side of the closet, and brought a sense of mystery to those on the right.

He looked down; saw a brown cardboard box at the back of the closet, behind two rows of neatly arranged shoes that ranged from low-heeled loafers to strapped sandals to a pair of high black leather boots. He stooped down and lifted the top flap of the box.

"John, there's a light switch to your right," Ralston said. "Why don't you turn it on?"

He flipped the switch and caught a glint of metal as he pulled both flaps of the box aside, and saw a pair of handcuffs, a gray plastic vibrator, and a piece of black cloth.

He pulled a pen from his pocket and used it to lift the black cloth, realizing that it was a hood, the kind that would be slipped over a person's face to hide it completely, and secured with a string around the neck.

He went back into the living room just as Niles came back in. Niles was noticeably pale, and nervously twisting his gold wedding band. His eyes were blinking quickly, *anxiously*, Caruso thought, as if he had had some kind of scare.

"You all right Niles?"

"Yeah, I'm all right." Niles' voice had a breathless edge.

"You look like you've seen a ghost."

"I'm fine." Niles paused, as if he needed to collect his thoughts, and then said in a quiet voice. "I ran into one of the neighbors in the hallway. You'll never believe what the lady did for a living."

Caruso thought of the tweeds and button-down shirts hanging in her closet, and the secret sex box on the floor below.

"Try me."

"She was a *teacher*. At Langford Secondary."

5

Stephen was troubled all day by Sara's phone call and grew more anxious as he made his way through the heavy traffic in the wet snow, which morphed into a blizzard by the time he turned onto Route 270, the first of several highways that would guide him to the roads that made up the final stretch. Some drivers became more cautious and others ignored the hazards, which lengthened the commute to nearly two hours of slow and precarious maneuvering. He met a minor traffic jam at the shopping center that housed the gourmet grocery where he bought the ingredients for dinner, and drove the rest of the way with extra care as he listened to the newscasters filling every moment of airtime with warnings about the worsening storm.

He sighed with relief when he finally pulled into the garage, and his mood lightened as he stepped into the house and thought of the night ahead; dinner with his kids, in the family room and warmed by the fire. He called out to them as he entered the foyer, then heard the shower running in the bathroom that adjoined Sara's room and got a dreary "Hey dad" from Kenneth answering from his own room.

Feel the love, baby. He shook his head as he imagined Lori, standing beside him, grinning wryly and making light of the fact that hanging out with "the parents" was the last thing Sara and Kenneth would want to do. But as he listened to the wind and the flicking of the wet snow on the window screens he was certain that the evening could be salvaged with a nice hot meal and a cable movie on the family room's big screen.

He headed back into the kitchen, turning lights on as he went. He took off his tie and filled a rocks glass with ice and a hefty shot of Wild Turkey, and then heard the ring of his cell phone, which was still in the pocket of his coat in the front hall closet. He knocked back half of the bourbon as he waited for the call to go into voice mail, then took his second pull as he listened to the message, from the principal at Langford. The man's voice was clipped and unemotional as he described the incident that sent Kenneth to the school nurse's office. He sounded as if he was reading from a script as he directed Stephen to the "school district's policy on school violence," which was posted online, and requested a call on Monday to discuss the matter further.

It was a bureaucratic response but the message was clear. Kenneth had been beaten worse than Sara had described; badly enough to warrant a call from the school's top brass.

"Ah Kenny…" Stephen muttered. The second floor of the house suddenly seemed very quiet, as if both of his kids had known the call was coming and wanted to avoid any discussion of what had really happened.

God, give me strength, he thought, as Sara came down the stairs.

❄ ❄ ❄

Sara sensed her father's unease as she stepped in front of the mirror in the foyer, and felt suddenly self-conscious about the curve of her breasts in the tight black top, the deep burgundy painted on her lips, and the high black boots that would lift her to eye level when Kieran O'Shea held her in his arms.

"Where are you going?"

She turned to find him standing in the archway that led to the kitchen. He looked exhausted and sad.

She took a deep breath and looked past him. "I'm staying overnight at a friend's house."

"You are? Who?"

So far she only had one "friend" who he had met.

"Madison," she said.

She saw a flicker of relief in his expression. Madison had come by a few times during their first weeks in the house, acting nice enough to charm both of her parents. The budding friendship had faltered when Madison started grilling her about how her mother had died (*"Doesn't it make you feel weird Sara? I mean, people are saying she* killed *herself"*), and had dissolved completely when Madison's on-again, off-again boyfriend decided that Kenneth was a geek who had to be taunted at every opportunity. Embarrassed and angry and knowing it would only invite even more scrutiny than she needed, she had never told her father about the way things had ended.

"You sure it's okay with her mom?"

"Yeah dad, she's fine with it."

"It's awful outside."

"We're staying in. We're going to watch a couple of movies and just unwind from the week."

"I'm making a pizza with seafood, the kind you and Kenny like."

"I already had a salad."

"I wish you'd stay home."

He looked strangely worried. *Like he's desperate to keep me here,* she thought. *Like I'm running away.*

She tried to laugh but faltered. "I'm only going to be a few blocks away." She stepped forward and hugged him. She couldn't remember the last time she had actually lied to him but she remembered Kieran telling her a few weeks earlier that it was "natural that there should be a separation" between herself and her father. *"You're under his roof, but you can't be a caged bird forever,"* he had said. *"You have to find your own voice, experience life on your own."* He had brushed her hair away from her face as he spoke, his fingertips lingering on her cheek. It was the first certain sign of where they were heading.

"All right," her father said. "Be careful."

She rolled her eyes, ridiculing the possibility that anything bad could happen during a simple sleepover at a friend's house. "I'll call you when I get there, okay?"

"Okay," he said.

There was an awkward moment of silence and a slight sway in her father's stance. His eyes were glazed, and she caught the scent of liquor on his breath.

"We need to talk about the fight Kenny got into at school today," he said.

She nodded, but looked anxiously toward the grandfather clock next to the stairs. Kieran had told her it would take at least forty-five minutes to get to his house on the mountain, maybe even longer with the snow.

"Can we wait until tomorrow?"

"What *happened*?"

"It's complicated," she said. "I promise I'll tell you everything I know tomorrow. But it's Friday and I'll go crazy if I don't get some time to chill out. Is that okay?"

He sighed with resignation, but offered her a slight smile.

"Yeah, it's okay."

The look on his face made her feel even guiltier about lying to him. She felt a nervous twitch in her cheek as she slipped her hands into the pockets of her coat, and realized she had forgotten her phone.

"Thanks—love you," she said, and went upstairs without looking back. Her bedroom was cast in a vague glow from the streetlamps and she saw nothing but a blurry whiteness outside the window.

She turned toward the bedside table where she had left the phone, and went back to the Facebook page she had been viewing moments before. It was a tribute to the teacher, Ms. Jenkins, who had been murdered in her apartment. There were already hundreds of postings, with students going on and on in typically tearful, morbid fascination.

Can't think about that now, she thought, and switched back to her own page and the photo she had taken after applying her makeup, an affirmation that it was one of her better days. And then she took one more look at the rest of her bedroom, appraising from a distance the pile of stuffed animals on the canopied bed, the ruffled teal curtains, and the girlish French provincial style dresser her mother had picked out in middle school.

The room felt familiar yet foreign, like a snapshot out of her past as she thought about the night ahead.

This is you before, but not now, she thought.

Not after tonight.

She opened the door and peered down toward the foyer to make sure her father wasn't waiting with more questions. Then she went downstairs as quietly as possible and slipped out into the night.

❄ ❄ ❄

She was halfway there when she realized something was wrong. The Jeep Wrangler had 80,000 miles on it and it had always run a little rough. But now the rumble in the engine was louder, and there was a noticeable hesitation as she climbed the hills. She remembered that it had backfired several times on the way home from school. Both she and Kenneth had noticed the scent of burning rubber but neither of them had said anything to their father.

She kept both hands on the wheel and thought about what a disaster it would be if she broke down and had to call him and explain why she was twenty miles away from Madison Reidy's house. She realized then that it had been at least five minutes since she had seen another car. Kieran had given her "easy back road directions" that were supposed to save her time but as the snow began to fall faster she felt a growing sense of anxiety.

The road up the mountain was getting steeper, and neither side had a shoulder. She slowed down, concentrated on the short stretch of pavement that was illuminated by the headlights, and reminded herself that four-wheel drive vehicles were made to grab the road even when it was icy and wet. She slowed again as she passed a sign indicating a sharp curve and a speed limit of 15 mph.

She tapped the brakes as a gust of wind brought a sideways shudder to the Jeep, and for an awful moment she thought she might be pushed off the road. She gripped the wheel tightly and slowed to a crawl. She had never tried to find out exactly where her mother had crashed but knew from what her father told her that it had been near a major curve.

Maybe right here.

She heard a small backfire and then a gurgling sound from the engine as she headed up another steep rise. And then she saw the turnoff Kieran had told her about.

She braked, and carefully made the turn. Kieran had never talked about the precarious nature of the roads that led to his house, but he had asked her a few questions about the accident—focusing mainly on whether all the "unresolved questions" made it difficult for her to "move on." She had admitted then that the whole night it happened still seemed terribly surreal, and that she had to deal with a shaky, scary feeling every time she thought about her mother's last few moments.

She could have driven right past here that night.

She knew it for certain by the sudden chill at the back of her neck.

Could have passed that sign right before she crashed.

A moment later she saw the landmarks—a dilapidated shed on one side of the road, the wreck of a backhoe at the entrance to a logging trail on the other—which Kieran had said were close to his house. Then after another bend she saw the lights in the front window of a building set far back amid the tall trees. As promised, Kieran had tied a bright red cloth around the mailbox to assure her she had arrived at the right place.

Kieran O'Shea kept a close watch on his phone, anticipating at any moment a text from Sara telling him she had decided not to brave the storm, or that her father hadn't believed the sleepover story, or that an attack of nerves or yet another slide into depression over her mother's death had robbed her of the courage to be with him.

With no message by 8 p.m., he knew that it was going to happen, and made final efforts to make the house as presentable as possible. 4334 Rolling Road had started out as a trailer but it now had an addition built on a cinder block foundation that faced the woods at the back. There were two bedrooms and a common living area that Kieran and Aidan shared; space that had enabled both of them to get away from the monster who brought them both into the world.

Nurlene

She was supposed to be his mother, and by the blackness of her hair and pale blueness of her eyes Kieran knew it was biologically true. But he had never felt that way as a boy who grew up cowering and silent. In his younger years the violence had been sudden and quick—most often an open-palmed slap that would send him into a stunned silence. But later it became much worse. Eventually he learned how to separate himself from the pain; became accustomed to the sensation of being *outside* himself, watching from a distance every time she beat him. He started thinking about the addition the year he miraculously grew five inches and became big enough to fight her off, and worked with a manic intensity into the nights and on the weekends to build it to completion.

He was sixteen when it became semi-livable, and from then on it became a place of security for himself and Aidan, reached through a solid wood door that he had deadlocked when he wanted to keep her away. He had always done everything possible to protect Aidan from his mother, and he had felt a certain solace in having the extra space. But in the end he could only do so much, and he was pretty sure the bitch would have killed both of them if luck hadn't intervened.

Nurlene was dead and rotting in the ground now, but they still spent almost all of their time in the addition despite the wear and tear of the years. He no longer had the energy to paint over the crayon and pen drawings on Aidan's bedroom wall, and he was often too exhausted at the end of the day to clean the place up. Dealing with electricity had never been his strong point, so after ten years there were all kinds of glitches because of the way he had wired the space. Window air conditioners flicked on and off on hot summer days, and worries about a short igniting the portable heater had forced him to install a woodstove to warm the main room where he and Aidan spent most of their time.

And yet tonight, after an hour and a half of cleaning, the space looked nice—the oak floors swept and dust-mopped underneath the colorful wool rugs; the pine table that he had built with his own hands polished and gleaming. There were Victorian candelabras mounted on five-foot tall pedestals on both sides of the large upholstered couch; black lace cloth over the side tables; more candles placed around the room. A cattail of incense burning a light and pleasant musk into the air.

Almost perfect, he thought, and stepped toward the kitchen in the original front part of the house. The sink held the dishes from Aidan's macaroni and cheese dinner. He filled it with hot water and poured in liquid soap, grabbed the sponge and began scrubbing…

And saw the glimmer of light at the edge of his vision.

The buzzing at the back of his head came next. A feeling of dread swept through him as he shut his eyes.

Look...

The voice was clear, and real, forcing him to turn around.

Nurlene was there, translucent and shimmering in front of the plywood he had nailed over the old closet near the front door, looking exactly as she had looked on the last day of her life, her flesh-colored bra barely containing her huge, drooping breasts; milky white rolls of fat on her arms and bare stomach; black jeans that she had yanked on as she had stumbled hastily out of bed.

He stared at her for several seconds, his breath trapped in his lungs as fat droplets of bright red blood trickled down her broad, pale face.

FUCKHEAD!

The plate slipped from his hands and shattered on the floor. He stood still, immobilized until she began to dissolve, the lights and darks reversing like a photo-negative image as she began to fade.

When she disappeared completely he was suddenly able to move. Without thinking he ran barefooted over the shards of the broken plate and into the main room and Aidan's bedroom at the back of the house.

Aidan was there, lying stomach-down on the bed, drawing race cars on the sketch pad that matched the crayon and marker images that covered the walls. He was humming to himself, lost in concentration, the tip of his tongue between his lips.

Your imagination, he thought.

She wasn't there.

He's okay.

But the uneasiness stayed with him as he backed away, his balance wavering as he stepped into the bathroom. He leaned against the wall and pulled a sliver of the broken plate from his foot. Several drops of blood fell onto the linoleum floor before he grabbed a towel and pressed it against the wound. He took a series of measured breaths, and concentrated:

Have to control this.

Make it stop.

He looked into the mirror; saw a doubled, vibrating reflection of his pale face and the long black hair that framed it. A wave of dizziness forced him to lean forward, with both hands on the sink to steady himself until the two images of himself slowly melded into one.

The good one.

He took another deep breath, remembered the 4 p.m. dose of Ativan, which usually quieted the voices even though it did nothing to help the lapses of memory, which had stolen several hours from the night before. He had admitted as much to John Caruso, who had surprised him with a visit to his office at school, asking him questions about Cherilynn Jenkins and how well they might have known each other, and looking skeptical when he had answered "hardly at all."

Caruso had stared at him then, tilting his head slightly forward, waiting for him to fill the silence.

He had resisted, saying nothing more, but Caruso's obvious suspicion stayed on his mind as he stepped back out into the original living room, testing his weight on the wounded foot, wondering if there would be yet another scar to add to all of the others that came from the worst of his childhood punishments—the raised lumps under the skin of his calves; the puckered skin from the surgery that repaired the compound fracture in his right arm; the clearly defined shape of a hot iron pressed against his back as he lay pinned, stomach down, on the floor.

All leading to the darkness. He looked toward the old closet, where he and Aidan had spent countless hours as little boys, their screams and cries ignored. Years ago Nurlene had affixed heavy metal brackets on either side of the closet, which held a 4 × 6 plank that kept the doors closed tightly enough to withstand their frantic, violent kicking. The doors were gone now. He had replaced them with a sheet of plywood, rough and slightly warped, a constant reminder of the old days in the original part of the house.

He heard the rumble of an engine, the sound of tires crunching the snow. He tensed at the thought of Caruso coming back to question him again. But the worry disappeared as he looked out and saw Sara, not Caruso, pulling into the yard and missing most of the driveway, which was completely concealed under the snow. She stepped out of her Jeep. As usual she was wearing all black, clad in a coat that looked a bit like a cape, and boots that went up past her knees. From twenty feet away he could tell she had ramped up the make-up; had probably freshened it right before she got out of the car.

Turning it all on for her big night with you.

He flipped off the overhead light in the front room to hide the old furniture and scarred walls and squalor of the old house, with its memories of darkness and pain, and thought about the best way to get her quickly to the newer rooms at the back. The happy places that brought out the *good* side of him, the one who would do her no harm.

7

Stephen switched from bourbon to Merlot and drank most of his first glass as he looked out through the family room's French doors at the rapidly falling snow. He was still unsettled by the icy commute home and felt a nagging sense of worry as he recounted the conversation with Sara. Her heavy makeup and tight clothes had set him off balance and he couldn't help the feeling that she wasn't being completely truthful with him.

His concerns intensified as he looked at his watch and remembered her promise to call him when she arrived. He picked up his phone and found a text message from her instead:

Got here fine. C u 2morrow.

He sighed, and relaxed. His daughter had yet to give him one single reason not to trust her, and he didn't want to start now.

His thoughts turned to Kenneth next. The distance between them had been growing for months and it had broadened into a chasm as the questions about Lori's death remained unanswered. On the way home he had decided to say nothing to Sara or Kenneth until he had another conversation with Detective Caruso about the mysterious addendum that may or may not have figured into the insurance investigators' verdict.

But you do have to find out what happened to him today, he thought. *Let him know you're in his corner, no matter what.*

He kept that thought at the front of his mind as he prepared Kenneth's favorite meal and headed upstairs. He knocked on his bedroom door twice before he was answered with a grudging "Yeah."

"Hey buddy. How about some dinner?"

He heard the squeak of bedsprings, and Kenneth clearing his throat. "Okay."

I guess that means I have permission to enter. He balanced the pizza on his forearm and grappled with a twenty-ounce bottle of Diet Coke, a handful of paper towels and his wine glass as he reached for the doorknob.

Which of course was locked.

"Ken, can I get a hand here?"

There was a long pause before Kenneth opened the door. He appeared to be free of bruises and cuts but his skin was mottled, as if he had been crying with his face pressed against a pillow, reminding Stephen of the Raggedy Andy doll that he had carried around until his first day of kindergarten.

Fortunately, Kenneth's eyes brightened at the sight of the pizza, topped with basil and broiled shrimp and clams from the gourmet market.

"I assumed you'd want to eat in your room," Stephen said. "God knows I'd never get you out of here."

Kenneth shrugged, but smiled as the scent wafted through the air.

"So let's clear some space." Stephen took the pizza over to the desk, then turned and gave Kenneth the Coke and made a toasting motion with his wineglass.

"Cheers."

Kenneth raised the bottle. "Cheers dad. Thanks."

"You're welcome, *tough guy*."

Kenneth frowned. The attempt at humor had obviously fallen flat. Stephen knew the talk wouldn't go well if his son was feeling the least bit defensive.

"I'm just kidding—joking about the fight you got into today." He made a nonchalant shooing motion with his hand. "Don't worry. We don't have to talk about it right now if you don't want to. Come on, dig in."

He saw the tension easing in Kenneth's shoulders as he took a slice and sat on the edge of the bed. As a baby and toddler Kenneth had been a fussy eater—a fussy kid in general—but over the years his appetite had become much healthier. Stephen felt good seeing the pleasure he got from the pizza, eaten now in the safety of his bedroom, the one room of the house that was fully finished. Kenneth had painted the walls a pleasant khaki and the trim a semi-gloss white two days after they had taken possession of the place. The ceiling fan and light fixtures had a nautical art deco design, and the carpet was a light tan and periwinkle plaid that tied in nicely to the slate blue bedspread and curtains. Two walls were covered with reprints of black and white photos made by twentieth century masters. Thanks to nearly twenty years with Lori, whose own talent had always amazed him, Stephen recognized the landscapes of Ansel Adams, the surreal arboreal compositions by Blossfeldt, the erotically charged Mapplethorpes, and the Diane Arbus works that had always reminded him of carnival sideshows, all the more striking because the odd people she photographed were real.

It was a highly personal space—a *private* place complete with a Mac computer equipped with more gadgetry than Stephen would ever understand. Lying beside him late at night at the old house, Lori had told him she was worried about what was "out there" in cyberspace and suggested that as parents they should establish their right to inspect Sara and Kenneth's computers at will. At the time Stephen had disagreed. He was already beginning to feel a distance between himself and his children and worried that laying down the law would only make it worse.

But now he thought he might have been wrong. Kenneth had been buying his own software and accessories for years now. Stephen knew that at a minimum he had a Web camera and enough know-how to find his way to pretty much anything the Internet had to offer.

All that and so few real friends. He took a long hit of the wine and looked closer at the bed. To Kenneth's right and left were several fabric samples, set out in what looked like an organized order around color strips from Behr paints. Months earlier Lori and Kenneth had made a pact to decorate the house together. "*Something that will be good for both of us,*" Lori had told him. "*So your son can prove his creative genius and I can find something to do with my time.*"

The statement had troubled him. It was a subtle reminder that Lori's decision to abruptly end her career "*for the sake of our family*" had been weighing hard on her mind.

Her decision, not yours.

He sipped some more of the wine, reminding himself to keep the guilt at bay.

You didn't force her to do anything.

He took a deep breath to gather his courage, and wished he hadn't started drinking so early.

"I actually do need to know what happened at school today Kenny."

Kenneth tensed. "You just said we don't have to talk about it."

Stephen squeezed his shoulder. "But we do."

"It doesn't matter."

"It *does* matter, because it isn't right."

"So *what*? There's nothing you can do."

"I need to know who did this to you."

"Some jerk named Marco Niles."

Stephen frowned, his memory jogged by the last name. *Detective Niles' son,* he thought, remembering the conversations that he had had with Joseph Niles after Lori's death.

Kenneth was blushing, as if he had been forced to relive the incident again.

"I know this is hard to talk about Kenny, but I have to meet with the principal at your school on Monday. I need to know how it started."

"It came out of nowhere. I was sitting there minding my own business and the guy walked up with a bunch of his dumb jock friends and beat the crap out of me."

"Just like that? For no reason?"

"Oh yeah, he had a reason. He called me a faggot."

Stephen felt a clenching in his gut. He did his best to maintain eye contact; to look unthreatening, non-judgmental.

"That's terrible, Kenny. I mean, hell, no one should be subjected to that. Someone—a teacher or whatever—should have stopped it right away. Someone should have dealt with it."

He realized he was stammering, talking around the issue instead of addressing it. His mind raced with questions: *Is it true? When did you know? What did we do wrong?*

"It's not true," Kenny stared down at the floor. Stephen remembered reading that denial was part of the initial process of self-acceptance that some adolescents went through, and said in a gentle voice:

"Don't worry...I'm not going to judge you."

"You didn't hear me." Kenny raised his head and met his eyes. "It isn't true. I'm not."

Stephen nodded, and wondered if the denial would make everything even more difficult. *Focus on helping him*, he thought, *giving him everything he needs to get through this.*

"So you're not," he said. "But I'll tell you right now that I'm extremely proud of everything that makes you different from other kids, Kenny. Your mom would have told you the same thing."

Kenneth's cheeks took on a deeper shed of red. "Yeah, right."

"I'm serious."

"I doubt she really felt that way."

Stephen frowned. "What do you mean?"

"Sometimes people say things because they want to believe them."

"Not in this case."

"She knew it wasn't easy."

Stephen stared at him, unsure of how to respond.

"What wasn't easy? Being an artist?"

"No. Being unhappy, like her."

"Your mom wasn't *unhappy*."

"Sometimes she was, dad." Kenneth's voice was quiet. "Sometimes you both were, together."

A chill shot down the back of Stephen's neck. "Where did you get that idea?"

Kenneth's shoulders slumped as he sat down on the bed and stared down at the floor. Stephen considered the underlying message in what his son was telling him. He had believed that neither Kenneth nor Sara had any idea of the troubles he and Lori had faced; believed their secrets had been safe.

"Did mom say something to you?"

"No," Kenneth met his eyes. "But I knew."

Stephen sat down next to him. The buzz from the bourbon and the wine made it more difficult to determine how to respond.

And then he answered, with the truth: "We did have some problems Kenny, but they were in the past. We *were* happy together in the last few months. You know that, don't you?"

Kenneth shrugged again. Stephen felt an urge to argue with him, to somehow convince him to agree, but he knew his son's mind was made up.

The silence lengthened, becoming awkward as the call with the insurance agent drifted back into his mind. Weeks earlier Sara had told him there were rumors at school about Lori's death. At some point soon he would have to tell his kids about the decision. And now, with Kenneth's state of mind, the whole prospect seemed more precarious.

You have to help him, he thought. *But you can't do it alone.*

"I'll do everything I can to get you through this Kenny. I'll find you a counselor or a psychologist, or just someone to talk to—"

"A *psychologist?*"

Kenneth's voice was hoarse, anxious.

"You think I need a *shrink?*"

"No, I didn't mean—"

"You think I'm some kind of *freak?*"

"Kenny." Stephen touched his arm.

Kenneth sprang back as if he'd been jolted by an electric shock. "Get away from me!"

"I'm trying to support you."

"You can't do anything to *support* me!"

"Yes—I'll talk to the kid's father. I know him. He's one of the detectives—"

"No!"

"Kenny."

"Leave…me…*alone*."

A visible shudder ran through Kenneth's upper body. He looked as if he was about to burst into tears as he crossed his arms, defensively tight against his chest.

Stephen stood up, his hands hanging awkwardly at his sides. He felt completely powerless to break through the invisible wall between them. But then from the back of his mind he heard Lori's voice in a conversation from the past—"*He's so vulnerable. So alone*" and without another thought he sat down on the bed and wrapped Kenneth in a hug.

"It's okay Kenny-boy. Really okay."

He felt the heat from his son's body and hazarded a kiss to the top of his head. He was suddenly immobilized by the gravity of being alone; one parent to take care of both of his children. He tried to summon the mantra *all you need to do is love them and they'll be all right* but the weight on his chest made it seem as if all three of them were doomed.

"I miss mom."

Kenneth began to sob, but remained stiff in Stephen's arms.

"I miss her so much."

8

Sara stopped worrying about the Jeep and barely thought about the winding mountain roads as she sipped her second glass of the lovely red wine Kieran had poured for her and went through the reading lesson she had pulled from the web site for teachers of autistic kids. Aidan was rocking back and forth in the bentwood chair across from her, the physical motion enhancing his ability to focus as he described key parts of the narrative in the book she held on her lap.

Aidan barely resembled Kieran. His eyes were a darker blue and his hair was sandy-colored and his stocky body had a doughy softness that she had felt tonight for the first time. He had surprised her first by *not* jerking away from her touch and then by actually allowing her a brief hug.

"The cows are low and they get scared," Aidan said, with a certainty that showed he almost understood.

"You mean what they *see* is low," Sara gently corrected him. Together, they had read through a chapter of a book written by an autistic—and highly accomplished—woman who designed cattle pens and routing systems for the beef industry. The book had been Sara's idea—reading to strengthen comprehension skills and reinforce the fact that people with autism could do great things. And although the idea still seemed to have merit, she couldn't help feeling queasy with the knowledge that the cows walked single-file through the woman engineer's brilliantly designed chutes so they could be killed.

Slaughtered humanely, the book said. As if that could actually happen.

"Remember what the engineer said about the cow's field of vision." She spoke carefully to keep from undermining his confidence. "They see straight ahead but not sideways. So the way the channels are designed in the pen makes them feel more comfortable as they move forward."

"Oh." Aidan's gaze shifted to a spot over her head, a sign he might be drifting.

"Do you understand, Aidan?"

"The cows are in a pen." Aidan's rocking slowed.

"That's right."

"With cowboys."

"Well..." she hesitated. "Sort of."

"Cowboys ride horses. Mustangs."

"Um yes, a Mustang is a kind of horse but—"

"The 1968 Mustang GT has a 157 horsepower with four-speed overdrive."

She sighed; the mental trajectory that took him from cow to cowboy to horse to horsepower was a sure sign she was losing him.

"Aidan?" She held up her index finger to focus his attention, and placed it just above the bridge of her nose, directly between her eyes. She had come up with the gesture at the tutoring lab at school and for some reason it had worked. "You're doing well. You understood a lot."

"I understood a lot."

The repeating means he's still off-task, she thought. *Get him back with a question.*

She held up the book, and pointed to the title. "What's the name of the book, Aidan?"

He narrowed his eyes, and focused on the cover.

"This book is named *Thinking in Pictures*. It is written by Temple Grandin. Temple Grandin likes cows."

"I think our boy's getting tired," Kieran said.

She sighed, and rested her left hand on Kieran's knee. He was lying back on the sofa, looking comfortable and pleased with the way she had handled the lesson. The slight stubble she had felt on his pale, beautiful skin this morning had thickened, and it gave him a soulful look in the light of the candelabra beside him. She gazed at the length of his body, imagined herself draped over him, her hands gently caressing the wonderful planes of his face as they kissed.

"You think so?" she asked.

"It's past his bedtime."

"No it's NOT past my bedtime!" Aidan yelled. "Today is Friday and I stay up late on Friday!"

"Hey. Aidan. Look at me." Kieran raised his index finger and used the same gesture she had used to get Aidan's attention, but he looked sterner, more authoritative. "We have company in the house. A beautiful girl. You have to use your manners around company. And around beautiful girls."

Kieran's words filled her with a sense of euphoria. He smiled slightly, from the corner of his mouth; then met her eyes as if they were sharing a secret. She looked past him as she remembered the almost unbearably erotic memory of her first secretive visit to his office, when he had slipped his hands up underneath her blouse, and touched her nipples, gently at first, until they stiffened.

"You okay Sara?"

Her face was hot, flushed. Kieran was still smiling at her, as if he knew exactly what she had been thinking. For a long, surreal moment it felt as if the two of them were already joined, already experiencing the inevitable sexual connection.

"I'm a good boy," Aidan said.

"Yes you're a good boy." Kieran stood up and placed his wine glass on the side table and then leaned over and laid his hands on Aidan's shoulders. "And a good brother. Right?"

"Right!"

"And good brothers always get along."

"Yes!"

Kieran made a growling sound deep in his throat. Aidan's face was suffused with delight as he mimicked it back.

Kieran growled again, and then playfully pressed his forehead against Aidan's. "And if we don't, we *rumble*."

"SO WE'RE GONNA RUMBLE NOW!" Aidan yelled, and then suddenly they were wrestling; Aidan playfully swatting his forearms against Kieran's face, then butting his head against Kieran's chest, both of them growling louder now, like dogs.

"No NO NO!" Aidan yelled, and Kieran suddenly froze, tilting his head forward so Aidan could pound him with more playful blows, his fists hitting Kieran's shoulders as Kieran lowered himself into a sitting position.

Sara recognized what Kieran was doing; sending a signal of calm retreat, easing out of the wrestling match by giving up his ground. After a moment Aidan got the signal and stopped the punching but kept Kieran wrapped in his arms. Kieran had told her once that bedtime was one of the most challenging points in the day. Aidan could be so full of nervous, pent-up energy that getting him into bed was "like pushing a Jack-in-the-Box back into the can."

Kieran's body language seemed to be working, at least temporarily; Aidan was standing still but looking tense, as if there were springs coiled in his body.

"You wanna talk about cars?" Kieran spoke quietly, his voice just above a whisper, another tack for drawing Aidan's focus.

"I know all about cars," Aidan said.

Kieran eased himself out of the embrace. "How about car movies? Tell me the best car movies—top three."

"Top three!" Aidan said.

Kieran nodded. "Sara Porter you're about to see something really amazing from my brother Aidan here. Aidan, tell us about the best car movies ever made, starting with *Thunder Road*. Ready…" Kieran palmed a rapid beat against the seat cushion. "Go!"

Aidan's voice rose to a theatrical level. "*Thunder Road* 1958 has the 1950 Ford Coupe V8 flathead engine with three-speed overdrive and a 1957 Ford Fairlane Skyline V8 190 horsepower."

"What about *The Fast and the Furious*?"

"*The Fast and the Furious* has a 1994 Toyota Supra custom T-66 turbocharged 544 horsepower and 6800 rpms in Lamborghini Candy Pearl Orange, with a Bomex front spoiler and a Gertag Six-Speed gearbox with a Stillway sequential adapter!"

"*Gone in 60 Seconds*!"

"*Gone in 60 Seconds* has a 1967 Mustang GT 500 Fastback with a 289 four-on-the-floor top loader transmission."

"YO AIDAN O'SHEA!"

Kieran raised his right hand for a high-five gesture that stopped in midair. There was a sudden change in his expression—a rapid, nervous blinking of his eyes. He tilted his head and looked toward the trailer section of the house, as if there was someone standing there.

And then he shook his head, with quick, jerking motions.

Sara felt a strange tension in the air, as if Kieran was suddenly unable to see or hear Aidan or herself.

And then Kieran flinched, as if he had been slapped.

She reached over and touched his arm. "Are you okay?"

The motion seemed to bring him back, but his eyes still looked dazed. After a moment he squinted, as if he was forcing himself to concentrate.

And then he looked at Aidan again.

"Nice job little brother."

"Thank you," Aidan said.

"It really was," she reaffirmed, and touched Kieran's arm again. "Are you sure you're all right?"

"Yeah." There was a tic in his cheek, another nervous blink of his eyes. "Why wouldn't I be?"

"For a minute there…it was like you kind of went away."

"Don't worry about it."

The testy tone of his voice made her sorry she had brought it up. "Okay…sorry."

There was a long moment of quiet, an undercurrent of agitation in the way Kieran was looking at her.

"I want to draw a picture," Aidan said.

"Aw not now. It's so late." Kieran yawned in a slightly exaggerated way.

"I want to draw a picture of Sara."

Kieran sat up, and headed toward the hallway off the living room. "I'm going to get your toothbrush and toothpaste ready and then we'll do good-night time."

Aidan stayed where he was, looking at her. When it was obvious he wasn't going to follow, Kieran came back and wrapped him in a tight hug.

"I'm too tired to rumble again little brother. Come on and help me get you ready."

Aidan squirmed but Kieran held him tighter. His face reddened. He looked distressed.

"Good night, Aidan," Sara said. "Thanks for hanging out with me."

Aidan said nothing, but lowered his head, looking as if he might cry as Kieran turned him toward the hall.

She felt sad as she watched them go. A lot of the literature about autism focused on the sense of alienation and inferred that some autistic people liked being in their own world. But she knew that Aidan truly enjoyed interaction with other people. Yet he was largely left alone and even shunned at school. And now he was being sent away alone in his own home.

The depressing nature of it stayed with her as she looked for the first time at a series of large drawings on either side of the television. She had glanced at them when she had come in and she realized now they were simply tacked to the wall, without frames.

She got up, looked closer. The drawings were of people she recognized: Ms. Carson, Aidan's English teacher. Melissa Carroll, another autistic seventh-grader at Langford. Ms. Bernard, a large black woman who managed the cafeteria.

She noticed the printed letters in the bottom right hand corner of each drawing: *Aidan O'Shea*, and felt an unexpected tremor of emotion as she stepped back and observed the nuanced shading and expertly rendered facial expressions.

He's gifted, like Kenneth, she thought.

She heard the sound of running water, then the murmur of voices behind the closed bathroom door; Kieran's gentle tone punctuated by a sudden *"No!"* from Aidan.

Kieran suddenly became more insistent.

"You have to get to bed buddy."

"I WANT TO GO OUT IN THE SNOW!"

"It's late. You need to brush your teeth and get to sleep."

"I WANT TO GO NOW!"

She nervously sat back down on the couch, her palms pressed between her knees. She had experienced one of Aidan's outbursts during a tutoring session a few weeks earlier and had been unable to say or do anything to stop it.

She looked anxiously toward the hallway that led to the bedrooms as Aidan yelled, "*NO*!"

And heard the *smack*, the sound of an open-palmed slap.

A low moaning sound came from the room. It was Aidan, sounding as if he'd been struck, and hurt.

"You'll be good now, right?" Kieran's voice was tense. "You'll listen to your brother?"

Aidan moaned again.

"Listen and do what I tell you to do? Come on. Brush your teeth. And tomorrow we'll go out in the snow for a long time."

She heard a sniffling sound, and then a change in the sound of the water, as if Aidan was finally sticking his toothbrush underneath it. She turned and went into the trailer section of the house, which Kieran had told her they no longer used. There was a short hallway that had a piece of plywood, nailed to the wall. It was yellowed with age, and slightly warped in the middle. She stepped closer and realized it was covering a space that must have been used as a closet.

It was a strange sight. Kieran taught people how to build things. If the closet door had been broken she would have expected him to fix or replace it. But the plywood was old and looked like it had been there for a long time.

She stepped into the bathroom. It had an ugly vanity cabinet that was a different color from the toilet and a cheap pre-fabricated shower unit with faucets that had been taken apart but abandoned, a screwdriver and wrench and a plastic container of nuts and bolts left open on the floor.

She shut the door and turned on the light and tried to make sense of what she had just heard. She didn't want to believe that Kieran had hit Aidan but the sounds were lodged in her mind now, as violent and ugly as the attack on Kenneth at school.

You must have heard it wrong, she thought. *Must have been the wine.*

Of course she had. Kieran lived for his brother. He had shaped his whole career as a teacher around the need to be at Langford, where Aidan had been mainstreamed, so that he would always be within reach.

He's a caretaker, like you. The conversation in Kieran's office drifted back through her thoughts, reminding her of everything they had in common. She loved Kieran and was coming to love his little brother. She would be good for Aidan; would help him find guidance for his talent. Soon Aidan and Kenneth would become friends, bonded by their artistic abilities.

The thoughts made her smile as she checked her purse for the condoms she had bought, just in case he didn't have any.

They were there, zippered into an inside pocket. She remembered one of the many conversations she had had with her mother about sex—something that *"shouldn't be taken lightly because of all those consequences that I'm going to make you uncomfortable lecturing you about,"* her mother had joked, both of them content to talk around the edges of any kind of promises or warnings.

The memory of that conversation was an uncomfortable intrusion—another sign of the forces that were meant to keep her apart from Kieran. Because of the age difference, which didn't matter, or his role as a teacher, which also didn't matter.

All that really matters is that we're meant to be together.

There was a sudden vibration in the floor, a thumping sound on the other side of the wall.

She opened the door and almost bumped into Kieran in the hallway.

"Whoops, sorry." He smiled down at her, seeming taller in the close space. "Had to put a load of clothes in the dryer."

She looked past him, into another shallow closet where the washer and dryer sat side-by-side, the dryer shaking and rumbling as if it was very full. The glimpse of domesticity, *Kieran O'Shea doing laundry*, was surprisingly endearing.

"I think we finally get to be alone," he said.

She smiled, *mysteriously*, she hoped, and they walked hand-in-hand back to the living room. The fire had burned down low and the candelabras sent shadows of their bodies flickering against the walls. The music was different now. There was a slow, rolling, electronic beat to it. During the past few minutes Kieran had brought out a large glass bong and put it on the table alongside a plastic baggie.

He placed his hand on her cheek when he saw her gazing at the bong, and then suddenly pulled her closer, his arm tight against her back. She felt a wonderful, anticipatory tension, like the last few moments before stepping onto a rollercoaster as he whispered "I'm going to take you so high," his hand moving downward, his fingertips pressing gently against the racing pulse in her neck.

9

Later, Stephen would wonder if the switch from red wine back to bourbon was prompted more by Kenneth's inconsolable sadness or his knowledge of Lori's unhappiness in the weeks leading up to her death. The excessive drinking was a bad move either way but it calmed his mind as he ate a solitary dinner at the kitchen counter and watched the snow piling up to the midpoint of the French doors that led out to the back deck.

And then, with only a brief thought about the ramifications, he went online.

The office email came first, and gave him a page with dozens of messages. He gazed at the subject lines without opening them, knowing that he was only killing time.

He went to Sara's Facebook page next, and skimmed through what he knew was a version carefully chosen for his eyes, a parental profile that probably obscured other content viewable to her friends. He followed with a visit to Kenneth's page, which likewise told him nothing he didn't already know.

He stood up and stretched and walked around the family room before continuing on; stood by the fire and told himself it was best to just shut the computer down and head up to bed even as he made his way back to the kitchen and filled his glass with fresh ice and another shot.

The screensaver image floated onto the computer as he sat back down. It was a photo of Lori and himself in front of the house the day they had moved in, the white siding and green trim gleaming in the late September sunlight. He squinted, noticing for the first time the tentativeness of Lori's smile in contrast to his own.

Should have taken this down, he thought, *found something better.*

His fingers moved quickly across the keyboard, taking him to the address ingrained to his mind. The screen seemed to freeze for several seconds, giving him the uncanny feeling that he was being warned not to continue.

And then he was there. At a screen filled with images of Lori from her childhood, teen, and adult years, right up to a week before she died. It was a multimedia collage created by Kenneth, which served as a homepage to the online memorial site created by Lori's parents.

He continued on to a page of videos that had been uploaded from friends and family, and watched a few minutes of two short clips from a Boys and Girls Club theatre production with six- and seven-year-olds that Lori had directed a few years before, and smiled at the sheer sweetness of the children riding an imaginary bus across the stage as his eyes filled with tears.

He knocked back most of the bourbon and went on to a page of tributes that had been spoken at her funeral, and clicked through and read the first few lines of each one. A few drops of the whiskey caught the back of his throat as he reached his own tribute and sent him into a minor coughing fit. He made his way over to the sink when it passed and grabbed a paper towel to wipe the moisture from his eyes, and then without much thought poured another shot over the melting ice before sitting back down.

There was a tab marked Photo Albums at the top of the page. He touched the mouse and clicked through. The albums had been uploaded by Lori's family and friends, and the page allowed photos to be added on an ongoing basis.

He skimmed over the titles, and landed on the one titled "Work," which had a notation, "2 New Photos."

The next click of the mouse brought up the entire collection, the page filling with rows of thumbnail photos of Lori from her last ad agency position, all of them from parties and office functions. All of the photos on the page were familiar, all taken during happier days as his wife rose to the top of her company through talent and drive and charm that made virtually every one of her colleagues a treasured friend.

The belle of the ball.

It was an expression he used time and again when he watched the way people responded to her; drawn to the same effervescent southern persona that had captivated him from their very first moment together.

He clicked through to the next page, yearning to see more of her wide, happy smile.

And then he saw the photos that had been added. Both showed her alongside the agency's creative director, seated at a banquette in a bar during the last holiday party she attended. The man had dark hair, dark eyes and what looked like a calculated two-day growth of facial hair. He appeared to be in his late thirties, which made him ten years younger than Stephen. His arm was draped over Lori's shoulder, and both of them were laughing with unmistakable camaraderie.

The ease of lovers.

He felt a sudden, unbearable tightness in his chest, and leaned backwards on the kitchen barstool, one hand gripping the edge of the marble countertop; one becoming a fist that he pressed hard against his lips. He looked at the "date added" tab; saw that both photos had been uploaded within the past few weeks, by the man who still grieved for Lori a full year after the brief series of sexual encounters that had riddled his wife with guilt.

He shut his eyes and took several deep breaths as he thought once again about her confession; his initial shock giving way to a feeling of pity as she stood in front of him, sobbing, begging him to forgive her as she told him of the man's unrelenting pursuit and her weakening resolve. Admitting, nearly outright, that none of it had occurred on the spur of the moment. Telling him, in a fit of complete truth, that for a brief while she thought she had loved him.

She had quit the agency the following day; then committed herself to a self-imposed purgatory in the months that followed, telling him of her gratitude for his "forgiveness," deciding to give up her career completely. In retrospect the slide into depression seemed as if it had been inevitable; a penance. She had told him—*promised* him—that she would never see the man again. He wanted to believe her. But he knew that the emotional cost had been supreme.

He stepped off the barstool and leaned forward, both hands on the counter, imagining his wife's lover loading the photos onto the page, thinking of her, missing her still.

As if he had a right.

His dinner threatened to come up, a sign of the gastric problems that were beginning to make him wonder if the acids were eating his stomach away. He grimaced and waited for the feeling to pass; reminded himself once again that Lori had told him she loved him nearly every day after the confession; that she really had been content to "start over and just stay home" with her husband and kids. Assuring him the relationship had indeed been a mistake and that it was completely over.

He did not want to think about the hours she spent alone on the laptop she kept in the spare bedroom. Or his certainty that she viewed the sex between them as a physical obligation while her mind went somewhere else. Or his suspicions about what he had seen on her computer, two days before her death.

He kept the lights low as he wiped down the granite counters of the kitchen and listened to the soft swish of the dishwasher and watched the snow pile up higher outside the French doors. And then to ensure that he really would fall headlong into sleep he poured one more drink. In a crystal shot glass; filled to the brim. Took it upstairs and sipped it in the bedside chair until his throat swelled and his eyes began to sting with images of the Lexus being pulled from the bottom of the flooded gorge, the questions drifting once again through his mind:

Why did you have to go out that night baby?

Why did you have to be on that road?

And then he was in the bed and under the blankets, his face turned toward the windows and the still-falling snow, his mind drawing down into darkness as he felt the soft pressure on his cheek, the touch of an unseen hand.

He wrapped his arms around a pillow, whispered *"Lori."*

And once again slipped into the nightmare of the summer thunderstorm and the mountain road as the phone began to ring.

❄ ❄ ❄

Sara had always wondered what it would be like to fly and now she knew. With her eyes closed she saw herself drifting over the rooftops of the houses in the neighborhood where she used to live and then soaring up the mountain to Kieran O'Shea's house in the woods. Here, in a room lit only by the fire and the candles as they reclined over a blanket and floor pillows, lying sideways, kissing. It was either hours or minutes ago that Kieran had slipped his hand up her blouse and unsnapped her bra and she had no idea how long it had been since he had unbuckled his jeans and pressed himself against her. That was where they were now, on the edge of being joined; everything moving so slowly and gently with the smoky-sweet scent of pot lingering in the air and the chanting voices on one of Kieran's special music mixes like an ambient force in the room.

"*Sara...*"

She loved the way he whispered her name; loved the feel of her rapidly beating heart as he slipped his hand down her skirt. *He's here*, she thought. *We're here. Touching*. His fingers were moving perfectly, as if they were somehow guided by the force and direction of her imagination on all of the nights when she had been alone. After a moment he took his lips away, pressed his chin against hers, and tilted her head upwards. And then he was kissing, then sucking, her neck, his mouth pressing firmly against the pulsing vein there, the sensation sending an erotic current straight through the rest of her body.

She tried to say his name but her voice was breathless as he drew her flesh even tighter against his lips and flicked it with his tongue. She opened her eyes and broke the kiss. But before she could speak he guided her face upward once more, exposing her neck, running the tip of his tongue along the length of it. Then he touched her again, just *right*. She moaned softly, feeling a surge of wonder at the pleasure that swept through her. The feeling lasted until the slight shift of Kieran's weight as he nudged the inside of her knee, opening her legs wider.

She smiled, encouraging him, then slipped her hand under the back of his shirt.

Her fingertips touched raised ridges of skin along his spine, the texture as coarse as corduroy.

He gasped, jerking upwards as if he had been shocked.

"What's wrong?"

He moved back, then sat up on his knees, and looked anxiously toward the front trailer section of the house.

"Kieran?"

She heard a faint grunt, and then his mouth opened and moved as if to say something. He looked down at her but the sockets of his eyes were shadowed above a strange grimace.

"Are you okay?"

He grabbed her wrist and yanked her arm upward, over her head. Bright red splotches appeared on his cheeks and his jaw was tightly clenched.

"Kieran —"

"I'm not ready for you to see me…like that."

"Like *what*?"

He held her wrist in a vise-like grip, his face twisted into a scowl. The pressure became painful. She was an instant away from asking him to release her when he grabbed her other hand and brought her other arm up over her head and clamped her wrists together against the hard floor.

"Kieran, that *hurts*."

He looked into her eyes, and nodded slightly. Then without relieving any of the pressure he lowered himself over her again. His penis was fully erect and pressing against her as he took one hand away from her wrists and yanked her underwear down, shifting his body a few inches to the side and probing her more deeply with his fingers.

Her breath came in gasps as he slipped his tongue back between her lips. She tried to look into his eyes but they were closed, as if he had gone into some kind of trance. She looked past him, toward the ceiling, where the pot smoke lingered. It seemed like half an hour ago that they had put the bong down but the smoke was denser and grayer than before.

It also had a slightly different smell, a vaguely familiar scent she could not place. She turned her head toward the low table where Kieran had set the bong down. The water in the pipe was low and there was no longer any smoke coming out.

But the smoke on the ceiling was still there, and thickening.

She shifted slightly, for a better look. "Kieran?"

He held her firmly down. The smell was stronger now. It made her think of the Jeep, the erratic rumble under the hood.

The smell of rubber, she thought. *Burning.*

All at once she realized what was happening.

Clothes in the dryer. Burning rubber from the dryer.

The air exploded with the sudden shriek of the smoke alarm.

Kieran jerked up, his eyes wide with confusion.

"I think it's the dryer!" she called out, her voice lost in the overwhelming loudness of the alarm. Kieran put his hands against his ears and squeezed his eyes tightly shut, as if the sound was causing some kind of unbearable pain in his head.

And then he was up and running, back into the hallway wearing nothing but his underwear, shirt and socks. She sat up as the acrid smoke scratched the back of her throat, and saw Aidan in her peripheral vision as he ran into the room with his hands covering his ears in a gesture that mirrored Kieran's, his mouth working in spasms as if he was screaming.

Aidan had on gray denim jeans and a bright red long sleeved thermal undershirt. Different clothes from what he'd been wearing all night. He was shaking his head from side to side.

"*Aidan!*" she called out as he dropped to his knees, as if he had been crippled by the sound. She started toward him, her arms raised, hoping to calm him down, then tripped over one of the floor pillows. Her arms partially broke her fall but her head struck the corner of the low table with the bong, toppling it.

Pain shot through her forehead as she slowly stood back up.

She looked back toward the hallway, where Kieran stood with a cylindrical fire extinguisher, looking enraged as he sent a rush of white foam directly into the closet that held the washer and dryer. There was another large poof of gray smoke. He waved his hands through it, took a closer look at the machines, and then disappeared down the hallway.

Seconds later, the alarm stopped. But the ringing continued between her ears for several seconds, vibrating painfully before fading away.

Kieran appeared in the doorway, and ran his hands through his hair. “Jesus fuck,” he said, then met her eyes. “What happened to you?”

She felt wetness on her forehead, and reached up to touch it. Her fingertips came away slick with blood.

“I fell,” she said. “But I think I’m okay.”

She looked into Kieran’s eyes, expecting to see concern, but the sight of the wound only seemed to make him angrier as he stepped back into the kitchen and came out with a towel and tossed it to her. She tried to catch it and missed. The room tilted and her legs felt weak as she leaned down to get it.

She stepped carefully over to the couch and sat down.

“The dryer is second-hand,” Kieran said. “I did some rewiring yesterday when I installed it. I must have *really* fucked it up.”

She tried to smile as she dabbed at the blood and imagined herself saying *Kieran you cuss like a sailor*, and wondering what it would be like to go back to school on Monday after this strange night of passion. *Plus a weird near-death experience.*

She would have laughed if not for the lingering rage in Kieran’s eyes.

“I’m sorry,” she said.

The look of disgust stayed on his face as he turned back toward the closet.

She remembered the way Aidan had cowered, his hands covering his ears, and looked toward the hallway that led to his room. “Is Aidan okay?”

“Why wouldn’t he be?”

"He ran in here for a second when the alarm went off. He looked terrified, and he was covering his ears as if he was hurt."

"He's sensitive to certain sounds." Kieran went into the hallway that led to the bedrooms. "High-pitched noises make him crazy."

"Is he back in his room?"

"He better be. Aidan?"

She heard him call out twice more, then heard the banging sound of a window being slammed down.

"Goddamn it!" Kieran yelled.

She stepped closer to the dying fire. "What's wrong?"

Kieran rushed back into the room, grabbed his jeans.

"Aidan's gone."

"What?"

"He crawled out his window—probably to get away from the noise. He's out there now. In the snow."

10

John Caruso worked the Cherilynn Jenkins murder deep into the night, reserving his last fifteen minutes alone in the small office that he normally shared with Detective Niles for a final review of everything that he did and did not know.

There were fingerprints on the outside of the first floor bedroom window, but they did not match any offenders in the FBI's IAFIS database. Caruso wasn't surprised. Given the level of preparation involved in the crime—the use of the stun gun, the wadded cloth, and the entry during what was probably the darkest time of night—he was certain the killer had worn gloves.

The footprints in the plush pile carpeting were only marginally more useful. They were from a common make of Timberland boots, men's size 11, available at thousands of retail and online outlets worldwide.

The initial autopsy results verified most of what he had expected. The victim had indeed been sexually assaulted, which was probably easier once she was immobilized by the Taser. Her cheekbones had been fractured by the brutal beating and the hyoid bone at the top of her neck had been crushed; most likely, the coroner suggested, because the killer had climbed onto her chest and put the full weight of his body into the strangulation. There were striations on the whites of her eyes, indicating she had managed to struggle in the moments leading up to her death.

Unfortunately, there wasn't any skin underneath her fingernails, and although semen was found on the bed sheets it would take at least a week before a DNA analysis came back. Which meant there was no physical evidence that could be readily matched to his leading suspect, a fellow teacher who was well-known to the Frederick County Sheriff's Department.

Of course that hadn't stopped him from making an impromptu visit to Kieran O'Shea's office at Langford Secondary. It had been predictably awkward, initiated with a handshake and small talk about Kieran and Aidan's well-being, followed by the direct questions that had triggered a nervous blinking of Kieran's eyes as he claimed no more than an acquaintance with Cherilynn Jenkins, and asserted he'd been home throughout the previous night.

Now, as the day drew to a close, Caruso wondered what might have happened if he'd been more direct with his questions. If Kieran—in a moment of emotional weakness—might have given in to the history between them and confessed to the crime.

Unfortunately, that hadn't happened, and since he was admittedly jumping to conclusions based on conjecture, he knew he had to keep his mind open to other possibilities; other men who might have had a reason to rape and murder a beautiful young woman in a carefully-planned crime driven by an obvious sense of rage.

Easier said than done, he thought, as he shut the computer down and looked out at the swiftly falling snow, then made his way down to the parking lot. The roads were icy despite the ample coating of salt and the early runs of the city's plows, but the snow tires on his Chevy Blazer gave him a confidence-boosting amount of traction as he headed up to his home on Short Mountain. Half an hour later he reached the fork in the road that gave him two alternatives: a straight shot to the left that would deliver him to his cabin just four miles away. Or a veer to the right for the more circuitous journey that would take him around the curve and the view of Brighton Gorge.

He had been taking the roundabout way more often during the investigation into Lori Porter's death; had become accustomed to slowing down and imagining her last moments before her car overshot the curve. Despite the seemingly intentional nature of what had happened and the suicide note that had been discovered afterward, he would never believe the woman had taken her own life.

In his heart he knew it was fear that had propelled her; fear of a car—or a truck—chasing her and the fear of what she had probably seen by the side of the road just moments earlier, less than two miles from Kieran O'Shea's mountain house. That was where the body of Danica Morris had been found.

There was nothing that overtly tied the two deaths together, no hard evidence to prove his theory that Lori had come upon the woman being attacked, or perhaps already dead, being seen by the killer, and then chased as she tried to drive away. But it made circumstantial and common sense as he thought of the steep, winding road that led to the sharp curve, the short and nearly useless guardrail, and the eighty-foot plunge to the swollen creek at the bottom.

Tonight, once again, he slowed and looked off to the right as he went around the curve even though he knew it was a waste of time. The guardrail was invisible in the rapidly falling snow, and at 12:30 a.m. he needed to be home sleeping, preparing for the next step in the investigation. It would happen tomorrow, with a request for Kieran O'Shea to come into the station and be fingerprinted and agree to another round of questions.

The questions would be tougher this time, and more focused on the absolute quest for truth, because he was almost certain that Kieran had gotten away with murder before.

11

Sara stepped around the foam on the hallway floor and looked at the narrow space behind the clothes dryer to make sure the fire was completely extinguished, then grabbed some towels from the bathroom and did her best to mop up the mess. Kieran's house looked very different with the lights turned all the way up. The paint was faded and there were cobwebs in the corners underneath the ceiling. With the upended bong and lingering smell of pot the whole place had a sordid, dirty feel to it now.

It also felt suddenly colder, as if the heating system had cut out. Anxious to get warm, she put all of her clothes back on, and then slipped into the bathroom for a glance in the mirror. She looked pale and tired. She doubted she and Kieran could recapture the mood that the shrieking alarm had blasted away. She thought about the Visine she kept in her purse, a must for countering those moments when the sudden sting of tears reddened the whites of her eyes; thought of the burgundy gloss that would bring some much needed luster to her bloodless lips—

And then she thought of her mother, watching her. The feeling intensified as she looked into her eyes in the mirror, the shape and shade of green being the main physical trait that they shared. She crossed her arms over her chest, remembered the last time her mother hugged her, on the last day of her life, which followed an afternoon of shopping for clothes. They had come home empty-handed;

everything she had tried on had felt awkward for her body. *"Don't worry baby, there are a lot of worse things than having such big boobs,"* her mother had said with a laugh. There had also been numerous disagreements about what to buy; Sara had already begun gravitating toward the blacks and maroons and the occasional dash of lavender, which her mother had pronounced as "depressing," and hours of perusing the racks turned up nothing to make her the least bit excited about starting the year at a new school, where she already knew she wouldn't fit in.

The hug had come as a surprise, just as she was turning to walk up the stairs. It had felt like an impulse, with a hint of desperation. Sara had hugged her back, acquiescing with a growing sense of melancholy as the embrace lingered. Her mother's eyes were teary when she finally let her go, and murmured, *"It's okay by me if you want to be your own person, baby. It's good to be different."*

It was a strange moment. From any other mother it would have sounded like a declaration of pride, but she had felt something behind the words; a reluctant reckoning of the distance between them. Then, because she had wanted nothing more than to be alone with her journal and her music, she had broken the embrace and was heading up the stairs when her mother called her name and suggested a "girls night" with carry-out Chinese and cards, a supposedly "perfect" way to spend the evening.

"Nah," she had answered, with an off-handedness that sounded unintentionally dismissive, and pretended not to notice the shadow of disappointment on her mother's face. Then in a moment that felt even more callous she had retreated without another word and shut her door as soon as she stepped into her room, putting up a barrier to halt any further discussion. She spent the next hour reading meaningless Facebook postings from friends at her former school who she knew she'd never see again, imagining how easy it would have been for her mother as a teenager to step into a completely new environment; how easily she would have connected with new people who would have *loved* to meet her. The thought had filled her with a mixture of envy and sadness that she knew, from experience, could only be dealt with by spending several hours alone.

She remembered only a few details of the night that followed: the note on the message board that her mother left about going to see her friend April, who lived up on the mountain. The sound of thunder and the rain battering the roof. Looking out her bedroom window and watching her mother's Lexus driving off into the night.

God, I'm so sorry, she thought, as if it mattered now. She rubbed her eyes and tried to ignore the knowledge that would always be with her; the dreadful fact that she had been at least partially responsible for her mother's death; that if not for her own petty jealousy and moodiness she never would have left the house.

As usual the memory brought a sudden rush of tears. She gripped the front edge of the sink, summoning the mental image of a thick marble wall stopping the sadness, like a giant dam holding back a flood. The image had come to her on the first day back at school after the accident. All day she had fixated on it, willing it to push her sorrow to the back of her mind. For the most part it had proven to be a useful mental device.

She *needed* it to work for her now. The last thing she wanted was for Kieran and Aidan to return and find her weeping uncontrollably.

"Just think of something else," she whispered, and looked out the window that faced the woods, seeing nothing but a snowbound whiteness under the night sky. It sounded as if Aidan had run out without a coat. If he were a normal boy he couldn't have gone far. Yet she knew that one of the afflictions of his autism was a bizarre insensitivity to cold—Kieran had told her that he had to remind his brother to wear his parka no matter how cold it got outside.

She crossed her arms over her chest and leaned closer to draw some warmth from the fading fire. Then to pass the time she cleaned up the pot residue and straightened the pillows on the couch to bring some sense of order to the room. Aidan would be half-frozen by the time Kieran brought him back, so she took two logs from the basket and put them on top of the embers.

She looked at her watch. It had been almost twenty minutes since Kieran had gone out. She thought of the landscape she had driven past on the way up to the house—nothing but thick woods and winding roads around the gorge—and hoped that he had had some idea of which direction to look.

You should have gone out with him, she thought. *You could have split up and searched different areas.*

But here she was, doing nothing.

So call him. Find out what's going on.

She went back into the main room and reached into the side pocket of her purse.

The phone wasn't there. She tried to remember what she had done with it after texting her father. She thought of Aidan, asking to see it a few weeks earlier; remembered his fascination with it and remembered Kieran telling her, *"He's crazy about 'em because he can't have one. He sees all these kids at school with them and it makes him feel more alone. I feel guilty but I know he'd lose it and I can't afford to keep replacing them. So I made a rule."*

She sat back down on the couch and looked toward the hallway again. There had been three doors besides the one that led outside. One for Aidan's room. One for what was probably a closet. One that had to be for Kieran's room.

It's probably just messy. That's why he didn't show it to you.

Right, she thought. *Keep telling yourself that.* She expected the real reason came down to privacy; Kieran wasn't ready for her to see his bedroom, not before he *led* her there, as a sign of his willingness to bring her even farther into his life. But now, in the wake of their intimacy, it was easy to believe they had crossed a threshold; easy to believe that was where they would have been at this moment if not for the interruption.

She held the thought firmly in her mind as she went back into the hallway and stepped toward the door.

Probably locked.

But with a turn of the knob, it opened.

The room was stark and colorless. The walls were blank and the small single window was covered with a Venetian blind. There was a twin bed topped with an Army-green blanket, a bedside table with a clock and a phone, a dresser and a desk with Kieran's laptop computer. The laptop was open on the desk, and the handles of the double-door closet were looped together by a combination lock that looked like it belonged on a bicycle.

The bed was tiny. She could not even imagine the two of them sleeping here, in a room that looked like a prison cell.

Outside, the wind moaned. She went to the window, and peeked through the blinds. The snow was almost up to the lower sill now, and the cold air made her shiver again as she looked down at a small wooden box on the dresser. She ran her fingertips across the inlaid design on top, and imagined Kieran leaning over a work-table, his eyes narrowed in concentration as he constructed it. With only a moment of hesitation she unlatched the small hatch and raised the lid.

The box was filled with bottles of prescription pill bottles of varying sizes. She read a few of the labels—*Olanzapine, Fluvox-amine, Ativan*—recognizing them as depression medications based on what she had learned online after coming across a bottle in her mother's purse.

But her mother had taken one prescription. The box contained six.

The thought made her uneasy as she looked around the strange, uncomfortable room again.

You shouldn't be here. You need to get out.

Her hip bumped the desk when she stepped back. The screen on the laptop bloomed with light. She looked down and saw the website for a television station. It was the same site Kieran had been viewing in his office at school. There was a video box at the center of the page under the headline "MURDER VICTIM IDENTIFIED AS LOCAL TEACHER."

She sat down at the edge of the bed, her mood darkening even more with the realization that she hadn't even bothered to ask Kieran about Ms. Jenkins, who might have been his friend.

And then she looked at the top of the screen. Kieran had used Google Chrome as his browser, which revealed tabs for three other web pages he had open, each identified by a line of text:

Frederick woman dies in crash.

Still no answers in roadside murder.

Detectives appeal to public for clues in death.

She felt a sense of foreboding as she leaned forward, and put the cursor over the first tab.

It was the story about her mother, one she had seen a dozen times before, the Lexus pictured upside down at the bottom of the gorge.

She went to the next tab, a story about another woman, Danica Morris, who had been murdered at the side of the road. She glanced at the date of the story: September 13.

The same night, she thought. *Up here on the mountain.*

On Rolling Road.

She switched back to the site that had first been on the screen, the story about Ms. Jenkins, and scrolled through it again.

"Seen enough Sara?"

She turned toward the door as Kieran's voice echoed through her mind.

But he wasn't there.

She went back into the hallway, which was empty.

Your imagination, she thought. *Playing tricks.*

And yet it had *felt* like he had been right behind her. Watching her. *Again.* For weeks she had been certain of the psychic bond between them, a mental and emotional connection that always told her she was about to get a text message, or when her phone would ring.

A connection that made her feel as if he was *still* watching her, right now.

Her legs wobbled as she went back into the main room, then sat down on the couch and leaned forward and thought of everything Kieran had told her about his childhood. The death of his mother. The abuse. The nightmares he suffered, even now.

Suddenly all she wanted was to get away, to be back in her own home, in the warmth and familiarity of her own room.

But you have to say something. You can't just run out.

She went over to the table, where Aidan had left his notebook and pencils. Scribbled a note: *Kieran, it's late and I need to go*. The pencil lingered above the page as she tried to think of something else to say. *I hope Aidan is okay. I'll call you in the morning.*

She knew she needed to write something more, like, *Love, Sara.*

She left it blank, and grabbed her purse and then her coat and stepped awkwardly around the jumble of old furniture in the front section of the house.

The cold seized her as she stepped outside. She sank up to her thighs in the snow and even though she wanted to run she could barely walk to the Jeep. She reached into her purse, pushed the button for the remote and unlocked the doors. The inside of the Jeep was as cold as the air outside and the windows were covered with ice. After three tries, the engine turned over. She turned the defroster on high and pulled the scraper from the glove box, then with another anxious look back at the house quickly swiped narrow swaths of visibility across the windshield and side and rear windows.

She pressed the accelerator to keep the engine going, then glanced in the rearview mirror and shifted into reverse.

The wheels spun through the loose snow, but after a moment she had the traction she needed to move. Back toward the house and then, with a grinding turn, toward the road.

But then with a loud backfire the Jeep shuddered. The lights on the dash flickered and the engine died.

She turned the key and heard nothing but a *click*.

Tried again. Heard nothing.

God don't let me get stuck out here. Her heart was beating quickly, erratically.

She thought of her father, hugging her, urging her to stay home.

Call him and tell him to come get you.

He would know she had lied to her about staying overnight at Madison's.

Tell him you changed your mind. Tell him you decided to help Aidan with his homework instead.

It was a poor explanation and she doubted she could carry it off.

So go back into the house. Lie down and pretend you're asleep. If Kieran left her alone she could simply stay on the couch, all night, then ask for a jump-start or a ride home in the morning.

But even then she would have to face him; would have to look into his eyes. Would have to pretend that she hadn't heard him *slapping* Aidan—

Stop—don't think about it. She got out and trudged back toward the house, her teeth chattering uncontrollably as she stepped inside, and suddenly saw the night for what it was. The lie she had told her father. The wine and the drugs. The carefully-chosen clothes and makeup that she had so desperately hoped would ensure her seduction by a man—a *teacher*—ten years older than herself.

And then an inkling of something worse as she remembered the look on Kieran's face after she had fallen, the *disgust* in his eyes as he tossed her the towel. The moment seemed terrible now, like a sudden unmasking, a glimpse at some kind of rage deep within him.

Her regret was overwhelming as she stared down at her wet clothes and reached for the phone. The dial tone was jumpy and there was a ticking sound on the line. It rang four times before her father answered:

"Hello." His voice was groggy and confused. She remembered the neediness in his eyes when he had asked her to stay home.

"Daddy," she said, as if she were a little girl. She looked down at the pillows where she and Kieran had almost made love and rubbed her wrists, which were still sore from the pressure he had put on them when he held her against the floor.

He wanted to hurt you. She knew it for certain as she remembered the anger in his face, the power of his strength.

Because he doesn't love you.

And he never will.

The realization hit her hard as she started to speak, the wall finally crumbling as she stammered on, telling her father she was stranded and scared of the storm, her voice breaking into sudden, uncontrollable sobs as she begged him to bring her home.

12

Goddamn it Aidan where did you go?

Kieran stood in the backyard, his mind addled by the lingering effect of the strong weed, his chest tightening with fear over the idea of Aidan being outside without a coat. He opened his eyes wider in an effort to adjust his vision to the darkness, his fingers tracing their way to the flashlight's "on" switch, and felt a dull and sudden pain at the base of his skull as Nurlene's voice came back.

He ran away.

Out the window in the snow.

The voice was louder than it had been during the brief episode inside the house.

Now he dies. I died and now he dies.

Freezes.

Dies.

"STOP!" He took a succession of deep breaths, drawing the icy air into his lungs.

He waited several seconds, then gazed up into the falling snow again and imagined himself slipping into his brother's mind, a dense mental jungle with thousands of footpaths that meandered into eternity. It was an ability that came from his own mental condition and it worked best in the last few moments before he drifted off to sleep, when echoes of the day's interactions made him feel as if he could access Aidan's thoughts.

He looked back toward the direction of the house, and imagined Aidan running out into the snow, desperate to escape the brain-piercing siren. When he looked down and ahead he saw the footsteps that verified Aidan's route and followed them, picking up the trail that went into the woods.

The footsteps became more difficult to read as the woods thickened, and then they seemed to disappear completely.

He stopped, leaned against a tall, thick tree, and looked at the path of the trail ahead. If Aidan had continued on he would have eventually come alongside the edge of the gorge. The thought was terrifying given the heavy snow and the likelihood of ice beneath it; the easy possibility of Aidan slipping and falling and tumbling over.

But maybe not. Aidan had grown up in the woods, and had always played in them as if they were his private sanctuary. His mind was odd in so many ways, but it was finely attuned to the wonders and dangers of the wilderness around him.

He looked back at the path he had traveled, switched the lamp from the flood setting to a focused beam, then walked back the way he had come, going no more than ten yards before he saw the strand of rare white birches; the sight instantly tapping into the not-too-distant memory of the "frontier game."

"Big Chief on the birch trail finds the road."

"Big Bear on the rock trail finds home."

The phrases were a call-and-response mechanism that he had created to give Aidan his bearings in the woods; the words like song lyrics that would act as a mental compass if he ever became lost. He heard the lyrics as Aidan might have as he approached the birches, which marked the trail that led back to Rolling Road. Five feet beyond, and covered almost completely by the snow, was a large boulder that marked a side trail that would meander through thicker trees and dense brush before leading back to the house.

The trail beyond the boulder looked untouched.

But there were footprints in the trail beyond the birches, the route to Rolling Road.

You came back down the main trail.

He thought about the altercation in Aidan's room.

You were afraid to go back home where I was waiting. So you went off on the birch trail, toward the road.

He considered following the same route, yet realized that if Aidan was walking in the road he needed to be there with the truck, so he could pick him up and bring him home.

The footsteps he had made in the trail made it easier to move back toward the house. He saw the vague light in his bedroom window, visible even through the closed Venetian blind, the level of light that would have crept in from the hall if his bedroom door was open.

Which meant Sara must have wandered in.

He thought of his laptop, tried to remember if he had shut it down before she arrived, and started to head back inside.

No, he thought. *No time.*

He took off his right glove; grabbed the keys to the pickup from his jacket pocket, slid into the truck and pulled out onto Rolling Road; ever more conscious of Aidan alone and freezing, somewhere in the night.

❄ ❄ ❄

Caruso was still thinking of Kieran O'Shea and the dead women as he carefully pulled the Blazer up to the drive to the cabin. Inside, he had set lamps on timers to bring late-night light to several of the rooms, partly for security reasons but mainly because he hated walking into a dark and empty house. The two fireplaces at the front of the cabin burned wood, but for practicality's sake he had installed gas jets in the hearth that anchored the beam-ceilinged room off the kitchen, a study that had once held the antlered trophies of deer killed by his father and grandfather.

He shivered as he stepped into the room now, a delayed reaction to the freezing gusts that had assaulted him as he'd moved from the Blazer to the front door. Once the fire was switched on he stood in front of it, feeling the intense heat at his back; his eyes moving, as always, to the console table along the wall and the photos of relatives both living and dead. The visit to Langford Secondary brought back memories of his own high school days as he looked at the 90s-era prom shot of himself and Cassie, his first and only love; a photo that had been taken two days before she learned about the tiny life growing within her.

Four months later they were married eighteen-year-olds; Caruso spending his days in college classes and nights on the EMT crew while Cassie babysat a neighbor's son and prepared for her own.

On darker days Caruso sometimes wondered about the wisdom of keeping that photo and so many of the others on the console table: his infant son Elliot in a red and green costume that made him look like one of Santa's elves; Elliot on a tricycle, with his beaming smile; the 5 × 7 studio shot of Cassie and himself and Elliot together, shortly before their lives fell apart.

In his sub-conscious mind the photos from his five-year marriage would always be bracketed by birth and death; the impending birth of Elliot the driving reason for walking down the aisle before being even old enough to have a drink; the boy's death triggering its end. Despite a handful of relationships in the years since, he remained alone to this day, a single man by circumstance more than choice, still throwing himself into work to keep sad thoughts of Cassie and the life they would have had together out of his mind.

The potential slide into the memories made him moderately grateful for the investigation, a diversion away from dark thoughts that would have ruined his sleep. After pouring an ample amount of Glenfiddich over ice, he logged on to his laptop for another look at how the media were reporting the story. A visit to the TV news stations came first. Two out of three did stand-ups from the gates of the apartment complex where Cherilynn Jenkins lived. The stories were brief, saying nothing that hadn't been reported at 6 p.m. aside from the fact that there would be a candlelight vigil for the "beloved teacher" in the days to come; the last one ending with a shot of teenaged girls crying into each others' arms.

Caruso felt a tight, scraping sensation at the top of his throat as the segment ended, an overdue reaction to the death as his cell phone buzzed with a call from central dispatch.

There was no real urgency in the dispatcher's voice and he was only half-listening until he heard the description of the Jeep, at a house on Rolling Road, where a teenaged girl named Sara Porter was stranded in the snow.

❄ ❄ ❄

"AI–DAN…!" Kieran slowed the pickup to a crawl as he called out through the open window. He had driven for twenty minutes along Rolling Road and was now searching back and forth along the narrower logging roads that crisscrossed it, feeling as if his brother had been swallowed by the storm.

But he had to be out there, somewhere.

He was certain that the tracks on the Birch Trail had been Aidan's. But from the truck, and with another inch of fresh snow on the ground, the tracks were no longer visible.

He found another trail.

The thought filled him with dread.

And walked back into the woods.

He hit the brakes. The truck skidded several yards before stopping at an angle in the roadway. Then after a long look behind and in front of the truck he shifted back into first gear and kept going, his arms and shoulders tense as he searched for a sign of movement amid the trees.

And then he glanced in the rearview mirror.

And saw the flash of red as Aidan emerged from the woods, stepped into the road, and started walking the opposite way, back toward the house.

He braked and turned around in the seat, his eyes straining to see through the sheeting ice on the truck's rear window. An hour earlier he had responded to Aidan's incessant pleas to go out in the snow by promising, *tomorrow. As soon as we wake up. We'll even get dressed for it now. So you'll be ready.*

It was a brilliant ploy, deferred gratification that *felt like* immediate gratification; allowing Aidan to put on the red thermal undershirt and heavy gray jeans and sleep in his boots so he was dressed to play outside even if it wasn't going to happen until morning.

Boy, you're gonna have hell to pay.

He shifted the truck into reverse for a U-turn. Aidan had been moving slowly. He was probably stunned by the cold even if he didn't feel it, and would be easy to catch, his legs too numb for running away once the truck pulled up beside him.

In a matter of minutes they'd be home with the fire blazing. Sara Porter would be shocked at Aidan's distress.

And to yours, he thought.

After being out in the cold, his eyes would be stinging and teary. Sara would assume that the intensity of his fear for Aidan had made him cry. She would be touched, and worried, and when her guard was down he would ask her what she had been doing while he was outside.

Did you go in my room, Sara? What did you find in there?

He tried to think of how he would respond if she had seen what was on his laptop.

You'll have to make her believe it's not you.

Could never be you.

The road curved. He tapped the brake, but the truck skidded instead of stopping and the right rear wheel slipped over the edge of the pavement. He slowed to a crawl and continued moving forward but the back of the truck veered further off the roadway, into the shallow ditch.

"Fuck!" he yelled, and hit the gas, expecting the four-wheel drive to pull him out. At first the treads of the back tires seemed to find the ground, but then there was another bump, and a whirring sound as the truck merely vibrated without moving forward.

He looked up the road. Aidan was heading back toward the direction of the house.

He lowered the window, and called out:

"AIDAN O'SHEA GET BACK HERE!"

Aidan reacted by walking faster. Seconds later he was no longer in sight.

He opened the door and started to call out again as the sound of a car coming from the opposite direction filtered through the trees.

He called out again: "GODDAMN IT COME BACK!"

And heard the whir of braked wheels against the ice.

He ran toward the sound but slipped after just a few steps, his legs flying upward as he fell, the back of his skull smacking the pavement as he came down.

❄ ❄ ❄

For the rest of his life Stephen would see the images in freeze-frame, a slide show of horror to be relived again and again.

His vision was still blurred from the booze; his hands like fists around the top of the wheel as he drove up the mountain, using careful pressure on the gas to get to the top of each rise and carefully pumping the brake just before each steep descent. His concentration was fixed on the icy pavement in front of him when he saw the faint glow of headlights at an odd angle beyond a bend in the road ahead.

The sight held his attention for an instant too long, dulling his reflexes and making him realize too late that he was cresting an incline. The skin on his arms tingled as the front wheels rose from the pavement and his breath caught as he came down hard and fast—too fast to handle the next sharp curve in the road. He tapped the brake but the car went into a sideways slide as he stared in shock at the figure suddenly in front of him.

A boy.

In the road.

Adrenaline shot through his heart as he smashed the brake pedal to the floor and jerked the wheel to the left. As the car went into a spin he remembered something about turning *into the skid* and turned it back, losing control completely as the wheels locked and skated across the ice. The boy disappeared from the headlights and he felt a flicker of hope that he was out of the way.

But then he heard the awful *thump* as the car came to a stop.

The headlights were pointing straight into the woods; the Explorer resting across both lanes of the road.

He opened the door, swung his legs outward, felt the restraints of his shoulder belt pulling him back. He groped for the latch, snapped free, and stepped out to a blast of cold wind, the snowflakes tinged with ice and hitting his face with a rapid-fire sting. He took a step and almost lost his footing on the slick pavement; put his hand on top of the open door and turned around.

The road was shrouded in darkness beyond the reach of the headlights but he searched—wide-eyed, yearning—for the boy. Standing up. Alive and whole. He tried to call out but his voice was trapped in his throat. He kept his hand on top of the car for balance as he walked around it, toward the rear where the field of vision was even shorter, the falling snow tinged red from his taillights.

And then he saw him. On the ground. Flung sideways; his back against a tree.

He rushed forward and dropped to his knees; the sight sucking the air from his lungs.

The boy's eyes were half-open and glazed. Fat drops of blood clung to his nostrils and a line of it dripped in a single trail from the corner of his mouth. Stephen took his wrist and searched for a pulse. His skin was unnaturally cold. He reached up, put his hand over the boy's heart, and pressed against the red thermal undershirt. The boy was as still and lifeless as a mannequin.

"Oh God," he whispered, and reached for his wrist again. The movement shifted the boy's weight against the tree and his head dropped limply forward.

Stephen gasped as the horror hit him full-force.

His neck is broken.

He's dead.

He staggered backwards, leaned against the car and moved around to the open door; sat back down behind the wheel as a wave of dizziness swept through him.

You killed him.

He lowered his head, covered his eyes with his palms. Snippets of the night came back to him. The drive home from work in the snow. Kenneth crying in his arms. Sara's voice on the phone, telling him she was in trouble.

Call 911. Tell them what happened. An accident.

But then his mind was suddenly, terribly clear.

You're drunk.

Driving.

Drunk.

The night was strangely silent, as if the air all around him had been shocked and stilled. He looked down at the phone, his heart pounding as he stared at the glowing screen.

13

Kieran opened his eyes to the sight of snow falling like a million stars from the night sky. He was sprawled out with his back against the frozen ground. He heard a rhythmic *swishswash* sound and turned his head toward it; saw his pick-up truck back-ended into the ditch, the front wheels angled on the pavement; the wipers still moving back and forth across the windshield.

He arched his back, slowly sat up—

And remembered. Aidan in the woods. Aidan on the roadway. The whirring of brakes on the ice.

Still out there out in the snow the cold.

Nurlene was back, a disembodied voice that came from all directions at once.

Racing car in the road racing too fast on Rolling Road.

He sat up; winced at the sharp pain at the back of his skull. It felt as if his brain had been knocked loose as he rose to his knees and grabbed the driver's side door and himself up to a standing position.

Snow cold reckless car.

"Stop." He shook his head and breathed in and out, pushing the voice away, and gazed dazedly in the direction he would have driven if he hadn't gotten stuck. He remembered seeing Aidan behind him. Remembered stopping the truck, backing up. Watching as Aidan trudged down the road, back in the direction of the house.

His whole body ached as he started walking, his legs heavy and still uncoordinated after the fall, realizing after a few yards that he'd left the flashlight in the truck.

Just keep going, he thought.

Find him—

He began moving more quickly as his balance leveled. And then he heard, in the distance, the faint rumble of an engine starting. He began walking faster, his feet and legs still unsteady on the icy surface as he rounded the bend.

The car was no more than a hundred yards ahead—a silver SUV. It sat at an angle across the road, as if it had spun out of control.

Even from the distance he recognized the man behind the wheel, from photos he had seen online.

Sara's father.

Stephen Porter.

He instinctively ducked, moved quickly off to the side of the road; then watched as the SUV backed up, straightened out, and drove away.

❄ ❄ ❄

Caruso poured the rest of the expensive scotch down the drain as he informed dispatch that he was heading out to check on the girl and the vehicle stranded at 4334 Rolling Road. Kieran O'Shea's address was embedded in his memory, and the thought of Sara Porter being there with him filled him with dread.

He shivered as he stood next to the back door and put his ski vest, coat, and gloves back on. His service weapon was where he left it, in the primitive pine bureau that had stood in the cabin for more than a hundred years. He slipped it back into the shoulder holster underneath his coat, and stepped back outside.

He had to brush another half inch of snow off the truck's windshield before he could pull out of the driveway and onto the road that would take him to Kieran O'Shea's house. It had been years since he had been in a church but he muttered a prayer as he got behind the wheel; a plea that Sara would be found safe upon his arrival, and that he would not be complicit in any harm that might have come to her.

❄ ❄ ❄

Sara was looking through the front windows of Kieran's house when her father pulled up in front. Then she was outside and trudging as fast as possible through the snow, desperate to keep him from coming to the door.

She gave him a short wave and rushed around to the passenger side of the car and got in before he could turn off the ignition.

"Oh my God, it's freezing!" She shivered. "I can't wait to get home."

She pulled down her shoulder belt and buckled it before looking at him. And knew then that something was wrong.

"Sara…"

His face was ashen. His eyes were glassy and his mouth was moving as if he was trying to speak but couldn't form the words.

She asked him if he was all right. He shook his head. She saw the rise and fall of his chest as he sucked in deep breaths.

And then suddenly he found his voice. "What are you *doing* out here?"

She pulled her collar up higher around her neck, and held it tightly with her hand as she told him the story she had worked out during the wait. An argument with Madison that made her change her mind about staying overnight. A call on her cell phone from the autistic boy she had been tutoring at school. A spur-of-the-moment decision to drive up to the boy's house and help him with a homework assignment.

He stared at her as she spoke, but his eyes were unfocused and she wasn't sure he was even listening. His breath smelled funny, as if he'd been drinking.

He looked at Kieran's house. "This is where you called me from."

"Yeah, but the storm messed up the phone lines. That's why you couldn't hear me."

He looked at her again. "I tried to call you on your cell. You didn't answer."

Something else to be in trouble for. She touched her collar again, self-consciously, and felt a nervous twitch in her cheek. "I might have lost it. It wasn't in my purse when I looked for it. But actually it's possible that Aidan has it."

"Aidan."

"Aidan—the boy I tutor. The autistic one. You're never going to believe this but he's actually outside somewhere, running around in the snow. Probably doesn't even have a coat."

Her father's mouth dropped open. His eyes were bulging and bloodshot. He looked like he was in shock.

"Dad, what's wrong?"

He was quivering now, and she heard him groan as a gust of wind rocked the car.

❄ ❄ ❄

Kieran ran toward the spot where he'd seen Stephen Porter's SUV. His feet and hands were numb and he had to move carefully to keep from falling back down as he called out to Aidan again.

And then he saw him; at the side of the road. Still and lifeless.

He felt the night collapsing around him as he moved forward and sank to his knees and gently placed his hands on Aidan's face. Aidan's skin was cold, his eyes half- open. Kieran knelt closer, used one hand to feel for a heartbeat underneath the red thermal shirt and the other to gently open his brother's mouth, which he covered with his own, blowing in, willing life to return to Aidan's broken body as Detective John Caruso's white Blazer rounded the bend.

❄ ❄ ❄

Stephen continued down Rolling Road, driving farther and farther away from the scene of the accident, until he came to another intersection, this one marked with a sign—FREDERICK—and an arrow indicating that a right turn would take him back down the mountain.

He felt Sara watching him as he came to a stop; saw the nightmare scene playing out in his mind, the handcuffs closing in on his wrists, bars and a cell, a courtroom and a judge—

"Daddy?"

He blinked, saw the boy in the road, his arms coming up in front of his face.

Your friend Aidan is dead. I killed him. And then I left him there—but only because my phone didn't work.

But now the phone *did* work. He had gotten a clear signal the moment he pulled up in front of the house Sara had called him from. But even then he had waited, thinking of how it would play out in the morning, knowing from his former life as a reporter how the media would swarm around the story.

"A local man has been arrested in connection with the death of a teenager. Authorities say Stephen Porter was driving while intoxicated when he lost control of his car and struck the boy—"

"We have to go back," he said.

Sara frowned, and visibly shivered despite the high heat in the car. "Back where?"

He stopped himself from answering, conscious of saying too much as he backed up and executed a three-point turn on the narrow road, then drove another two minutes before coming to the top of another rise, and saw the accident scene in the distance. He abruptly stopped, leaned forward and squinted as he gazed through the rapidly falling snow. There was another SUV stopped in the middle of the road, its hazard lights flashing.

Sara leaned forward in an effort to get a better look. "What's going on down there?"

"I don't know," he said too quickly, realizing that whoever had arrived at the accident scene must have already called 911. And then he remembered the sound of the man's voice he had heard just an instant before he hit the boy; the vague glow of light he had seen in the woods.

"Dad, can we please just go home now?"

From a distance, just barely audible underneath the moaning wind, he imagined that he heard the sound of a siren, somewhere down below them on the mountain, approaching slowly, with no need to rush.

❄ ❄ ❄

Kieran was sitting with his back against a tree, looking toward Aidan's body in the snow. Caruso had pulled him away from his brother as soon as he had driven up. He had then checked Aidan's pulse, then put his palm against Aidan's chest, then shaken his head, a confirmation that Aidan was gone.

And now Caruso was standing a few feet away, talking on his phone. The snow was falling heavier and faster—in thick, white flakes that swirled around them in the frigid wind. Kieran's face was numbed by the cold but the back of his head was wet, bloodied by the fall on the ice. He imagined that a vessel had ruptured underneath his skull; imagined the blood clotting, halting the flow of life to his own brain. He gazed at Aidan's profile—the pallid skin, the soft blond hair tousled by the wind—and began to weep, his mind fixated on the image of Stephen Porter getting back into his car, and driving away.

Cold and dead.

Ran him over.

He shivered, conscious of another presence close by, and watched as it took shape just beyond the illumination of Caruso's headlights.

It was Nurlene, standing just behind Aidan's body, looking just as she had hours before, the blood rolling down from the top of her head.

With me now—

"*Kieran*, look at me."

Suddenly Caruso was in front of him, squatting down, face to face.

"Tell me what you're doing out here."

Caruso's voice was gentle, but his eyes were hard.

"Tell me what you saw tonight."

PART TWO

14

Stephen made it all the way home without saying another word. His whole body was rigid with tension as he navigated through the storm, and the need to concentrate kept both he and Sara from having to talk any more about what had happened.

As expected, it took two attempts with the remote to get the garage door open. When it rose high enough he pulled halfway in and stopped.

"Go ahead and get out," he said.

Sara frowned. "Aren't you going to pull all the way in?"

"Please Sara." His voice was tight. He had to be sure she went straight into the house without noticing the damage to the car. "Just go inside, okay?"

She gave him a sullen look and stepped out.

He waited until the door to the family room was completely shut before driving all the way in to the garage. The remote that controlled the door was clipped to the visor. He pressed it before getting out, and when the door grudgingly squealed closed he walked around to look at the damage.

The dent was located on the rear passenger side. It was about six inches wide and extended from the edge of the rear bumper. The location of the damage showed that he had almost succeeded in avoiding the boy—that with a few more inches…

But he *had* hit him, probably somewhere near the waist, Stephen thought, given the way he had been flung backward against the tree.

He stooped down, looked for blood near the dent, and saw none. The taillight cover alongside the dent had been fractured. Most of the glass stayed in the frame but a triangular piece had fallen out.

It's probably still up there, right where you hit him, he thought.

Proof it was your car.

He knew there would be other signs of the accident—skid marks on the icy roadway, tracks that would be matched to the Explorer's tires, his footprints.

But then he thought about the snow. It had been falling heavily when he had hit the boy, and it was still coming down fast and thick. He wondered: How much snow does it take to cover tire tracks? How long would it take investigators to get up on that mountain? Was it possible that the storm would conceal all of the evidence?

God, what are you doing? A feeling of shame swept through him. Through the eyes of a cop or any everyday citizen he was nothing more than a criminal. A drunk driver who killed a teenage boy and drove away.

No, he thought. *You never would have gotten in the car tonight if Sara hadn't been in trouble. Never would have driven after all that drinking.*

And now he had to do everything possible to keep from getting caught.

❄ ❄ ❄

The clock over the stove read 2:45 a.m. when he stepped inside the house, which still held the light smell of pine from the cleaner he had used to wipe everything down after dinner. Sara had gone straight upstairs and probably wouldn't be down until the morning, and by then the death of the boy would be a leading item on the local news. For once he was gratified that neither of his kids read the morning paper.

But he knew it would only be a matter of hours before they learned what had happened. He thought about the first short conversation with Sara in the car. He had said nothing to incriminate himself, nothing about the boy. And yet it seemed impossible that she wouldn't eventually realize the truth. If she asked him he would have to lie. And if she didn't believe him he would have to stick by the lie. And if the police ever did connect him and she was questioned...

Stop. One thing at a time.

He looked at the note he had written to Kenneth on the message board: GONE TO RESCUE YOUR SISTER IN THE SNOW. Kenneth had been asleep when he had left and it was doubtful that he had gotten up and seen it.

With a swipe of the eraser it was gone.

He sat back down at the counter. The Jeep was still parked in the yard of the boy's house. When the police investigated, the boy's family would report that Sara had been there, and that she had called and asked him to pick her up.

Which would probably lead them here.

So he had to be prepared to admit to it.

She told you the Jeep broke down and she was stranded at a friend's house. You'll tell them you drove straight there and back without seeing anything.

But he had also called 911, and there would be a record of that call. If questioned, the dispatcher would probably mention his confusion, his slurred speech...

Groggy, not slurred, he thought, *because the call had happened in the middle of the night.* He heard the defense as if it had been spoken by an attorney representing him. As if he was already being judged, a jury listening to fact after incriminating fact.

Yet he knew that physical evidence would be the most important connection. Tire tracks. Damage to the car. *Footprints.*

Pressed by the urgency of Sara's call, he had left the house in the shoes that were closest to the door of the mud room—a pair of loafer-style Dockers. The shoes had a light tread on the soles that would probably have made an impression in the snow. He had taken them off just minutes ago, and had left them by habit on the mat to protect the family room's maple floors.

He felt the skin tingling on the back of his neck as he went into the laundry room; felt as if there was an invisible camera watching him as he grabbed a plastic garbage bag from the closet and dropped the shoes inside.

After living in the house for only four months, he had managed to keep the garage tidy, with built-in storage and a workbench lining one wall, and the kids' bikes hanging from the ceiling next to one another. For the moment he stuck the bag in a corner behind two big bags of mulch, then went back into the mud room and saw the L.L. Bean boots he had only worn a few times.

If you're questioned you'll tell them that you wore these when you went out tonight, he thought. *The footprints won't match what they find at the accident scene.*

He stepped into them and went out the side door to the yard. He sank up to his knees in the snow. His teeth chattered as he walked in a slow circle, making sure the boots were good and wet. He then left the boots on the mat in the mud room and went back inside and tried to think through everything else that would incriminate him.

The damage to the car was the worst. There was nothing he could do about the dent. But the taillight cover could be replaced.

He went upstairs, stood at Sara's door long enough to know she had already gotten into bed, then went back into the study. The computer was still on and the Mapquest page of directions filled the screen. Stephen moved the cursor to the browser and typed in Advanceauto.com.

A mistake.

He took his hands away from the keyboard an instant before going to the page. If he did become a suspect the computer might be seized, and evidence that he had visited the site of an auto parts store just hours after the accident would be one more strike against him.

He cleared the browser, stepped away from the computer, and went back downstairs for the hard copy of the Yellow Pages. Advance Auto was a mega-store for do-it-yourself mechanics, and there were nearly a dozen locations in and around the cities of Rockville, Frederick, and Baltimore. The stores opened early—6 a.m. on Saturdays. If the roads were halfway passable it would be possible to get a new cover for the light and get back home before Kenneth and Sara even got out of bed.

You can replace it in the garage. Put the broken pieces in the bag with your shoes. Take them to the landfill, or toss them into a trash can somewhere.

He sat down on the couch. He was still wearing his coat, but felt as if the night's chill had worked its way inside of him. He crossed his arms over his chest, then reclined back, wide-awake and eerily alert to the sound of the ticking of the grandfather clock in the foyer and the moaning wind outside. In the middle of the night the family room felt familiar, yet strange. A territory between two very different realities. Hours earlier he had stood here by the fire, an ordinary law-abiding suburban father. Now he was waiting to be arrested and jailed. Yet even if he escaped that tangible, real-life punishment, he knew his conscience would haunt him, like a curse.

And everyone who sees you is going to know.

Lori had told him long ago that his face was a mirror of his emotions, and that she could always tell what he was feeling by the look in his eyes. There were so many times in his adult life when those feelings had very nearly overwhelmed him. He had wept with happiness in the operating room when Sara and Kenneth were born, and had cried like a five-year-old boy in the intensive care ward at the hospital where his father had squeezed his hand, closed his eyes, and died.

"Oh God. I am so sorry. Please help me."

He folded his hands into a fist, pressed it hard against his chin.

You're praying for help because you killed a child. Someone's son.

The utter wrongness of it filled him with a new fear: the damnation of his soul; the certainty of judgment that would doom him at the end of his mortal life.

He reached into his pocket for his phone, tried to imagine what he would say if he called the police now, an hour and a half after the accident. Even if the alcohol was no longer detectable in his blood he would still be charged with hitting the boy and then driving away.

Sara and Kenneth have already lost their mother.

The reality was the same now as it had been at the scene of the accident.

And now they'll lose you.

He wondered if that would make any difference when the judgment came; if there was some kind of spiritual check-and-balance that could justify what he had done. It was a frail wish, sustainable by nothing but hope.

Somehow, you'll make up for this. Do something good with the rest of your life.

The thought rang hollow, like the cry of a coward. A man trying to justify a crime. But he held on to it as he thought through everything that would have to happen in the next few hours, the tactics that might protect him from the inevitable questions to come.

❄ ❄ ❄

A few days after moving into the new house Lori had spoken of throwing away the things they no longer used nor wore, including old denim and leather jackets from the years before the kids were born, and dresses and suits from her days at the ad agency. But her death had disrupted the plan, so they had all stayed in the basement, right where the movers had placed them. The box marked "costumes" was tucked into a corner, behind several others. The seam was still sealed with strapping tape and Stephen had to use a carpet knife to slice it open. In earlier years Halloween had been one of Lori's favorite celebrations, usually commemorated with costumes she had assembled herself. She had saved most of them over the years, right down to the action hero and princess get-ups that Kenneth and Sara had worn when they were in elementary school.

It took a bit of sifting to find the smaller box that he was looking for. It was from a company called StageEffects. Lori had found the company through her volunteer work with a local theatre group run out of the Silver Spring Boys & Girls Club, and had utilized quite a few of its offerings through the years.

He took what he needed and resealed the box with a new piece of tape, but put it back exactly where he had found it, thinking once again of the need to have everything as it had been hours before.

He then opened the boxes of clothing that had been slated for Goodwill. There was an old navy-blue jacket made of poly-fiber that had been a gift from his parents years earlier. The coat had been way too large and had never been worn. In the same box were half a dozen baseball caps and hats. He took the most non-descript—a black knit that could be folded down to his forehead and over his ears.

He went back upstairs and into his bedroom, where he put on two heavy sweaters and a hooded sweatshirt to be worn underneath the jacket. In the bathroom he turned the halogen lights all the way up and stood in front of the mirror and put on the glasses he had taken from Lori's box. They had an outdated tortoiseshell frame. The lenses were non-prescription but thick. Stephen vaguely remembered them being worn by a teenager in one of the plays Lori had directed. She had evidently saved them on the off-chance that she could talk him into actually dressing up for one of the costume parties they were always invited to at Halloween. She had given it a try every year, and every year he had begged off.

The sweater, sweatshirt and jacket made him look twenty pounds heavier. The knit cap completely covered his scalp and came down over his ears. The glasses didn't feel quite right, but without them he was almost certain that the shape and color of his eyes would give him away.

He checked his wallet to ensure he had enough cash, then turned out the lights and crept as quietly as possible back down the stairs. It was 4:30 a.m. now, probably the quietest time of the night. The squeal of the automatic door sounded like it would awaken every household on the street as it shuddered open and closed with a slow grinding sound behind him.

The closest Advance Auto store would have taken him a mere half hour to get to, even with the snow. But he had shopped there too often in the past. It took twice as long to reach the next location, in a neighborhood of strip malls and garden apartment complexes at the edge of Montgomery County.

There were only a handful of cars parked in the lot, most halfway buried under the night's snow. He parked between a white van and a pick-up truck, kept the engine running for warmth but turned off the headlights and waited. At a minute after 6 a.m. the store lights flickered on and a large black man unlocked the main doors from the inside.

Stephen got out of the car, realizing then that it was the worst possible time to be in a store. As the solitary customer there was a far greater chance that he would be remembered.

But he had no choice. He forced himself to keep walking toward the entrance.

A bell over the door announced his arrival. In his peripheral vision he saw the security camera pointing directly at him. With a visible shiver, he pulled the collar of his jacket a bit higher around his neck, and ducked his head, a gesture that hopefully made it even less likely that his face would be recognizable on tape.

The aisle marked LIGHTING had well-stocked shelves of headlight and taillight lenses and bulbs. He selected the lens cover that he needed and moved quickly to the register at the front of the store. With the box in his hand he considered the possibility that buying a singular item would also make him easier to remember, and turned toward the aisle containing waxes and cleaners.

The aisle ended in front of the store's large windows, which revealed a police car, moving slowly through the parking lot. He stood frozen in place as it pulled to a stop just a few feet from the Explorer.

He awkwardly stepped back and turned around. His thoughts raced as he walked back through the store. *They already know it was you. They have your license plate and your name. They're going to arrest you with the taillight in your hand. Right now. Right here.*

The aisles ran perpendicular to the front of the store, and he now stood at the front of the one that was farthest from the door, enabling him to view the police car less conspicuously. He watched as it made another slow circle of the parking lot and then drove on.

He took a deep breath, felt rivulets of perspiration sliding from his armpits and popping out around his neck. It was still dark outside. The store was probably seen as an easy target for robbery at this time of the morning. He told himself that the cop in the car was probably just going through his rounds, on patrol.

The clerk was now behind one of the registers, and was picking up the phone to make a call. A welcome distraction. Stephen pulled out his wallet and waited until he heard the man engaged in a conversation before moving quickly forward.

He was at the register, with his back to the door, when the bell announced another customer. Without thinking he turned around, and looked straight into the face of the cop.

His face flushed with heat as he jerkily looked away.

"Yeah we'll be open till five," the clerk was saying into the phone, and fumbling with a ring of keys at his belt. Stephen kept his back to the door and shifted his weight from one foot to the other as the clerk took a key and inserted it into the register. The clerk was nodding and listening intently to whatever was being said on the other end as the countertop scanner slowly pulsed with light. The monitor was tilted mostly toward the clerk but Stephen saw the words WARMING UP on the screen.

From the corner of his eye he saw the cop walking toward an aisle that was just a few feet from the registers. The muscles in his legs twitched as he reached into his wallet and pulled out a twenty-dollar bill.

The register screen was unchanged, the machine still not ready to work. He looked toward the door, contemplated the possibility of simply leaving without the cover, but put the cash on the counter instead.

The motion finally drew the clerk's attention. Stephen pointed to the price tag and briefly tapped his watch. The clerk frowned in annoyance. Stephen mouthed "sorry" and attempted a good-natured grimace and then said, "Keep the change. I have to go."

The clerk glanced down at the money and looked confused, the phone still at his ear, the register still warming up. Stephen looked for the cop and didn't see him, then took the box with the taillight cover and headed toward the door.

He felt as if he was floating as he stepped out into the cold, as vulnerable as a target in a shooting gallery with his ear cocked and ready for the voice of the cop telling him to stop and turn around. He managed *not* to run as he headed for the Explorer. The windshield had started to freeze over again. He cranked the heat and the defroster all the way up. It took a lifetime for the hot air to start melting the ice on the front windshield and rear window. He gunned the engine, flinching at the loudness of it in the near empty lot, his shoulders hunched forward as he drove toward the exit of the parking lot.

The sudden, shrill ring of his cell phone filled the air. He thought immediately of Sara, knocking on his bedroom door, finding his bed empty, and wondering where he would be. He had no sense of what he could say to her. No way to explain where he was. But he reached for the phone deep within the pocket of the oversized coat anyway, pulled it out and glanced at the incoming caller ID.

John Caruso

He stared at the screen. He remembered Caruso telling him that he lived in a cabin up on the mountain, which probably wasn't too far from where the boy had been struck; remembered trading cell phone numbers during their first conversation after Lori's death. Caruso was calling him at 6:15 on a Saturday morning, which could only mean that he knew about the death of the boy, and had already connected him to it.

He dropped the phone on the passenger seat without answering, forced himself to breathe as it continued to ring. The snow was falling heavier now, blowing in an onslaught at the front windshield, obscuring his vision of the pavement as he drove up the entrance ramp to the highway, still expecting the red revolving lights of the cop to appear in his rearview mirror. But after what felt like several miles he realized he had somehow escaped. He was driving alone amid the sparse early morning traffic, without any sense of direction at all.

He acted on reflex as he came up on the exit sign and made another hard right. The ramp emptied onto a road lined with office buildings. He turned into the first parking lot he saw.

He cut the lights as he came to a stop, then picked up the phone. There was no message from Caruso. But the man's name on the "missed calls" screen proved he was already in the detective's sights.

He leaned forward, with an iron grip on the wheel. The sensations of the last several minutes cycled like a nightmare through his mind. The straight-on eye contact with the cop; the twitch in his cheek as he gave the twenty to the clerk; the fear that one or both men would see his car racing away from the parking lot.

He glanced up at his reflection in the rearview mirror, and saw the alien reflection of himself in the glasses. Once again he felt cast-off and adrift, with every action taking him further away from the decent man he had been *before*—

He sat back, wiped the sweat from his forehead with his sleeve. Looked at the taillight cover in the passenger seat. The evidence of his criminality. His *guilt*.

You can't do this, he thought.

You have to stop it, right now.

❄ ❄ ❄

But there was no stopping. No going back. Stephen knew it for certain as he watched the first frail daylight in the eastern sky. The next steps were vital and he had counted on the cover of darkness to pull them off. Now every minute of the approaching dawn put him in greater danger.

It took more than ten minutes to find another strip mall. He drove back to the rear service entrances and saw the large dumpster, then scanned the one-story building's cinder block wall, checking for security cameras, and saw none. He stayed inside the car and quickly took off the coat, sweatshirt, knit hat, and sweaters and wadded them up and stuffed them into the black garbage bag that contained his loafers, then tied a knot at the top to keep it closed. He stepped out of the car wearing only his shirt and jeans and kept his gloves on as he opened the dumpster's heavy door. The dumpster was nearly full and the smell of the garbage inside made him gag as he leaned inside. There were several cardboard cartons on top. He took time to shift them around so they would cover the bag, and then tossed the glasses farther back. He pulled the heavy door down and flinched at the crashing sound of metal on metal as it shut.

He slipped into his barn coat and pulled on a new pair of gloves and drove as quickly as he could manage across the icy parking lot to get away. An hour later he reached the parking lot of the shopping center where he had stopped for the dinner ingredients the night before. There were just a handful of stores—the food market, a drycleaner, an art gallery, and two vacant spaces with For Lease signs in the windows. Tall old oaks and a low fieldstone fence that had been designed to give the center a rural ambiance also shielded it from easy view of the adjacent boulevard.

He pulled in. The lot was lit by replicas of Victorian lampposts, set in concrete bases. There were no visible cameras on the lampposts or on the building, and he was relieved at the absence of cars in the parking lot. Chances were good that in just a few hours a cop would be standing right here, checking his story, and it would be only natural to talk to the shopkeepers in search of any recollections that worked against it.

For now the storefronts were still dark, and he could only hope that he wasn't being watched as he backed up to within inches of one of the concrete bases that held a lamppost, realizing how inexact his measurements were going to be. He then set out to create the fender-bender exactly as it might have happened, visualizing himself driving across the already-slippery surface of the lot for his last-minute shopping, turning the wheel and backing up without gauging how close he was to the lamppost, tapping the brakes, sliding on the ice…and hitting the gas.

He barely heard the impact against the concrete, but looked anxiously back toward the storefronts, half-expecting to see someone at a window. After several seconds of silence he stepped out and checked the damage.

The dent was now twice as large, and it was impossible at a glance to tell which damage might have been caused by the impact against the boy's body and the impact with the concrete.

He heard the sound of a bus approaching from the distance. Traffic on the adjacent boulevard was picking up. Saturday mornings were busy in the surrounding neighborhoods—a catch-up time for errands that couldn't be completed during the week. Traffic wasn't heavy yet, but there would be plenty of other vehicles, driven by other potential witnesses, on the road home.

He was nearly overcome by fatigue as he slipped back into the driver's seat, the exhaustion weighing on his eyelids and numbing his mind. He briskly rubbed his cheeks as he restarted the engine and headed out of the lot. He drove with extreme caution at the edge of the speed limit, anxious to avoid suspicion with so much of the evidence against him right there in the car.

His neighborhood was a still life when he arrived; the wide streets empty of traffic and the houses buried up to the first floor windowsills in fresh white snow. He stopped looking in the rearview mirror as he approached his own street, focused only on what he needed to do now.

Pull in the garage. Close the door. Replace the taillight cover and stash the old one in a trash bag.

He tapped the brakes and drove carefully into the garage and pushed the button on the visor to close the automatic door. The squeal of the damaged motor made him wince as the door started down, and descended no more than two feet before coming to a stop.

He stepped out of the car and pushed the button on the visor again. Instead of continuing down the door went back up.

"Come on." His teeth were clenched as he hit the button once more. There was another sharp squeal and a slow grinding of gears as the door started down and then stopped again. This time when he pushed the button there was no reaction; nothing but the slight smell of burning oil in the air.

Groaning, fighting another wave of fatigue, he hit the door with his fist. It had stopped six inches above the rear bumper, leaving the broken taillight cover exposed to the street.

He heard the crunch of tires on the snow, and without thinking squatted down.

Headlights flashed into his eyes as a Frederick County Sheriff's car pulled into the driveway, with John Caruso behind the wheel.

15

Caruso spotted Stephen Porter's car as he turned onto the street, but he was a block away when Porter turned into his driveway. Even so he was certain that he saw damage to the side panel near the vehicle's rear end an instant before the garage door came down.

For a long moment he stood in the cold air and tried to imagine what Stephen was doing inside the garage. And then he sensed movement at one of the second floor windows, and looked up to see Sara Porter looking down at him.

Caruso had met the Porter kids twice—first at Lori Porter's funeral, where he had simply said hello, and then during an official visit to the Porter house, where, in the presence of their father, he had asked a handful of questions about their mother and what she had been doing on the day that she had died.

This morning he caught only a glimpse of Sara before the curtain fluttered shut. And then the front door opened and Stephen Porter looked out, appearing gaunt and exhausted, as if he'd been up all night.

❄ ❄ ❄

Stephen was trembling uncontrollably as he went from the garage to the family room and then to the foyer, where he opened the door and watched John Caruso step up to the front porch.

"Hello Stephen."

Caruso's voice was quiet, with a reluctant tone.

"John—hi."

The detective's first name was a stark reminder of the rapport during the interviews after Lori's death, when he had been the innocent widower, and Caruso had been the supportive cop.

"I'd like to talk with you," Caruso said.

He shifted his weight, so that his body took up more of the open doorway; then looked down at his watch and noticed that his hands were still shaking. "It's seven in the morning."

"I know that," Caruso widened his stance, as if to send the message that he wasn't budging.

Stephen nodded, knowing he had to acquiesce, and stepped aside. Caruso carefully wiped his snow-covered hiking boots on the mat before coming in. He was wearing jeans and a ski jacket and there were dark circles under his brown eyes. His posture and bearing made the visit feel official but when their eyes met again Stephen saw no sense of aggression.

Caruso looked past him, toward the stairs, and then nodded toward the first floor study. "Can we step in here? I need to ask you some questions."

"Questions about what?"

Caruso went in without answering. Stephen followed, and shut the door.

"I called you about an hour ago," Caruso said. "Aren't you curious about why?"

Stephen turned and tried to meet his eyes; tried to look confused as he absently reached into his coat pocket and grasped the phone. "I didn't know that. I must have the ringer off."

Caruso looked as if he was waiting for him to say something more.

"So why *were* you calling?" he asked.

"At 12:39 this morning you called 911 and reported that your daughter was at an address on Short Mountain. You wanted the police to respond. I need to know what happened next."

Stephen cleared his throat, and answered the question as he had planned.

"That's right. Sara called me and said she was stranded at a friend's house and wanted to come home. I was worried. She sounded like she was in trouble and I wasn't sure I could make it through the snow. So I asked for help. But I wasn't sure if the police could get to her so I went out to pick her up myself."

Caruso nodded. "What happened then?"

"*Nothing*."

The response came out too quickly. He took another breath, his mouth as dry as cotton. "I went to the house where she called me from. I picked her up and brought her home."

Caruso continued staring at him.

"Her Jeep wouldn't start, so we left it there. I went out this morning to try and find a store where I could get salt for the driveway. I didn't find anything open this early, so I came back home."

"What about the damage to your car?"

"Why are you asking?"

"It's a simple question. What happened?"

He frowned, doing his best to look confused. "I'm not sure what's going on, John. My daughter's home. She's okay. Why are you here?"

"Your daughter was at the home of a teacher from Langford Secondary last night. Kieran O'Shea. Has she ever discussed him with you?"

A teacher? "No, she hasn't."

"What time did you pick Sara up?"

Stephen paused. "I don't...remember exactly. It was the middle of the night. I had to drive through a blizzard to get up there. I wasn't paying much attention to the time."

"I need to know exactly what happened on the way there and the way back."

He thought again of the heavy snow on the mountain, the absence of traffic and witnesses, and the steps he had taken since arriving home, and allowed himself a small measure of hope that Caruso was putting on a bluff; that he wasn't already *trapped*—

"I told you, nothing happened. I picked Sara up and brought her home. She's still asleep upstairs. Everything is fine."

Caruso said nothing, but with the slight shake of his head and the sagging of his shoulders he made it clear that the story wasn't holding up.

"John..." His voice was a strangled whisper. "What's going on here?"

"Kieran O'Shea has a younger brother, who was a student at Langford," Caruso said. "His name was Aidan. A few hours ago he was hit by a car. The driver of the car left the scene. Aidan's dead."

He exhaled, feeling suddenly lightheaded. He had known it was coming but Caruso's declaration hit him like a punch to the gut. He stood as still as a statue, still grappling with how to respond as the study door opened.

Sara stood at the threshold, her eyes filling with tears.

She's been standing at the door, he realized. *She heard all of this*—

"Oh my God...Dad!"

"Sara—" He stepped toward her, and pulled her into an embrace.

"I need to take a look at your car," Caruso said.

He held her tighter, as if she could save him from the walk into the garage, where Caruso would immediately see the damaged bumper, the broken tail light cover, and the replacement, still in its new packaging—

And realized in an instant how to stop it from happening.

"John, my daughter is very upset. This is a shock. Please, can you come back later?"

"No," Caruso said. "I'm sorry Stephen. I need to see your car now."

He shook his head. "No, I need to take care of my daughter now."

"I'm not stopping you from *taking care of your daughter*." Caruso sighed and crossed his arms over his chest. "I'll come back with a warrant if I have to."

He willed his voice to be steady. "All right, if that's what you have to do."

Caruso looked gravely disappointed. "I could have seized your car already based on what I know. But I wanted to have this conversation—to give you a chance to tell me what happened first. I'm asking you now to please cooperate with me. You're only going to make it harder on yourself if you don't."

He continued holding Sara; fearful that she would break the embrace and leave him alone, with no excuse to push Caruso out. He also knew that telling Caruso he would *have to* have a warrant to inspect the car was the worst possible move; an acknowledgment that he had something to hide and would use his legal *rights* to do so.

But you can't let him in there.

He tightened the embrace, and stared down at the floor.

Have to get him out of the house.

"I'm sorry John, but you need to leave. We need to be alone."

Caruso's posture stiffened. There was no longer any sense of friendship in his eyes.

"All right Stephen, but you know I'll be back. Soon."

Sara looked up at him, her mouth moving soundlessly, as if any second she would blurt out something to doom him completely.

Stephen stared back at her, silently imploring her to remain silent.

After several seconds the moment seemed to pass. Sara turned around to face Caruso. For an instant Stephen thought that she might openly defend him, but she said nothing as the tears rolled down her face.

Caruso backed reluctantly into the foyer, and left the front door wide open as he stepped outside. The frigid air swept into the study as Sara turned and walked silently back to her room.

16

Caruso went back to his patrol car and did what he had to do. It took ten minutes with his laptop to finish typing up the request for a warrant to seize Stephen Porter's Ford Explorer, but less than two minutes to get a Frederick County Sheriff's Deputy to the scene. Caruso stayed in Porter's driveway as he instructed the deputy to park in front of the Porter house until the warrant came through, and to follow Porter if he left the house and report back if he saw visual damage to the vehicle.

And then he sat for several more minutes, massaging his temples, running back through the conversation inside the house and trying to imagine how Stephen Porter could have struck a teenaged boy and left him at the side of the road; his thoughts bringing him back once again to the same conclusion.

He knew Aidan was dead, and panicked.

And then he went to rescue his daughter—

From Kieran O'Shea.

Who might have been involved in the death of his wife.

He sat back, remembering O'Shea's dilated pupils and delayed, slurred speech at the accident scene. Instincts and circumstances told him that Kieran had seen it happen. But Kieran had claimed otherwise—and said he had simply discovered Aidan lying beside the road. So instead of being able to tell Porter there was a witness, he had merely been able to refer to the circumstances that had put

Porter there—and hope that he fell apart under the pressure of their suspicion.

Which might have happened, Caruso thought, if Sara Porter hadn't broken his rhythm.

He thought about the 911 recording that he had listened to several times before heading out to Porter's house. He had heard the desperation in Stephen's voice, and understood Stephen's obvious belief that he had no choice but to drive out into the storm to rescue her.

Because you would have too, he thought, knowing it for certain as he thought of his own son. As often happened when he was exhausted from the job, his thoughts went immediately back to the days when the illness was first revealed: Elliott's fainting spells at preschool; the pale skin that began to bruise at the slightest touch; the all-too-frequent complaint—"*I'm ti-werd daddy*," in Elliott's hoarse little-boy voice.

Caruso had just turned twenty-three when the diagnosis was made, an age of transition from college graduation to induction as a Frederick County Sheriff's Deputy. He had purposefully developed a mindset that reflected the stoic, disciplined bearing that deputies were expected to project. Life was all about the conveyance of law and order on the job; the can-do spirit at the scenes of traffic accidents and natural disasters; the ideals of public service. It was a mindset that carried over into his reactions to the diagnosis—the commitment to be emotionally impenetrable.

Looking back, he recognized the self-protective value of that mindset during the nine months of searching for new and better treatments for Elliot's condition, insisting all the while to Cassie and everyone else that their son would "beat this" even though he knew it wasn't true; telling no one but God that he would have driven a knife into the center of his own heart if it would have saved Elliott's life.

So, yes, Stephen, I understand, he thought.

You did what you had to do for your daughter.

He looked at the closed garage door again, a temporary protection of the evidence that was bound to put Stephen Porter away.

But it won't stop me from doing what I have to do now.

He sighed, feeling sadly aware of Stephen's plight, a sense of weakness making him question his true ability to maintain the law-and-order responsibility of the job.

And then he felt the vibration of his phone in his pocket, conveying a text from Niles, who had been sent up to the mountain to be there as the techs processed the scene:

All kinds of problems here.

Will wait for you to come back up.

17

Kieran drove the pickup down the mountain with the speakers blaring, the windows vibrating with the crash and bang of heavy metal; the screaming lyrics fueling thoughts of retribution as a cacophony of voices—like hundreds of people shouting in a crowded, cavernous room—filled his mind.

He leaned forward, clenching his jaw until the voices faded away, then reached into his pocket and pulled out Sara's phone, which he had found beneath the cushions of his couch where she had been sitting during Aidan's reading lesson. He thought about calling her. Telling her what he had *not* told Detective John Caruso. Telling her what her father had done.

Caruso had clearly been confused about why he hadn't said anything about Stephen Porter running Aidan down, even after Caruso had mentioned Sara, telling him he somehow knew she had been at his house. But from the moment he had seen Porter drive away he had known that simply turning him over to Caruso would never be enough.

That little girl of yours was really getting hot when we were lying there, Stephen.

I had three fingers up inside her—had her squirming like a bitch in heat.

He stared out through the windshield, tears blurring his vision, and felt cold pressure at the back of his neck, knowing what was happening but desperate to *stop* it from happening as he heard the sound of short, rasping breaths in the back seat.

No.

Not there.

But Nurlene *was* there when he looked into the rearview mirror, the blood flowing down from the top of her misshapen head; a righteous, angry smile on to her face.

Cold and dead and cold and dead.

I can hurt him hurt him HURT him...

He shook his head with a violent motion that sent the truck into the oncoming lane. Nurlene's image vibrated and then vanished as he hit the brake and swerved back and then came to a skidding stop on the shoulder of the road.

His heart pounded with an erratic rhythm in his chest, his mind going back to the medical tests he had gone through years before; the memory of an MRI view of the top of his brain; identical twin hemispheres of gray against the black; two separate forces battling for control of his mind:

Killer.

Savior.

He felt the buzz of his phone, and knew it was Sara calling even before he glanced at the number on the screen. He turned down the noise from the speakers, and spoke in a near-whisper as he answered.

❄ ❄ ❄

Sara found it hard to breathe as she reached the top of the stairs and stepped into her room. She shut the door and locked it, her mind still fixed on the image of her father staring at her, silently *begging* her to say nothing as the detective grilled him about what had happened when he went to pick her up.

Moments later she was on her bed, in a fetal position and clutching a pillow as she remembered the scream of the smoke alarm and the sight of Aidan's empty bedroom. The detective—John Caruso—had said Aidan had been hit by a car and it was all too easy to imagine him lying in the road; her father standing over him—

No.

It must have been someone else.

The detective had said that Aidan had been killed "a few hours ago," so it could have been after her father had picked her up. And even if it had been in the middle of the night there had to have been other cars on the road—other drivers who could have hit Aidan and driven away. And yet she had known there was something wrong when she had gotten into the car and seen the stunned, *shocked* expression on her father's face.

She also remembered his absolute silence on the way home.

He couldn't even look at you.

Knowing what he had done.

She remembered the smell of alcohol on his breath and the dazed look on his face when he ordered her out of the car before they even went into the garage. Remembered feeling like something terrible had happened as she went up to her room and slipped underneath the covers of her bed.

She also remembered Kieran and Aidan wrestling, and Aidan running out without a coat into the snow. Kieran going after him, calling out his name.

And then she thought of the photos on his computer, which had worked their way into her dreams. She had awakened with a terrible feeling of loneliness, and had held the pillow tightly as she remembered the longing in Kieran's eyes as he held her in his arms, the slow, sensual touching…

She imagined him coming back into the house and finding her gone; imagined him alone, weeping over Aidan's death.

You need to be there with him, she thought. *Right now.*

Her legs shook as she got out of bed and checked her laptop. There were no instant messages. She still had no idea what had happened to her phone, but she had memorized Kieran's number months before. She tapped it into the landline phone alongside her bed.

It was answered on the second ring, but she heard only a raspy breathing sound.

"Kieran?"

She heard the rumble of his pick up truck, and then: "Sara."

She thought of her father, looking directly at the detective, *lying* to him.

"I know what happened," she said, without thinking. And when Kieran didn't respond she knew they both knew the truth.

She looked back at her bedroom door to make sure it was still closed, so neither Kenneth nor her father could hear what she said next.

"Oh God I'm so sorry Kieran. Please...*please* tell me what I can do."

❄ ❄ ❄

Stephen took two steps toward Sara's bedroom door and then stopped, his hands were hanging limply at his sides and his knees were so weak he had to lean against the wall for balance. He had planned to knock on her door; had planned to ask her all kinds of questions about Kieran O'Shea but now the whole conversation seemed futile. Any questions he asked would be followed by questions of her own. Questions seeded by the visit from Caruso, none of which he could answer with the truth.

He turned away from the door and headed toward his own bedroom. He gazed at the empty crystal glass on the table beside it and nearly collapsed on the bed.

And then he was praying, his hands clenched into a fist and pressed against his lips. Praying that John Caruso would not be able to prove he killed the boy. The room began to turn slowly around him and he heard the sound of his own heavy breathing as more images of the dead boy flashed through his mind. Once again he felt his palm against the boy's cold, still chest, heard the cry from the back of his throat as the boy's head tilted…

And then suddenly he was sitting up, his spine ramrod straight as he stared into the dresser mirror across the room. He barely recognized the terrified old man who gazed back. From somewhere outside the window he heard the rumbling growl of an engine being revved in the driveway.

He got up and went to the window. There was a Frederick County Sheriff's car parked like a sentry across the street. And a black pick-up truck was pulling into the driveway. Its windows were filmed with salt from the roads but the driver was visible behind the wheel. It was a man with long black hair and pale white skin and he held a cell phone to his ear.

Stephen leaned forward, angling for a better look. At that instant his own cell phone began to ring. The sound was distant, surreal.

He went back to the bedside table and picked it up. The call was coming from Sara's cell phone, which she had lost.

He answered, "Hello."

He heard loud rock music, and a slow, labored breathing sound. He kept the phone at his ear as he went back to the window.

"You killed my brother."

He felt the blood rushing from his face, leaned against the wall to keep from falling down.

"I saw you," the caller said. "I was right there."

He heard the front door of the house open and shut, and then watched as Sara stepped out from the front porch and trudged through the snow. She was wearing the black cape-coat she had worn the night before. Her long black hair was loose and uncombed. She looked as if she had dressed quickly, haphazardly.

As Sara came closer the driver reached over and opened the truck's passenger side door. Screaming rock music from the inside of the truck filled the air.

Stephen slapped the window with the palm of his hand then frantically reached down to try and open it.

Sara pulled the passenger door shut, blunting the music's volume. The driver glanced up again as he revved the engine, then backed the truck into the cul-de-sac, spinning dirty snow beneath its wheels as he took her away.

PART THREE

18

Kenneth sat up in bed and listened to the muffled voices downstairs in the foyer. He still felt groggy as he went to the window and peered outside.

His heart jumped at the sight of the Frederick County Sheriff's car parked across the street.

And then it all came rushing back; Marco Niles' grip on his shoulder; Marco slamming him back against the wall; the talk with his father the night before.

And now the police were at his house. Getting a statement, probably. Something the Langford Secondary principal would review on Monday before deciding what to do with Marco Niles, whose father was a detective.

So it will be his version against yours.

He sat back down on the edge of the bed and thought of how everything would escalate in the hours ahead. By now there would be messages all over Facebook and Twitter, a whole new torrent of comments to follow the message Marco had sent out some time last night, the last thing he had read before the burst of tears that led to just a few hours of troubled sleep.

Stay away fag boy Porter

Far far away

Marco had hundreds of friends online; including plenty at Langford who had probably seen the message and were already sharing it all around.

Deciding you're an even bigger freak now. Someone to hate forever.

He touched his nose, which was still sore from Marco's punch, the culmination of weeks of glaring looks in the hallways of the school. Like Sara, he had almost known something was going to happen and for weeks had been determined to stay out of Marco's way; using back hallways or trudging outside and walking around the back of the school to get to his classes; making sure he was never alone or out of sight of at least one teacher when he stayed after school to work on the Art Wall; packing his own lunch and staying clear of the cafeteria where Marco would be sitting, surrounded by his crowd.

But the simple avoidance hadn't been enough. And now it obviously never would be. Tears spilled from his eyes and rolled down his cheeks, making him feel as *weak* as he had the moment Marco slammed him back against the cinder block wall.

His father was right. He was falling apart, like some kind of mental patient; like the reject that he was. So unlike Marco Niles, a boy who could bench press the entire stack in the school's weight room; a boy who already looked like a man as he moved through the hallways, commanding friends and followers. The most popular guy in school.

His head felt light, disconnected from his body as he sat down on the edge of the bed. He felt a tightness at the base of his throat; the threat of more crybaby tears.

You can't live like this. He reached for the pillow, brought it close to his body, and pressed his face against it to stifle the sobs. He knew from experience it was the only thing he could do—crying till his tear ducts were emptied and the memories loosened their grip on his mind. He became barely conscious of the minutes slipping by as his eyelids grew heavy, and felt himself slipping into the netherworld at the edge of sleep as the rumble of a heavy engine in the driveway filled the room.

The sound was loud, jarring, drawing him back to the window, and the sight of Sara getting into a black truck, with Mr. O'Shea, the teacher, behind the wheel.

❄ ❄ ❄

Madison Reidy woke to needling pain in her temples and a sour taste in her throat. Her sleep had been sporadic and filled with images of what had happened in the hours before she had trudged home in the snow and locked her bedroom door and crawled underneath the blankets. Alone now, as the late morning light filled her room, she hoped the heaviness in her head would keep the memories deadened, tamped down. Yet they twitched to life as the vestiges of sleep faded away.

Memories of early evening: the spur of the moment decision to stop by Marco's house without texting him first. The shock of seeing him at the door, his face swollen, his left eye surrounded by a horrible purple-black bruise. For one surreal moment she thought of the fight with Kenneth Porter, which Marco had walked away from unscathed, before realizing that, once again, he had been beaten by his father.

The desire to simply comfort him had come to her first. A fresh towel filled with ice for the swelling. One of the Percocet that she had lifted from her mother's prescription drawer and hidden in the aspirin bottle in her purse. A half hour of peace as she rubbed the back of his neck before he decided he needed something more.

The coke had come out next; Marco evidently deciding his supply was endless as he laid out four long lines on the table and snorted three before offering her the last. And then suddenly he was wide awake and alert and interested in nothing more than a night of drinking when his friends Darrell and Sean dropped by with a bottle of tequila, both of them telling Marco to "chill out" over and over, which only made him more anxious as the night wore on.

Darrell and Sean's surprise arrival had made her angry even before Marco had decided to ignore her. She had first tried to get his attention by being pouty, and when that didn't work she had tried whispering into his ear, promising him a night he would never forget once he told Darrell and Sean to leave.

Yet he had continued pretending she wasn't even there, even when she went over to Darrell and sat on his lap and then asked him if he wanted to go upstairs, assuming that Marco would see it happening and realize then that she wouldn't be taken for granted. But Marco had barely noticed Darrell grabbing her ass and didn't even seem to hear her loud laughter on the stairs that went up to the bedrooms. Then, because she had already basically committed to it, she had followed through with the implied promise by gripping Darrell by the belt and leading him into one of the second floor guest rooms, where he had immediately started in with slobbering, open-mouthed kisses. Then he had started fingering her, roughly, before a few seconds of premature humping and then cumming in his underwear.

Followed by an uncomfortable silence as he left her on the bed and went into the adjoining bathroom to clean himself up.

She remembered going into the same bathroom after he went downstairs and looking into the mirror and feeling like she wanted to shatter it. But instead she had touched up her makeup and brushed out her hair and started to go back to the basement.

The sounds of explosions and screams had stopped her, the volume of whatever video game Marco and his friends were playing turned so high it hurt her ears as she stood at the top of the stairs.

She thought about going home but hated the idea of walking through the cold night and into an empty house, so she had wandered toward Marco's room instead. At first glance it looked the way it always had—there were clothes piled into every corner, posters of his favorite athletes on the walls, the unmade bed triggering erotic thoughts as she imagined him lying there, naked. But then she saw the things that were so clearly wrong: the cratered wall next to Marco's desk, which looked as if it had been hit with a sledgehammer; the wooden desk chair that was now missing a leg; the full-length mirror with the jagged vertical crack.

She stood in the doorway, knowing that she was probably the only person in the world who knew about the things that happened here. Marco had told her a few details about the last time his father had "lost his mind," and had fantasized about calling the police to turn him in. But they both knew that would never happen—knew that his father, a cop—would know exactly how to manipulate the legal system to save himself.

So instead he suffered, doing his best to get through his days and stay out of his father's way and channeling all of his energy into the things he could control. She knew that like all of the upper echelon athletes Marco lived for that big rush—the need to conquer, a need she felt just as strongly as she and the rest of the cheerleading squad cartwheeled and leapt through their routines; facing the crowds, rewarding whomever they chose with fetching glances and moments of eye contact that showed they were *noticed* by the popular girls everyone wanted as their friends…

Bitches.

In the end that's pretty much what they were. And despite the knowledge that she and the rest of the truly popular women of Langford Secondary lived under a well-deserved spotlight there were more and more moments, like this one, when she absolutely hated the person she was. She had still felt the semen of a boy she didn't even like clinging to her underwear and felt like gagging from the memory of his tongue in her mouth. She only felt sicker knowing that Darrell had almost certainly gone back to Marco and told him what he had done. It wasn't hard at all to imagine them laughing, jeeringly, and quickly turning their attention back to whatever filled the giant screen in Marco's basement.

She had intended to walk out of Marco's bedroom right then, had planned to just grab her coat and stomp out into the night without another word, but had stood in front of Marco's laptop instead. He was still logged on and the temptation to spy had been overwhelming. With one more glance at the door she had given in—

And seen the messages he had posted on Kenneth Porter's Facebook wall.

Stay away fag boy Porter

Far far away

She wanted to laugh about it now, but felt a sense of shame as she thought of Kenneth showing both her and Marco through his house a few days after the Porters had moved in. She remembered Kenneth telling them he wanted to be "an artist" and the nervous twitch on his face when Marco jokingly asked "You're not a fag, are you?" She had realized then that Sara and Kenneth would never have what it took to be popular, and that any semblance of a friendship with them could seriously threaten her own standing. From that point on it had been easy to find reasons to shun both of them and make sure that anyone else who mattered did the same, especially after Sara and Kenneth's mother killed herself, which basically proved there was something wrong with the whole family.

But Sara hadn't left it alone. Yesterday, after months of being blatantly ignored, she had finally snapped, sending the text message that fired back.

You really are a whore Madison. I never even wanted to be your friend.

Which had immediately prompted her revenge. The few words about Kenneth Porter that she had guessed, correctly, would fill Marco with rage. The accusation that led Marco to beat Kenneth up.

And now, as she stared at her tired face in her own bathroom mirror, she thought that maybe it had all gone too far. The fight had been a big deal—something people talked about for the rest of the day. Marco's father would be enraged—an especially scary thought since Marco already believed that one day the man might lose control completely and actually murder him. "You'll hear about it afterwards," he had said. "Some kind of terrible accident, but there's no way in Hell anything will happen to him."

The thought gave her a chill as she wrapped herself in her heaviest robe and went down the hall, past the doorway to her mother's bedroom, which was shut and would remain that way until noon or as long as it took to forestall yet another hangover.

The espresso machine was built into the cabinetry of the kitchen that her mother had had redesigned and upgraded with stainless steel "restaurant grade" appliances after her last divorce. It took just a minute to craft a double-sized cup. She took a sip and felt an instant jolt as she thought of Darrell Deane with his pants around his ankles while Marco remained downstairs, so totally oblivious…

"Oh Hell," she muttered, and went to the freezer and pulled out the bottle of Stoli, then poured and knocked back a quick, ice-cold shot. *For clarity*, she thought.

She took the espresso with her to the couch that faced the big flat screen TV. By habit she went straight to VH1. A video starring the latest pop sensation was on—featuring a girl who couldn't have been more than nineteen, gyrating in a weird dominatrix costume, surrounded by dancing men.

Queers, she thought, *like Kenneth Porter.*

There you go again.

She took a long hit of the espresso, felt it burn down her throat as she thought of Kenneth being thrown against the cinder block wall. Poor defenseless Kenneth, who still smiled shyly at her in the hallways, and still looked into her eyes with dumb confusion over why she shunned him.

The sudden sense of shame was overwhelming.

Nothing you can do now. She finished the espresso, and felt the first slight buzz from the liquor. *Get beyond it.*

She clicked through to MTV, which was showing a boring interview of another teen star, then kept clicking through Saturday morning cartoons. She landed on a local news station and started to keep going, but stopped at the sight of Aidan O'Shea, in a yearbook photo that filled the screen, and the sound of the news anchor's voice.

"Police sources say the boy was struck during the night by a hit-and-run driver."

She leaned forward, and set the empty cup on the coffee table.

"He was pronounced dead at the scene."

The video switched to a shot of police cars on a snowy mountain road. She gazed at it for several seconds, her thoughts dulled by the vodka buzz, before her mind filled with the memory of Aidan O'Shea with Sara Porter, in the tutoring center at school. She had seen them there for the first time on her way to cheerleading practice just two weeks after Sara's mother drove her car off a cliff on the mountain. Sara was helping Aidan with homework, and Kieran O'Shea was watching them. Kieran's smile was easy and relaxed as he leaned down and patted Sara on the shoulder then kept his hand there; a paternal gesture. The *good* teacher acknowledging the *good* girl; Sara looking freaky as usual in her gothic black and tinted hair but undeniably *sweet* for all the time she was spending with Kieran's autistic brother.

But now Aidan was dead; run down by a car in the middle of the night.

The screen filled once again with Aidan's photo from last year's yearbook. She tasted the bitterness deep in her throat; glanced at her reflection in the vague early morning light in the panels of the French door and had the strange sensation of seeing herself as someone else might have; haggard and ugly and at the edge of falling apart as she stared at the dead boy's photo.

But she wasn't crying for Aidan…not really. She was crying—nearly *weeping* now—because of the image looming bigger in her mind: *Sara* and Aidan, in the tutoring lab. Sweet, shy, awkward Sara, who spent her own time trying to make an autistic boy's life better simply because she cared about him. Sara, who was loyal enough to her loser brother to walk into a fight and try to save him.

The opposite of you in every way.

The tears were coming faster now, and with them the hiccups that always gave her a panicky feeling as she tried to catch her breath.

She brought her knees up to her chest; covered her face with her hands, felt powerless against the sobs that wracked her body; felt completely alone.

She cried for several minutes, until the room became a teary blur around her, and then in the back of her mind saw herself walking home alone, trudging through the knee-deep snow without once looking back at Marco's house behind her. At the time she had been certain that he hadn't even noticed that she had left. And hadn't cared.

But maybe he did. She grasped at the idea like a lifeline, let her mind form an image of Marco going back upstairs, looking for her, *missing* her.

Of course it was possible. The last time they had had sex he had come twice; and had covered her face with kisses when it was over. A reaction completely at odds with the way he had treated her the night before.

He was drinking, tooting up. That's the only reason why.

She let herself imagine the idea of him being alone—and lonely. Thinking of her as she was thinking of him. And then without allowing herself to think anymore she pulled the phone out of her pocket tapped a text message:

I'm alone. Downstairs at my house. I WANT you. Come now PLEASE.

In the memory of the phone she had a photo of herself, her breasts exposed, her hand beneath the waist of her panties. Marco had taken it just a few days before, and then, minutes later, had made love to her standing up, against the wall of her basement family room.

She attached the photo to the message.

And hit *send.*

19

Caruso drove carefully over the slick road that led back up the mountain, his thoughts fixated on the text from Niles, which affirmed that the crime scene was compromised by the weather, the remote location, and the more than two hours it had taken for the tech team to get there.

Which made it all the more crucial to obtain physical evidence, which could include Aidan's blood, or fibers from his clothing, or flecks of paint that could be matched to Porter's vehicle.

The sign marked "Rolling Road" was nearly concealed by the heavy snowfall. He slowed and started to make the turn when he saw a white vehicle crest the steep hill a hundred yards ahead. There was a brief moment of eye contact with the driver before the vehicle abruptly slowed. Caruso instinctively did the same.

He then lowered his driver's side window and stuck his left hand out, his palm forward, motioning for the vehicle to stop.

The driver wore glasses in a tortoiseshell frame, but even from the distance Caruso saw the wariness in her eyes. He responded with what he hoped was a calm, disarming look. *Keep it friendly*, he thought. *As if you're nothing more than a helpful cop*.

As directed, she stopped when they were parallel, and lowered her window. Up close her eyes were bloodshot, as they had been a week before, when Caruso had questioned her for the third time. Her name was April Devon, and she was the woman Lori Porter had planned to meet with on the night she died. The interview, like the one before it, had left him feeling certain that she was holding something back.

He faced her through the open window, feeling momentarily invigorated by the cold air.

"I guess you heard," he said.

She nodded. "I saw the story on the news this morning. It was a hit and run?"

"Looks that way." He glanced down at the logo—A STITCH IN TIME—on the driver's side door of her Kia Sorrento, a cross between an SUV and a minivan, suitable for delivering pieces of furniture and fabrics and for navigating the steep mountain terrain. According to what April had told him, and backed up by what he had researched online, she had run the business from her home in Fairfax, Virginia for several years before recently moving to a home on the mountain. She advertised in local circulars and online and did most of her work in the house's large living room, which had a panoramic view of the valley below the mountain.

That house was less than a mile away.

"I don't suppose you saw anything," he said.

"When?"

"Last night. When it happened."

She lowered her hands from the steering wheel. "No. I was snowed in like everyone else up here."

His mind skipped through her answers to his previous questions about Lori Porter, who had hired April to make curtains and slipcovers for the Porter home. April had first told him they were merely acquaintances, but her eyes had filled with tears as she recounted her movements on the night Lori died.

She glanced to her left, toward the Rolling Road intersection. "Do you have any idea who did it?"

"Maybe. We're still investigating."

He paused, and waited until she looked at him again.

"This is the third bad thing to happen on the mountain in five months," he said.

She looked down at her lap.

"So far the death of Lori Porter's the only investigation that's been concluded."

She looked up. "What do you mean?"

"It's a suicide, officially. Because that's the only option I have."

Her jaw tensed.

"You look like you don't believe it."

"No."

"But you're sure there's nothing else you can tell me."

She shook her head, which left him with the same odd sequence of events he had grappled with from the beginning—that Lori Porter had left her home at 8 p.m. and driven up Short Mountain in the middle of a torrential thunderstorm simply because she wanted to take a look at some fabric samples.

April brought her hands back to the wheel, and flexed her fingers in a nervous gesture. "I heard about the teacher at the high school."

"Yeah. Another tragedy," he said, watching her carefully as he added. "And so similar to the murder that happened the night Lori—"

"I *know* that."

He nearly winced at the sharpness of her tone.

"So…" he said, and paused.

"What?"

"There's still nothing else?"

She shook her head again, looking annoyed now. "I need to get going. Have to take some pieces into town."

"Didn't mean to hold you up," he said. "Just want you to know the door's always open. If you think of anything more."

"I've told you everything I can think of."

"You sure?"

His tone was more accusatory than he intended, but she met his eyes with a stoic expression, and nodded.

"All right then," he said. He stayed put as her window came up, and then proceeded toward the turn off to Rolling Road. He slowed to a crawl as he approached the scene, now blocked off by the van used by the tech team and patrol cars from the Frederick County Sheriff's office, and one of the Hummers that Niles drove.

Niles was sitting inside the Hummer, watching as the technicians finished up. He stepped out as Caruso pulled to a stop. There was a prominent bruise on his cheek that hadn't been there the day before, and his balance was a bit unsteady as he walked toward the car. Caruso might have believed his awkward gait and red eyes were a result of being up all night, but he caught the faint whiff of booze when Niles was two feet away.

The conversation that followed wound its way through everything that was wrong with the scene, including the techs' inability to get decent tire prints from the skid marks that Caruso had tried to protect, and the lack of physical evidence—paint, plastic, glass or metal—that could be tied to the striking vehicle.

"So without a witness..." Niles said, as his eyes strayed farther up the road, toward Kieran O'Shea's house. He had one hand resting on the top of the patrol car, as if he needed it for support. The other was deep within the pocket of his parka. Caruso wondered if there was a bottle of liquor in there, or if it was sitting underneath the driver's seat, because there was no doubt about Niles' condition.

As a higher-ranking detective he considered asking Niles for his gun and insisting he ride down the mountain in the passenger seat of the patrol car. But then Niles derailed his train of thought:

"So what did Porter have to say?"

Caruso took a moment before responding. Because they were partners in the investigation of Aidan O'Shea's death, he had had no choice but to tell Niles about Porter's middle-of-the-night 911 call about his daughter being stranded at the O'Shea residence.

"He's scared," Caruso said.

Niles gave him a wry smile. "Ya' think?"

He felt a flash of anger. "It's nothing to joke about."

The smile became a sneer. "Relax man. Just tellin' it like it is."

Caruso paused, making conscious effort to breathe, knowing he needed to be alone with his thoughts, and away from Niles. He glanced toward his Blazer, which he had parked over the skid marks in the effort to protect them from the falling snow hours earlier. It was now parked farther up Rolling Road. It would be up to a deputy to bring it back down to town once the processing of the scene was completed.

"I want you to stay up here until the guys pack everything up," he said.

Niles flushed. "That an order?"

Caruso felt a twitch in his cheek. "Yeah," he said, and hit the button to roll up the window, then did a three-quarter turn at a speed that was a bit faster than it should have been and headed back down the mountain.

The deputy he had placed in front of Porter's house called two minutes later.

"You wanted me to check in if anything happened," he said.

"That's right. Has he tried to leave?"

"No, but he had a visitor. In a black Ford F-150 pickup. It pulled into the driveway and sat there for a couple of minutes before a teenaged girl came out of the house."

Caruso's hands tensed on the wheel.

"The driver was a white male, late twenties. I ran the plate—"

"I know who the driver was. What did you do next?"

"You told me to stay here. But I thought it looked a little funny, and wanted you to know."

"Smart," Caruso said. "Anything else?"

The deputy paused. "Not really. Except the vehicle's registered to a residence on Short Mountain but I thought the driver was headed to another place in the development. Instead of going out toward the front gate he went farther down the street and turned toward the part that's still under construction."

Caruso vaguely remembered the layout of the new subdivision where the Porters lived. The front entrance was built around a grand stone gate. The other entrance was at a section with several vacant lots still for sale.

So he went out the back way, Caruso thought.

But to where?

He had planned on going back to headquarters and waiting there until the warrant to seize Porter's car came through, but quickly changed his mind.

"I'm going to put a BOLO out on the 150," he said. "The girl might be in danger. Stay put and let me know if anything else happens."

He hung up. Twenty minutes later he was back in Stephen Porter's neighborhood again. A road crew had given the subdivision's streets one run of the plows, which had piled the snow up high enough to block in most of the cars parked at the curbs, but the road surface was still slick. He drove cautiously as he passed the big houses, toward the street where Stephen Porter lived.

Half a block ahead, a wide, boxy SUV was approaching the intersection from a side street, moving way too fast for the icy pavement. The driver ignored the stop sign, and the car's back end slid sideways as it turned into the intersection, the driver just barely in control.

"Whoa," Caruso said, and watched as the car continued on, down the center of the road.

He turned on the flashing red lights. The driver was slow to react and maintained his speed. It took two blasts of the siren before the vehicle pulled over.

It was a Hummer, tricked-out with extra chrome and a three-tone silver-gray-blue paint job.

He stepped out and approached from the driver's side. The driver was a teenaged boy. He scowled as Caruso approached. His right eye had a massive shiner—with a black crescent at the top of the cheekbone and a smattering of burst capillaries beneath the yellowed skin.

Caruso stopped four feet from the driver's side door and motioned for him to lower the window.

The teenager waited several moments before complying. Caruso caught the sweet, heavy smell of marijuana driving out of the car's interior as the glass came down.

"Step out of your vehicle," he said.

The boy's stare drifted forward. He looked as if he was gauging the distance between his front bumper and the patrol car's back end; as if he was an instant away from ramming the patrol car and trying to pull away.

Go ahead and try it, Caruso thought, but said instead:

"You heard me. *Out*."

The boy waited just a few more seconds before opening the door, and slowly complied.

20

Stephen sat on the bed, his hands gripping his knees as Kieran O'Shea's last words cycled through his mind.

"You killed my brother."

"I saw you..."

He turned away from the window and went into the second floor study. The computer was in sleep mode. He powered it up and went to Google and typed in Kieran O'Shea. The web site showing the Langford Secondary faculty was the first page that came up. O'Shea faced the camera in his head shot. His skin was pale. His eyes were blue; his hair black and long, and parted at the center.

There was minimal text underneath the photo: just "Kieran O'Shea is a teaching team leader of Langford Secondary's Trade and Technical Academy."

Stephen scrolled through the rest of the site. He saw nothing beyond the short bio. And then he went to the first of several stories from the *Frederick News Post.*

WOMAN DIES AFTER FALL ON ICE.

He clicked the link. There was a photo with the article, a shot of a woman's face, staring straight at the camera, unsmiling, looking angry. She looked very much like Kieran O'Shea—with the same pale skin and black hair. Her eyes were lighter, and they looked puffy and red in the photo, as if she had been crying.

The text of the story was written like Associated Press copy, with short sentences that simply listed facts. Nurlene O'Shea, aged thirty-seven, had died from a head injury at a house located at 4334 Rolling Road. Frederick Sheriff's deputies and paramedics had responded to a 911 call placed by her son, Kieran O'Shea, and had found her on the concrete steps outside the kitchen door. The stairs were slick from an ice storm. She was pronounced dead at the scene.

The story had a quote from John Caruso, who was a deputy at the time, and who was the first responder to the call from Kieran.

Stephen gazed at the quote—"*Both boys were shaken up, and it wasn't the first time*"—which made it clear that Caruso and O'Shea had known each other for years.

He focused on the photo of Nurlene O'Shea next. She looked like a big woman, and only slightly more feminine than Kieran O'Shea. The story was dated—her death had occurred on a January night ten years earlier. Kieran O'Shea looked to be in his mid twenties now, based on the Langford Secondary teacher page photo. So he had been a teenager when she died.

He went back to the search page. Typed Nurlene O'Shea into the box, and gazed at links to several more newspaper stories.

FREDERICK WOMAN CHARGED WITH DUI

SOCIAL WORKERS ALLEGE CHILD ABUSE IN FREDERICK HOME

MOTHER PLEADS NOT GUILTY TO ABUSE CHARGES

Stephen's agitation intensified as he read through the nightmarish depictions of the things that had happened at the house on Rolling Road. He felt a line of sweat dripping down his right temple as he thought about the call from O'Shea; the implied threat in O'Shea's words and tone.

You have to call him back. Find out what he wants.

He went to the last incoming number, from Sara's cell.

It was answered on the third ring, but without a greeting; just the sound of steady breathing.

"Hello?" Stephen said.

The breathing sound continued.

"Is someone there?"

"What do you want?"

He looked down at the driveway, and at the pickup tire tracks in the snow.

"Is my daughter with you?"

There were several seconds of silence, and then, "Yes, I have her."

"Can I talk to her?"

Silence on the other end.

"Please?"

"That really isn't possible."

He felt a rush of blood from his head, and grasped the woodwork at the edge of the window to steady himself.

"What do you want from me?" Stephen asked.

There was no response. After several seconds, he sat back down on the bed.

"Please, just *tell* me."

"I guess we should talk."

"All right. When?"

"Now's as good a time as any."

"Okay."

"But not on the phone."

"Where?"

"You know where I live."

"Yes," he said.

"Near there. Go on, a quarter mile or so past the house. There's a clearing at the side of Rolling Road. Be there in an hour, by yourself."

"Please tell me Sara is okay."

There was a long pause, and then:

"I can't tell you that."

He shut his eyes, and begged:

"Please don't hurt her."

"Like you hurt my brother?"

He felt a swelling at the back of his throat; fought to breathe. "Please—don't," he said.

"One hour. I'll be waiting."

❄ ❄ ❄

Kenneth was sitting at the breakfast bar when Stephen came down the back stairway that led to the open family room. He was drinking black coffee. His eyes had the puffy look Stephen recognized when his son had stayed up too late.

"Morning, Kenny." He glanced at the clock on the wall. He had less than fifty minutes to get to the meeting place, but he took the time to come around Kenneth's back and wrapped his arms around his shoulders.

Kenneth stiffened but did not break away. Stephen looked toward the door that led to the garage, and thought about the Explorer being seized and examined.

What would an innocent man do? He tightened the embrace, and said:

"Something terrible happened last night. A boy from your school was hit by a car. He died."

Kenneth turned around. Stephen released him, and let his arms drop to his sides.

"His name was Aidan O'Shea," he said. "He has a brother who teaches there."

Kenneth nodded. "I know who Aidan is."

"I'm sorry Kenny."

It sounds like you just admitted something, he thought. He looked down at the floor, and then forced himself to meet his son's eyes again.

"Detective Caruso came by this morning. He wanted to talk to me because I had to go out last night and pick up Sara. She was at the house where the boy lived. The Jeep broke down and she needed a ride home."

He paused, and tried to concentrate on the storyline he would have to stick to.

"He knew I was in the area when the accident happened, because I had to get her, so they questioned me to see if I knew anything about it."

Kenneth gazed back at him, and frowned.

He's going to know you're lying, Stephen thought. *Once it all comes out—*

"I have to go out for awhile. There's cereal in the cabinet and milk in the fridge."

Kenneth looked distant, as if he was questioning everything Stephen had just told him.

"Are you okay Kenny? Feeling better this morning?"

Kenneth shrugged, and turned back around.

The silence lengthened.

"All right, I'll be back soon." Stephen headed toward the door to the garage.

"Where did Sara go?"

Stephen stopped walking, and slowly turned around.

"What do you mean?"

"She…left." Kenneth gave him an uncertain look, as if he had just ratted his sister out.

Stephen was once again conscious of the need to hold his tongue, knowing that at some point Kenneth might be asked to provide a statement about the conversation.

"I don't know Kenny." He stood very still, barely breathing. "Did you see her leave?"

Kenneth nodded. His bedroom windows looked directly out over the driveway. He would have seen the black truck, and perhaps a better view of the driver.

Stephen wondered how much Sara might have told him. His kids drove back and forth to school together every day and it was entirely possible that Kenneth knew something about his sister's relationship with Kieran O'Shea.

He was an instant away from asking when he glanced up at the wall clock again. He now had forty-five minutes to reach the meeting place. He shifted his weight from one foot to the other, and thought of O'Shea driving away before he got there, then telling Detective Caruso everything he wanted to know.

"Kenny, I have to leave, but I'll be back as soon as I can, all right?"

Kenneth stared at him, his posture still stiff and awkward on the barstool, a questioning look in his eyes.

"All right," he said, as Stephen headed out the door.

❄ ❄ ❄

Stephen replaced the tail light cover behind the closed door of the garage. The remnants of the old cover went into the box from the new one. For the moment he had no choice but to hide the box in the small attic space reached by the steep pull-down ladder.

His balance wavered as he stepped back down the ladder and he had to lean against the Explorer for half a minute to regain it. He cringed at the rumbling sound as he shoved the ladder back into the attic space, knowing that Kenneth could probably hear it inside the house.

He pushed the button for the automatic door, which rose normally this time. There was a Frederick County Sheriff's Department car parked across the street. The deputy behind the wheel looked directly at him with absolutely no expression on his face.

Stephen quickly turned away, thinking of Caruso's last words about the warrant to seize the Explorer, and knew that the deputy was there at Caruso's direction, guarding him. He thought of calling O'Shea back, pleading his inability to drive back up the mountain, but knew he wouldn't care.

He started the engine and backed slowly down the driveway, expecting the sudden illumination of the light bar on the deputy's car. It didn't happen, but he watched as the deputy spoke into his hand-held radio mike.

He straightened the wheel and drove on, his heart pounding as the Sheriff's Department car pulled out and followed him. He stayed just short of the speed limit through the housing development and then along the highway that took him toward the mountain. The deputy stayed a few car lengths behind him, close enough to be intimidating but far enough to stop if he hit the brakes.

The highway that led to the turnoff to the mountain had been plowed, but it was slick from the still-falling snow. The deputy stayed with him as he took the exit, wearing the same grim expression as they moved together up the winding, climbing roads. Stephen glanced at him through the rearview mirror every few seconds, and noticed as he pulled out the hand-held mike once more.

And then he saw a line of police vehicles, coming toward him. The cars weren't speeding; just driving at a normal pace, steadily approaching.

They're coming from the accident scene. He knew it for certain as they drew near; a white SUV in front, with two cruisers behind it. He looked into the rearview mirror again as they approached, and at that same moment the grill and light bar of the deputy's car lit up. Two short whoops of the siren followed.

He tapped the brakes and pulled off onto the narrow shoulder, and watched as the SUV passed, noticing the state of Maryland seal and the writing on the side:

CRASH ANALYSIS RECONSTRUCTION TEAM

Two Sheriff's Department cars followed. The car behind them was a Hummer, being driven by Detective Joseph Niles.

Niles made eye contact as he slowed and approached, then raised his right hand in the shape of a gun and pointed it at Stephen's face and pantomimed a firing motion before making U-turn and coming up behind the deputy's car.

21

Sara anxiously leaned forward in the passenger seat of Kieran's truck and silently willed him to slow down and turn into the shopping center ahead. It housed a Starbucks and a McDonalds and plenty of other places where they could sit and talk; safe places where there would be other people watching them. That was what she had agreed to, and what Kieran had told her would happen.

But once again he kept going, past the entrance, the truck picking up speed.

"Kieran we have to stop."

He stared straight ahead as if he hadn't heard her. She turned in the seat and touched his forearm.

He swatted her hand away.

"Kieran—*please*."

"Shut up Sara."

His tone took her back to the night before—the hateful look on his face after she had stumbled and fallen in his house, the alarm still ringing in her ears. She saw the exit to Route 15 ahead of them, and gripped the strap above the window as he took it.

We're going back up there, she thought. *Back to his house*.

The road narrowed to two lanes and began to climb. Kieran was still driving way too fast for the winding curves. The driver's side window was down, despite the cold. The wind was whipping his long hair across his face. On the brief phone call his voice had been thick with anguish as he pleaded for her to talk to him about what had happened to Aidan, but he radiated nothing but anger and refused to speak to her once she was in his truck.

And now he was accelerating again—his heavy booted foot pressing the pedal to the floor.

"KIERAN—*PLEASE!*"

Her voice was lost in the wind. She leaned slightly forward and touched his forearm again. He shook her off but the motion seemed to have some impact as he tapped the brake and made the next curve. The woods rushed by in a blur, giving her a momentary glimpse of a small sign reading Alternate 5.

She realized they were heading up the mountain on a different route than he had told her to take the night before. It was narrower and lined with snow that had been pushed by the plows into steep banks on both sides. It had been several minutes since she had seen any other cars. She gripped the strap above the window again as the road broke free of the trees and gave her a view of the gorge below.

The thought that Kieran wanted to kill both of them hit her with a sudden, debilitating force as she thought about the pill bottles in his bedroom.

But then the road curved once again into the woods. The trees were massive here—big enough to split the truck in two if they hit one at the speed Kieran was going. But then she felt the truck slowing, as if the prayer had been answered.

They reached Kieran's house. She thought back to the odd route they had taken up the mountain and knew that he had purposely chosen to stay off of the main roads. *As if he was afraid of being caught*, she thought.

She knew that her father would be angry that she left without telling him where she was going. It wasn't difficult to imagine him running down to the garage and coming after them in the Explorer; his face strained with tension and worry.

Or fear, she thought. *Because he's scared of what Kieran knows.*

The truck's suspension bounced over the uneven ground as Kieran pulled into the yard. He drove up to the Jeep and cut the wheel to angle the truck sideways in front of it. The Jeep was now covered up to the bottom of its windows in snow. It looked as if it had been permanently immobilized. She felt a lead weight on her chest—a claustrophobia that squeezed the breath from her lungs and sent her back to the moment she had called her father and asked him to drive up the mountain and take her away.

She felt the same way now—afraid of what Kieran would do once they were inside the house. She tried to think of some way to convince him to take her somewhere else but before she could speak he turned off the ignition and abruptly opened the driver's side door, and said "Get out."

He stepped out into the snow and slammed the door behind him, then turned and stared at her through the window. His wind-whipped hair now hung in oily strands over his face and his eyes were bloodshot; his full lips tight and twisted downward. She stared at him—taking in his pale skin and the fine shape of his face—but had the sudden sense that she did not know him at all; that overnight he had become a different person.

She heard the ring of her phone—an eerie tinkling of bells. The sound was faint and came from outside. Kieran reached into his coat pocket and pulled it out, looked at the incoming number, and turned his back to her and stepped away from the car.

She turned halfway around in the seat and looked back toward the road and tried to imagine running away from the house instead of walking in; wondered how far she might get before Kieran came after her.

But it wasn't your fault; he can't blame you.

Or could he? The accident wouldn't have happened if she hadn't called her father; if she had simply stayed in the house and waited for

Kieran to bring Aidan back. Which she would have done if not for the Web sites on Kieran's computer, the stories about her mother's death and the murder of the other woman on the same night.

She wondered what he would say if she asked him about what she'd seen; wondered if he knew something about her mother that she didn't as she looked toward the door to the house, where Kieran now stood, staring out at her, waiting for her to follow him in.

❄ ❄ ❄

She stood at the threshold for several seconds with the door open, feeling the cold outside air on the back of her neck.

The original living room in the trailer portion of the house was narrow and only slightly more illuminated than it had been when she had left the night before. There was a dark, open space in the short hallway, where the plywood had been.

She stared at it as a gust of wind blew a spray of flakes over the threshold and sent a shiver down her back. She shut the door, cutting off the pale daylight and deepening the gloom inside. She flicked the light switch on the wall. It turned on a lamp atop a small table that sat next to the door.

Her phone was there, where Kieran must have set it down after coming into the house. She picked it up, and saw that the call he had received outside the car had been from her father. She slipped it into the pocket of her coat as she heard the sound of cabinets being opened and closed and the sound of Kieran talking to someone.

She tried to decipher words amid his frantic, hushed tone of voice.

And then suddenly he yelled. "NO!"

She shivered from another chill up her backbone.

"STOP!"

She went to the kitchen doorway. Kieran was alone, with his back to her, his hands covering his ears.

"Kieran?"

He jerkily turned around and gripped the edge of the kitchen counter behind him and stared at her. He was still wearing his black leather coat. There was a ruddy brown blotch at the center of his chest, which had a faint sheen under the harsh overhead light.

After a moment he seemed to be calm again.

"Are you okay?"

He gave her a blank look, then turned to open the cabinet over the kitchen sink. There was a bottle of amber-colored liquor there. Scotch or bourbon, she thought, like her father drank. He poured it into a glass and took a long gulp.

His eyes became teary from either the burn of straight whiskey or from the emotions he must have felt as he stared at her.

"Do you want something to drink Sara?"

Her stomach rolled with the thought of alcohol. She shook her head and her voice croaked as she said "No."

"Sure you do," he responded. "I'll get you some water. Go into the back room."

She stayed in the doorway, wishing once again that she had never gotten into the truck, and that she was back home with her father, and Kenneth, safe in her room.

But you need to know what happened, she thought. *And what he's going to do now.*

She turned away and went into the addition. It was much colder this morning. Her arms were stippled with gooseflesh as she crossed them over her chest. The air still carried the scent of last night's fire. The sight of the bong on the coffee table only deepened her regret.

Kieran sat down on the couch, seemingly unconcerned over the wetness of his boots and the snow he had brought into the house.

He set the water on the side table, and watched her as she walked forward and sat down next to him. She took a long drink. It was lukewarm but tasted good sliding past the dryness in her throat. She felt as if she was supposed to wait for the conversation to begin, but when she looked over at Kieran he was staring at the wood stove, looking as if he had been shocked into silence by his grief.

"I guess you found my phone," she said. "Where was it?"

Her voice pulled him back. He met her eyes.

"You dropped it when you were sitting here last night. I found it between the cushions."

She wanted to ask him why he still had it. Wanted to ask what her father had said to him a moment before.

"I saw the note you left," Kieran said. "I want you to explain it to me."

She had known he would bring it up, and had planned her response.

"I didn't know how long you'd be gone. I knew Aidan would be freezing when you brought him home and didn't want to be in the way when you tried to get him back into bed."

He frowned. "Is that really true?"

She nodded.

"It felt like you were trying to run away."

A rush of heat came to her face. She looked past him, toward the bedroom wing where she had seen the laptop.

"No...I wasn't running away."

"Do you want to tell me why you *really* left?"

"That *is* why...I didn't want to bother—"

Color filled his cheeks. "Don't *lie* to me Sara."

"I'm *not*." She brought the glass to her lips, drank the rest of the water, and managed to meet his eyes again. "I would never lie to you."

"Is that right?"

"Yes." She looked down at the braided rug on the floor, and told him the truth. "I heard you trying to get Aidan to calm down so he could sleep. I heard you slap him. It shook me up. I tried not to think about it but later, after you left, it started to bother me."

She waited for him to respond, heard him sigh.

"I didn't *slap* my brother Sara."

She looked at him. "I heard you."

"No you didn't. I told you about the way we grew up. The way *our mother* beat the shit out of us, usually right before she barricaded us in the closet. She boarded us up in there for hours, in the dark. Ignoring us no matter how hard we kicked and screamed."

She glanced toward the front of the house, thought of the closet where the plywood had been. "That's horrible."

"Yeah, it was. And it's the kind of thing you never forget. So when I needed my brother to cooperate I *reminded* him of how she would hit us—that horrible fucking sting from her palm smacking his face. It was a sound I made with my hands, to get his attention."

She frowned, unable to hide her reaction as she remembered the whimpering, sorrowful sounds from Aidan that had followed.

"That's a harsh way to get someone's attention," she said. "It sounded *mean*."

"I knew how to take care of my brother."

He was glaring at her now.

"What were you doing when I was out looking for him? Did you go back into my room?"

She tried to shake her head, to tell him *no*.

"Don't you think that if I *wanted* to show you my personal space I would have?"

He held her eyes, as if he was daring her to deny it.

"You violated my *trust*."

"I'm sorry," she said.

He slowly shook his head and then slipped the tips of his fingers inside the braided bracelet on his right hand. She saw the pained emotion in his eyes, and thought of the matching version on Aidan's wrist and the depth of the devotion between them.

Devotion that now seemed dangerous.

She looked toward the wood stove. She thought she saw embers burning from last night's fire but when she blinked the sparks looked as if they were suspended in the air.

"Is there anything else you want to tell me, Sara, as long as we're being completely *honest* here?"

She looked at him again, and realized for certain that he already knew everything that she might have admitted. She turned toward the window and the gray, snowy light, felt an inkling of the same fear that had gripped her the night before. The need to escape.

"I should go."

She stood up and felt strangely lightheaded as she remembered the way Kieran had angled his truck in the yard, blocking her from exiting even if the engine hadn't been dead.

She turned back toward him. "Can you please take me home?"

"No, I don't think I can do that." There was a strange echo behind his voice. "Not in this condition."

Condition? She gazed back at him. He was still sitting in the same position, still watching her, *observing*, she thought. *Like he's waiting for something.*

"I don't know what you mean," she told him. "I'm fine."

But she knew that she wasn't. Knew it from the wavering of the wall behind him and the wobble in her knees.

Kieran stared at her, his expression still radiating a steady, controlled anger.

"Aren't you feeling tired?"

She tried to swallow the dry lump at the back of her throat, and tasted a bitterness on her tongue. She remembered the cloudiness of the water he had brought her. *He put something in it*, she thought, and reached for the back of the couch to steady herself. She felt an acceleration in the beat of her heart and beads of sweat on her forehead, and knew that she had to get out of there.

But with the leaden feeling in her legs she knew she couldn't move quickly; knew she had to do something else.

"Can you get me some more water?"

Kieran was sitting completely still on the couch, still watching her closely.

"Please?" She used the back of her hand to swipe at the sweat on her brow. "With some ice?"

Kieran nodded and placed both of his hands on his knees and stood up, then turned and walked with what looked like deliberate slowness back toward the kitchen.

She waited until she heard the cracking of the ice tray before she stepped back toward the front door and took her phone from her pocket and slipped outside.

She stood on the concrete landing and scrolled as far as "Dad" when the door slammed open behind her and Kieran grabbed her by the hair, then kicked the back of her knees to drop her to the ground, then yanked her back inside. She screamed as the pain tore through her scalp; screamed again just before he put his hand over her mouth and nose, cutting off her oxygen as she shook her head from side to side. She reached up but he swatted her hand back down. The room spun around her in a blur as he pulled her away from the door, the edges of her vision going black as she made one last attempt to shake herself free.

"Had enough?"

His voice was a soft whisper in her ear—confident, dominant and stifling her will to resist as he abruptly turned her around so she was once again facing the front room. He kicked the door shut behind him and then took his hand away, still holding her firmly at the waist as she leaned forward and caught her breath.

And then suddenly he moved her aside, raised one of her arms so that it rested against the back of his neck and across his shoulder.

"You should be able to walk all right, if you *really* try."

She struggled—or meant to struggle—but could only slump against him as he led her toward the back section of the house. He steered her toward the right, the direction of Aidan's room.

Aidan's door was open. He led her in and pushed her down onto the tangled sheets of Aidan's bed.

She tried to sit back up but found that she couldn't; tried to talk but couldn't seem to move her mouth.

The bed began to move in a slow circle underneath her. She tried again to sit up, but could barely raise her head. Her eyes were drawn once again to the stain on Kieran's coat. The streaks were ragged and vertical and led to a splotch just below his sternum.

He looked down and then looked back at her, and nodded.

"It's blood," he said.

She felt a tremor in the muscles of her abdomen as he slowly lowered himself, so his knees balanced on the edge of the bed and the coat was just a few inches from her face.

"*Aidan*'s blood."

She winced and shut her eyes, turned her head toward the bedroom wall.

Kieran reached down and put his palm firmly against her cheek, then forced her to look at the stain again.

"I tried to save him, but he was dead before I got there."

She imagined her father standing over Aidan, then stepping back and driving away.

And then Kieran, holding Aidan against his chest.

She tried again to sit up, but could barely raise her head.

"Don't try to leave, because you won't be able to," Kieran said, then stepped out into the hallway and shut the door behind him.

She looked toward the window that Aidan had crawled out of the night before, saw that plywood had been nailed over it, from the outside. *Plywood from the closet*, she thought, where Kieran and Aidan had been locked away.

The walls floated around her. She tried—but failed—to sit up again. Tried to speak but managed nothing more than a whispered "Kieran, *don't* —"

She heard the heavy, metallic click of the deadbolt and then the chain, locking her in.

❄ ❄ ❄

Stephen stayed behind the wheel of the Explorer as Detective Niles stepped out of his Hummer and gave a short wave to the deputy who had followed him, who remained in his car.

He lowered the driver's side window as Niles approached, but Niles veered toward the passenger side of the car and went straight back to the area that had been damaged by the impact with the boy's body. Stephen watched through the rearview mirror as Niles squatted down and tilted his head in a stagy, self-conscious appraisal, playing up every bit of drama in the moment. Niles then stepped back, pulled his phone from his pocket and took several pictures of the damaged area.

Stephen opened the door, and started to step out.

"Remain in your vehicle Mr. Porter." Niles' tone was cold and official. After snapping several more photos, he slowly walked around and stood in front of the open driver's side window.

"License and registration," Niles said.

Stephen took his license from his wallet and the registration from the packet of documents in the glove compartment and handed them over. Niles smirked. He looked like a schoolyard bully, out to settle a score.

"You have a new cover on your right rear taillight," Niles said. "All clear and shiny."

Stephen gave him a blank stare, noticing there was an ugly bruise on his cheek.

"Replaced this morning, I suspect." Niles looked down at the registration. "So where are you off to?"

You can tell him you're going to try and get the Jeep started, he thought. *You have jumper cables in the back.*

But a sudden instinct warned him to say nothing.

"Nowhere," he said. "Just driving."

"Really? That's dangerous, on these slick roads. You could *hurt somebody* out here."

Niles was staring intently at him.

"You want to tell me how your ass end got damaged?"

"I had an accident in a parking lot yesterday."

Niles frowned, clearly indicating his disbelief. He then glanced back toward the deputy and said: "Stay put."

He looked in the rearview mirror again as Niles went to the deputy's car. There was a short conversation, and then Niles was back.

"Detective Caruso asked for a warrant to seize your vehicle. It just came through. So you need to step out."

He glanced at the dashboard clock. He was due at the meeting site in five minutes. Niles was watching him closely, looking highly alert to his reaction as he thought through the steps he had taken; the careful cleaning of the damaged area, the replacement of the taillight cover, the disposal of the shoes he had worn when he had gotten out of the car.

"Unless you have someone who can come pick you up I suggest you ride back into town with one of us," Niles said.

Like I'm being arrested already. He glanced toward the deputy's car and saw himself riding down the mountain and missing the meeting. And then he imagined Kieran O'Shea sitting in front of Caruso's desk, telling Caruso and Niles what he had seen.

"I can't," he said.

Niles looked at him as if he had lost his mind. "What are you going to *do*, stay up here?"

The excuse came to him quickly, and he knew it would probably only damn him further.

"I'm going to the house where my daughter was stranded last night. I called for a tow. I have to meet the driver there."

"Kieran O'Shea's house," Niles said.

He nodded, and felt the cold air drifting through an opening at the top of his coat. He tightened the scarf around his neck and turned around, and looked at the winding upward slant of the road ahead of him. The house was at least another half mile away, and O'Shea had said the clearing was another mile beyond.

No way you're going to get there in time now.

He turned his back and started walking.

"Enjoy the cold," Niles said.

He looked over his shoulder, saw the smirk that had come back to Niles' face, then broke into an unsteady near-run, heedless of the hard-packed ice underneath his feet.

22

He was still running when he slipped. His arms dropped too slowly to break his fall and his chest and chin slammed against the frozen ground.

He stayed still for several seconds. His limbs were numbed by the cold and his balance wavered as he made the effort to get back up. He touched his chin with a gloved hand that came back dotted with blood. He opened his eyes wider to the snowbound landscape around him—saw pulsing shadows at the edges of his vision—and felt as if he was going to faint.

"I really need to get out of here."

Sara's middle of the night phone call echoed through his mind, taking him back to the fear in her voice, and the memory of her near-breakdown in front of Caruso.

The intensity of her emotions; like her mother, he thought. *After the truth had come out.*

He continued walking, faster now, thinking of the suspicion he had felt when Sara had left the house the night before. Suspicion he had wanted to ignore in the hope that he could simply trust his daughter to be completely truthful with him.

Even though it's become your nature. The past and present clashed together as he again thought of Lori, before the affair and after, the complete transformation of her personality as she tried and failed to deal with her guilt and the distrust that he had not been able to push away. He had started trying to read her emails long before the accident; had become accustomed to going to her computer minutes after she left it to see if she was still logged on; had checked the browser again and again to see what Web sites she had visited, always finding the "history" cleared.

Until the night when he had heard the muffled sounds of her whispering into her phone behind the closed door of the den. The same night she finally forgot to clear the history, which enabled him to see the Web site she had been logged onto. A site for online chats about all kinds of sexual dysfunction.

Sadomasochism. Incest. Pedophilia.

Hours of sleeplessness had followed, as the questions churned through his mind, working their way into his dreams when he finally drifted off. He had never asked her about what he had seen—hadn't wanted her to know of his snooping. Two days later she was gone.

The feeling of dread stayed with him as he rounded a bend and saw Kieran O'Shea's house. It was set back within the trees as he remembered. The Jeep was still parked in the front yard, embedded in the snow. There were at least two sets of footsteps leading up to the front stoop. Closed curtains on all of the front windows blocked the view of the inside as he approached, and knocked, and prayed that Sara would come to the door. Everything he had done during the past several hours was at complete odds with the *tell the truth; take responsibility* messages he and Lori had always preached. Just a few weeks earlier he had told Sara that he trusted her to *never* drink and drive and had made her promise that she would call him if she was ever out with friends who wanted to drive under the influence of alcohol or drugs.

Call me, he had told her. *No matter what.*

The conversation now seemed like it had taken place between two different people. A man who still yearned for the days when his little girl would rush into his arms as he came home from work. A daughter who had always been a model student, who spent virtually all of her free time during her sophomore year of high school volunteering at the nursing home where Lori's father had spent the last weeks of his life. *A pleaser*, as Lori had called her.

He stood still in the freezing air, and stared at the drab, faded white house, which he now realized had been formed by a trailer in the front and an addition in the back. Slats were missing from the ornamental shutters that flanked the four front windows and the top of the downspout that led from the gutter along the roof had come loose. It looked inhabited but ignored, as if its owner had decided to let it gradually succumb to the wear of weather and age.

The forest beyond the house was dense even without foliage; a wilderness.

Miles and miles of woods up there.

Stephen thought about the recent conversation with a neighbor who had grown up on the mountain but happily forsaken it for a big, comfortable modern home.

People have gotten lost for days.

He started walking again, his feet numbed by the cold, trying to resume his pace despite the treacherously slick road surface. O'Shea had said the clearing was a quarter of a mile past the house, but it was difficult to gauge his progress as the fatigue took a greater hold on his muscles. The first sections of the mountain road had been plowed, and when he had stepped outside of the Explorer he had been able to hear the faint din of traffic on the highway below. Now the air was silent and still, the landscape frozen in place by the heavy snow and capped by a low, leaden gray sky. He remembered looking at the online map the night before; remembered the indistinct charting of the road; the sense that it simply ended at a random point beyond one of the curves that came every hundred yards.

And then suddenly the clearing was there, and marked by the black pickup truck on the shoulder. At the center of the clearing he saw blackened cinder blocks that made up the foundation of a burned-out house and the remnants of a collapsed chimney. There were lean-to outbuildings behind the foundation and the ground was smoothly covered by an expanse of snow.

He tightened the scarf around his neck, crossed his arms over his chest, looked over at the black pickup and saw footprints. They came around the front of the truck and led around the perimeter of the clearing, indicating the driver had gotten out and gone straight into the woods. He stepped closer. The footprints had been made by boots that had sunk knee-deep in the snow. He put his gloved hands back into his pockets, peered back over the clearing, and then started walking, following the footprints. The ground was covered with brush underneath the snow and became more challenging as he stepped into the woods.

After a few feet he stumbled and fell forward, his arms sinking up to his elbows.

He stood up quickly and awkwardly, feeling clumsy and certain that O'Shea was watching him from a hiding place within the forest.

That feeling was confirmed a few steps later when he saw movement from the corner of his eye and heard: "All right you can stop now."

He turned toward the sound, and the sight of a man, just barely discernable twenty feet deeper into the woods. Stephen recognized his pale face from the glimpse he had gotten from the second floor window.

For a long moment they both stood very still, and then O'Shea said: "Walk toward me."

He complied, his eyes focusing on the uneven ground, his hands touching the trees to keep his balance. After a few unsteady steps he looked up. O'Shea was standing on slightly higher ground, looking down at him.

"I didn't tell you to stop."

He resumed walking toward O'Shea, who stood completely still. The scarf around Stephen's neck shifted as he moved and the cold again found its way through the opening at the top of his jacket.

"That's close enough."

He shivered as he met the man's eyes. They were blue-gray, and bloodshot. His cheeks were unshaven.

"Where's my daughter?" His voice was a whisper from his parched throat.

O'Shea tilted his head slightly down but kept his eyes locked on Stephen's as he stepped forward, his right hand was thrust deeply into the side pocket of his coat.

In one smooth motion O'Shea pulled out a gun.

"*No!*" Stephen shouted and ducked, his hands raised in a feeble gesture of self-protection.

The gun was pointed at his face.

"Get down on your knees," O'Shea said.

He stayed still, frozen in place, felt sweat trickling from his armpits.

"DOWN!"

He squatted, just barely balancing in the heavy clothes and uneven ground, the icy snow swallowing his thighs.

"I'm sorry," he whispered.

O'Shea pressed the gun against his cold-numbed skin.

"It was an accident!"

His eyes were squeezed shut, but he imagined the bullet smashing through his skull, blowing his brains and blood out into the snow.

"Please..."

Suddenly the pressure was gone.

He opened his eyes. O'Shea was still standing over him, with both hands on the gun. But the gun was pointed at an upward angle now. O'Shea was looking up toward the sky, his mouth moving soundlessly as if he were praying, and as a tear trickled down his face. Stephen remembered the tone of his voice on the phone; the sense of menace he had felt. But now he thought he might have heard something else. The sound of grief.

You lost Lori. He lost his brother.

So talk to him. Connect with him.

"I can't even *express…*" His voice faltered.

He sucked in a deep breath, tried again.

"I can't express my *shame*, and my sorrow, for this."

O'Shea was standing very still. Stephen saw the muscles of his eyelids flickering, as if he were watching dream images in a half-sleep.

And then suddenly O'Shea's eyes opened and stared down at him. Then without looking away O'Shea flicked the safety on the gun and put it back in his pocket.

Thank God. Stephen exhaled, felt the tension draining from his body. He was still kneeling, his legs numbed by the snow. He shakily stood up, knowing how it would end. The confession had already happened; he had admitted being at fault, and now he would reveal the terrible but unavoidable circumstances. *Sara sounded scared when she called me. I thought she was in trouble. I couldn't get anyone else to help her. I skidded on the ice; couldn't stop—*

"Turn around," O'Shea said.

"What?" Stephen asked. "Why—"

"Walk away."

He stood still, trying to think of something else to say. And then O'Shea tilted his head slightly forward and reached for the gun again.

"All right." He held up his hands.

"Go," O'Shea said.

He turned around and took a step and heard a grunt behind him as a hard kick knocked him forward. His head snapped backwards in a whiplash and his arms flailed as he slammed face-first into a tree.

The impact stunned him; spots of red flashed in front of his eyes. He turned halfway around before the next punch, which landed deep into his abdomen and knocked the air from his lungs.

He dropped to his knees and looked up an instant before O'Shea kicked him in the chest. He fell backward; his skull striking something hard and sharp underneath the snow, then scrabbled sideways just a few feet before O'Shea stepped behind him and grabbed the back of his coat collar and yanked him back up, then kicked him once more at the center of his back.

He shot forward and fell on his face, his teeth cutting into his tongue as he hit the ground. In his peripheral vision he saw O'Shea's leg drawing back; shut his eyes and pulled his arms and legs into a fetal position as O'Shea kicked him in the ribs, shooting pain through his upper body.

Warm blood from his tongue filled his mouth and trickled into his windpipe as O'Shea stooped down and put his knee against his chest and pinned him to the ground.

He coughed violently, spraying blood into the air. O'Shea's eyes were red with rage, his teeth bared as he clasped his hands together in a double fist. He imagined that he screamed *NO* as O'Shea said "Your turn now, *fuckhead!*" as the fist came down in a blur; smashing the soft cartilage of his nose and sending a jolt of pain through his spine.

23

Caruso put Marco Niles in an interview room at headquarters and then called his father. Joseph Niles was predictably angry that Marco was being charged with a DUI, even more so when Caruso told him he wanted to question the boy alone about the source of the weed that had been in the car when he was arrested.

He didn't mention the reason he wanted to get to Marco by himself, but worked it into his opening questions as he stepped back into the room.

"So what happened to your eye?"

Marco glared at him but didn't respond. His hair was sandy-blond and his broad face looked older than his years. He bore no real resemblance to his father except that he was big and tall and sporting a broad chest under his Langford Secondary letter jacket. Based on the scent that filled the small room Caruso guessed he was sweating beneath it.

"Must hurt like hell," Caruso said. "I can get some ice for it."

"It's nothin'," Marco muttered.

"Or type up a complaint against the guy who did it. Who was it—a kid at school? The guy you bought the drugs from? Someone else?"

"I don't know anything about any drugs."

Caruso frowned. The weed had fallen from Marco's coat pocket the moment he stepped out of the car. It was now in a plastic evidence bag, and was undoubtedly covered by fingerprints that would match Marco's once they got to that step in the process.

"We both know that's not true. But I'm still interested in your face. What happened?"

"It's none of your business."

"Just want to make sure you don't claim it was some kind of police brutality, just because you think things like that actually happen."

Marco's good eye widened a bit.

It was the sign Caruso was looking for. "Your dad has a bruise just like it. Maybe not as bad. So what happened—did you fight each other?"

The boy sat back slightly, and looked past Caruso, toward the camera affixed to the wall.

"It's not on," Caruso said. "So he's not watching."

Marco's shoulders dropped a bit.

"So is that what happened?"

Marco looked down at the floor; his lips still tight. *Still holding it in*, Caruso thought. It only took a moment for his mind to go back to encounters of child abuse in his own past: the numerous visits to the run-down mountain residence owned by Nurlene O'Shea; the memories of both Kieran and Aidan O'Shea, battered and bruised from her beatings; the meetings with the social workers who tried but failed to bring it all to a halt.

He leaned slightly forward with his hands clasped on top of the table, a move to make his body language less threatening. As a twenty-three-year-old deputy he had failed to help either Kieran or Aidan. He wasn't going to fail again.

"You need to talk to someone about this, Marco."

The boy pressed his lips into a tight line and shook his head, clearly conveying he had nothing else to say.

Caruso sighed, and thought about sliding his card across the table, repeating the offer, but decided to first tend to the matter at hand.

"I know you're a senior at Langford. I expect you're looking forward to graduating and going off to college. But now you've been arrested, and regardless of what you say or what you want to believe you're facing serious charges that aren't going to go away. With the DUI your license is as good as gone. Add to that the reckless driving that led to the accident, the running of the stop sign *and* the drugs—you're screwed."

"I told you—I don't know anything about any drugs."

"Your clothes reek of pot. I know you'll come up positive for that once the results of your urine test come back."

Caruso paused, thinking of another way to come back to the abuse, and lowered his voice.

"I can guess how your father feels about all this."

There was a noticeable tensing in the boy's posture. His Adam's apple bobbed as he swallowed.

"But maybe you do have a way out," Caruso said. "If you want to tell me where you got it—who you bought it from and who else you know who's dealing or doing drugs to kids at your school—you might be able to—"

"I can't."

Caruso watched him carefully. "Can't or *won't*?"

Marco stared down at the tabletop. Caruso sensed his mind moving, debating his response.

"Talk to me," he said.

There was a brief knock at the door, and then Joseph Niles stepped in.

❄ ❄ ❄

Caruso's fragile professional rapport with Niles fell apart completely in the ten minutes that followed, with Niles ordering his son to say nothing about where he obtained the drugs and even insinuating that the offer of lower charges was a ruse. Looking absolutely terrified,

Marco did exactly as he was told, leaving Caruso with no choice but to charge him with possession on top of the DUI.

Caruso pulled Niles aside for an explanation, reminding him that the charges would have to be reported to the principal at Langford Secondary, which would lead to an automatic expulsion. Niles' response only intensified his suspicions.

"Fuck it, I don't care."

"How could you not *care*?"

"Kid's been a fuck-up his whole life. One thing after the other."

"He's your son."

"Doesn't matter. He brought it on himself."

"What about that black eye? He bring that on himself too?"

Niles bristled, looking as if he was about to throw another punch, then turned and walked away. Caruso watched until he reached the end of the hallway, feeling glad that Marco had gotten at least one solid hit back.

And then he went back to his desk, his mind skipping through everything that had just happened between Joseph and Marco Niles. Niles had said little about his son in the year that they had worked together, but he had no doubt that they had fought each other, with Marco obviously suffering the worst. Perhaps it was none of his business, except that Marco was a juvenile, which made the physical assault an act of child abuse.

Has to be a reason, he thought, and went online. Social media had become one of the most reliable tools in investigations of crimes involving teenagers, so there was a good chance Marco's Facebook page might provide some evidence of the troubles with his father.

Unfortunately the initial scan didn't tell him much. There were hundreds of mobile phone photos chronicling Marco's daily life as a busy athlete and more than a few taken at parties where alcohol was obviously readily available. Marco was a big fan of the selfie, usually with his arm around attractive teenage girls and "look at me" smiles.

Caruso scanned quickly through the photos, and then moved on to Marco's recent posts. Once again there was nothing to indicate emotional stress, and no reference to problems with Niles; nothing more than boasts about his athletic feats in football during the fall and in basketball over the winter along with taunts about opposing teams. Taken together, the photos and posts painted the picture of a typically self-centered teenager, without a hint of the vulnerability exhibited in the company of his father.

He opened another browser window, intending to go next to Twitter and Instagram when he noticed the link for "Albums" in the photo section of the Facebook page. There were several identified in the "Profile" "Mobile" "Timeline" categories, all with similarly narcissistic but innocuous images. Caruso clicked through them quickly, and was just about to move on when he came to an image that had been scanned from a print photo. It was a class of young children, posed and standing on bleachers in a gymnasium. The photo was labeled THIRD GRADE, MRS. KELLEY, and the coloring made it obvious it was several years old.

He scanned the faces, and found it easy to pick out Marco, in the back row, already bigger than the rest of the kids. The listing of the students' names was in the right hand margin of the page.

It listed him as MARCO DEVON.

He leaned forward, peering closer at the boy's light hair and pale skin, remembering his last encounter with April Devon behind the wheel of her SUV.

And then he sat back and thought some more about Niles, who had mentioned an "ex-wife" only once as far as he could remember, and in a disparaging way that had made him disinclined to learn more.

He went back to the open browser, and did a search for Joseph Niles. The second link that appeared was an article from *Classic Car* magazine. Niles was one of several people interviewed in an article about Hummers, which the magazine predicted would become collectable treasures. The article was anchored by a photo of Niles standing alongside the two that he owned.

A perfect match to an outsized ego, he thought, and then went back to the search page. This time he entered Niles and then Devon.

Several new links appeared; all of them from news media sites. He took them in all at once. And then he read them, one at a time. After two minutes his heartbeat quickened. After two more he moved on to the password-protected law enforcement databases, his voice a near-whisper as he muttered "son-of-a-bitch" and began to put it together.

24

Your spine is broken.

You're dying—

Stephen saw himself in his mind's eye, lying limp in the snow. He felt as if he had left his body but was still tethered to it, still bound by the signals that continued to fire through his brain. He thought that he was alone—he had a memory of Kieran O'Shea looking down at him and then turning and walking away; remembered hearing the sound of snow crunching under boots and the distant creak of the door to the old pick up truck as it was opened and slammed shut; the rumble of the engine as O'Shea drove off.

Fight it.

Get up.

His eyes fluttered open to the sight of tall trees and a whitish blur of sky. His back and legs were numb; it felt as if he had frozen into the ground. His face was also numb but he felt an inkling of pain underneath the bones of his nose and the trickle of blood at the back of his throat. He took shallow breaths through his mouth; there was no feeling in his nostrils. He turned his head from side to side, saw his motionless arms, and concentrated on moving his fingers. For several seconds he felt nothing—it was as if the connection between his brain and muscles had been severed.

But then he felt a twitch, in the right hand and then the left. And then a tingling in the tendons behind his knees.

Thank God.

You can move—

He sat halfway up before the explosion of pain in his ribs knocked him back. He felt the blood flowing faster down the back of his throat. A panicked gagging reflex sent him into a coughing spasm; the pain like a pulsing, electrified force through his upper body. It felt as if every one of his internal organs had been ruptured, as if every bone in his chest had been cracked.

He managed to draw air into his lungs as he turned sideways and coughed again, sending a spray of bright red blood into the snow. He rose up on one elbow, the pain lessening slightly as he eased into a sitting position.

He stayed still for several seconds, fighting the terror brought on by the pain.

Have to calm down.

Think—

He took a deep breath of the cold air, fortifying himself for the agony as he stood all the way up and peered through the trees, searching for his bearings, and saw the foundation of the fire-ruined house and the road beyond. He managed two steps before his legs buckled. He dropped to his knees, the pain of simple movement pushing him to the edge of a dead faint.

Can't—Have to stay awake.

His mind flashed on the memory of Sara getting into O'Shea's truck.

It's not over.

He's going to hurt her.

He thought of the lies he had told Caruso, and now the consequences.

Call him, tell him everything. Get him to send someone up here.

He reached into his coat pocket for his phone. It wasn't there. He put his palm on a tree for balance as he looked down at the ground, his line of sight drawn to O'Shea's footprints in the snow.

And then he saw it. The screen was shattered, as if it had been stomped.

His lungs tightened with panic. It had been several minutes since O'Shea had beat him unconscious. His balance wavered as he staggered toward the road. He stumbled again but remained upright, gasping into another coughing spasm as more blood hit the back of his throat.

PART FOUR

25

Joseph Niles signed the papers that granted the release of his stepson into his custody, and then stood in the small waiting room of the station, his hands in the pockets of his coat, his back against the wall, doing his best to look tired and disappointed and give nothing else away. The deputy at the desk glanced at him as Marco emerged from the back hallway and went to the counter, where he received the rest of his valuables in clear plastic bags. Marco had grown up fast and big and was now tall enough to meet Joseph eye to eye, although that rarely happened. The sight of his stepson was barely tolerable on the best of days. Today it got him thinking of murder as Marco turned and gave him a defiant look.

"*You useless fuck...*" Joseph muttered under his breath,

For an infinite moment there was nothing but the compressed tunnel of vision between them as Marco stood completely still. Joseph stared back at him, conveying every bit of the rage he felt, thinking for the hundredth time what it might be like to simply abandon the boy, to escape the charade of being a normal suburban father with nothing to hide.

After several seconds, Marco shifted his weight from one foot to the next, and then stepped out into the waiting area. Joseph said nothing as he turned toward the main doors. Marco followed, several steps behind, well out of range of the sudden, debilitating punch that Joseph wanted to throw at him.

Not here.

Not until you can do it right.

His Hummer was parked at the curb, within open view of people coming in and out of the station. With measured breaths, he affected a downtrodden set of his shoulders as he unlocked the doors and waited for Marco to get into the passenger side. Then for the sake of anyone watching he made a backhand swipe at his eyes—the motion of a big, strong cop grappling with shame—then opened the driver's side door and slid in behind the wheel.

He pushed the button that locked all the doors with a soft *click*.

Marco flinched as if he'd been slapped.

He let him sit for half a minute and started the car.

"Looks like you're in the middle of a real shit storm, *son*."

He felt Marco tense, and prolonged the moment by resting his right arm on his knee, flexing his fingers and then forming a fist. Marco saw the motion in his peripheral vision and sucked in a quick, audible breath, as if he was already bracing for what he would face in the hour to come.

"You need to tell me exactly what you told him," Joseph said. "Every fucking word."

❄ ❄ ❄

Madison had waited for over an hour for Marco to come to her back door. Despite his "on my way" response to her text message, every minute made her more certain that it wasn't going to happen.

After three more texts and an attempt to get him on the phone, she had been forced to accept that he had found something else to occupy his time. Something better, obviously. What made it all so much worse was her attempt to ensure the visit would have been worth his while. She had taken a short, hot shower and pulled on a pair of tight jeans, without underwear, and a clingy silk T-shirt. Then to take the edge off of her thoughts she had downed two more Stoli shots and stood at the door that led from the laundry room to the backyard and smoked half of a joint, shivering in the cold and swatting the aromatic fumes into the outside air.

The buzz was more intense than she had expected it to be. There were yawning gaps from one thought to the next, and images flashing in an annoying, random way in her mind. Memories of how she had been the night before, her makeup mussed by Darrell's slobbering, open-mouthed kisses, the skin on her breasts blotched by his pawing hands; flickering mental snapshots of her clumsy trudge through the snow as she made her way back home and stared at her phone when she got there, desperate to see a text from Marco suddenly pop up on the screen. The images had made her feel pathetically lonely earlier but they were triggering something else now as she looked into the mirror in the powder room, her mind working through the mechanizations she had gone through—mechanizations Marco had *put* her through. All to end up alone. The feeling made her want to slide down the wall and weep into her hands.

She gazed out through the narrow window alongside the door and waited for the moment to pass. The yard was buried in several feet of snow, but the driveway that led to the garage behind the house had been shoveled by the neighborhood boy who did all of their yard work. He was only twelve, and she had often enjoyed standing just a little too close to him when they talked, watching him blush and stammer as he tried to carry on his end of the conversation. Her mother was still asleep and Madison doubted she had had the wherewithal to call the boy and request his services. More likely he had just jumped into action, knowing that he would be paid. She hated the idea of him knocking on the door to collect his money now, seeing the way she was dressed; hated the idea that he might somehow be able to look at her and know that she had gone to such lengths only to be ignored.

She stepped away from the window and went through the family room to the kitchen. The keys to the Rover were on the counter. She grabbed them and reached for her coat, which was draped over the barstool where she had left it the night before. She imagined Marco texting that he was on his way to her house and then blithely changing his mind.

You can't keep this up, she thought. You *need to deal with it now.*

Seconds later she was behind the wheel, backing out into the driveway, the Rover's tires finding loose traction on the icy street as she headed for the confrontation that was bound to come.

❄ ❄ ❄

Kenneth managed to eat a few spoonfuls of corn flakes before his stomach cramped. He sucked in a deep breath and hoped the food would stay down as he thought of Aidan O'Shea being hit by a car.

Last night, he thought. *During the blizzard.*

His father had sounded strange in the conversation before he left, as if he was acting, speaking lines he had rehearsed. The hug had been strange too. A bit too tight. Too long.

Desperate, he thought, with a sense of foreboding as he looked out into the family room. The French doors were covered up to the midpoint by gray-white snow, making the room feel like a tomb. He headed up the stairs, suddenly yearning for the brighter light on the house's second floor and the comforting colors of his room.

He went back to his unmade bed, his mind weary from the few hours of fitful sleep but wired from the coffee. He turned his head toward the dormered window, remembering the sight of Sara getting into Mr. O'Shea's truck, at seven in the morning, looking as if she was sneaking away. But it had to be all right, because Sara had been tutoring Aidan for months, and making it a point to walk alongside him to his classes and sitting with him at lunch, always pretending she didn't notice the stares of other kids who didn't want to have anything to do with either one of them.

"Misfits."

The voice came from the back of his mind as he looked at the fabric and paint swatches that were still laid out on the dresser and thought of the many conversations with his mother during the first two months in the house. After she had quit her job, and become a different person. The alteration of her personality seemed even more sudden, and more troubling in light of the way she confided in him, telling him she had done something "terrible" and was "atoning."

Telling him enough to make him worry, despite all her feeble attempts to laugh off her unhappiness. *"Don't worry—I'll be all right. In the meantime, you, me, and Miss April will decorate this McMansion together,"* making it sound like some kind of subversive adventure.

Which it was for awhile, at the end of summer and during the first couple of weeks of fall, despite his depression at not fitting in at the new school. There were trips up to April Devon's house on the mountain, where they looked at fabrics and catalogues and April's bizarrely impressionistic paintings—all laid out in the amazing workspace and gallery that overlooked the valley below. And there were other trips, to the museum in Baltimore on a school day, and to the antique stores in the historic part of town— "*Getaways to your destiny*," as April had put it, after seeing his own work.

Now more than ever he wanted to remember those good times—to pretend they completely overshadowed the depression that seemed to cling to his mother. But again and again she had assured him she was fine.

"Don't worry baby. There are people with far bigger problems than mine. People with secrets that'll damn near kill them."

He remembered that conversation vividly, it had taken place after she had spent a long afternoon at April Devon's house.

He went back to the window. The neighborhood had been emptied of trees before the houses had been built. His house sat on a slight rise that gave him a view of the main avenue. From a distance of two blocks he saw Madison Reidy's midnight blue Range Rover pull up to the stop sign. He felt a familiar twinge in his chest as he thought of their first meeting in the front yard the week they moved in; Madison introducing herself and Marco Niles, bright-eyed and smiling with her promises of how much he and Sara were going to *love* life at Langford Secondary. Her casual stroking of his upper arm as she spoke to him; the earnest way she seemed to be listening as he took her and Marco through the house and showed them one of his portfolios of work.

And then came the *change*—the night-and-day difference the first week of school, when he came toward her in the hallway, assuming her face would light up again; anticipating that she would introduce him to her friends. He had been shocked at the blank look in her eyes and then the way she glanced beyond him, as if she was looking for an escape, and then the barest acknowledgment as she passed by with a muttered *"Hey Kenneth—busy day."*

The change was staggeringly unexpected—like being doused with ice-cold water as he stood alone in the hall—and made all the worse by the feeling that everyone around them had seen the snub.

Months later the whole exchange remained a mystery. He had absolutely no idea what he might have said or done to bring it on. His reaction was also a mystery. He knew that he should have been angry—knew that he would have been stronger in the long run by simply writing Madison Reidy off as a shallow, self-centered enemy.

Instead he simply struggled with the *hurt*, still imagined day after day that she would somehow change back; that the distance in her eyes would suddenly vanish and she would smile at him again.

Stupid, stupid, he thought, feeling like a voyeur now as he watched the Rover turn the corner. Madison was driving too fast, as if she didn't realize how slick the pavement was. From the distance he saw her hands on the wheel and then the familiar shape of her face as she came closer. He was about to step back when he saw the slight upward tilt of her head and knew that she saw him, standing at the window, watching her. There was a sudden change in the Rover's speed—as if she reflexively hit the brake—followed by a sideways shift in the back end as she hit the brake again.

And then the Rover was spinning, missing the parked cars by inches as it smacked the curb, bounced and came down in a hard stop across the sidewalk.

He stood still, his breath trapped in his throat, the curtain wadded tightly in his hand. After several seconds he saw the front wheels turning backward, the SUV shuddering slightly but staying in place, then heard the muffled gunning of the engine, as if Madison, out of frustration, had the accelerator pushed all the way to the floor. But it wasn't working. The back wheels were lodged in the deep snow that had been pushed aside by the first run of the plows.

He stepped back from the window, feeling embarrassed for her predicament; embarrassed because he had seen it happen. Then he pulled the curtain aside and looked down at the Rover again, watching as she stepped out and walked unsteadily toward the front of the vehicle, looking for whatever was keeping the wheels from turning. Her skin had a grayish hue. She looked exhausted, beaten down as she brushed back her soft blonde hair with a bright red gloved hand, then glanced upward, as if she knew he would still be staring at her from his bedroom window.

"Misfits."

The word was stuck in his mind now, and with it the image of Sara and Aidan walking to class, and himself, knocked to the floor at school.

His mood lifted instantly as Madison met his eyes, and didn't look away.

Another chance, he thought, and after a quick wave and a nervous smile he turned and moved very quickly down to the entry hall closet to grab his coat and then into the garage for the shovel, stepping lightly with the prospect of coming to her rescue.

Kieran stood in front of the desk in his bedroom. He was still wearing his wet coat and boots; still feeling the icy outside air on his ears as he stared down at the laptop.

He touched the keyboard. The screen came to life with the stories about the murders and with a still image of Lori Porter's car in the gorge. He remembered sitting in the same place the night before, obsessing over Caruso's suspicions as he waited for Sara to arrive, and thinking about being charged with murder and sent away from Aidan, who would never have survived without him.

He sat down and stared at the screen; imagined Caruso seeing it and realizing that years of *normality* as Aidan's guardian were nothing more than a mask for the sickness in his mind.

He did what he had intended to do the night before, deleting his history of the online stories on the murders, knowing that it was probably useless if Caruso arranged to have his computer confiscated.

Only one way to destroy the trail for good.

He turned the laptop over. The compartment that held the hard drive was clearly marked, and secured with four small screws. He paused, his thoughts slowed by fatigue, and then got up and went to the room's small closet. He had secured the door with a combination lock around the pulls that opened it. Inside, he kept ammunition for his gun and a small box that contained the tools with sharp points and edges that he had to keep away from Aidan.

The tiny screws that held the panel dropped to the floor as he loosened them. The hard drive slid easily out of the side of the computer. He held it in his palm and imagined pounding it to bits against the cement step in front of the house, but shivered at the thought of going back outside so soon.

He stepped into the hallway and stood at the door to Aidan's room, which was still secured by the deadbolt, and listened for sounds of Sara moving about. He heard nothing, and wasn't surprised. He had given her a capsule of Rohypnol, enough to keep her dazed for hours.

He went to the living room and kneeled in front of the stove and slipped the hard drive into a space between the grate and a small piece of charred but still-burnable wood. He pulled two pages from the stack of newspapers in the basket next to the stove, wadded them up and stuck them under the wood and lit them. The flames shot up around the edges of the hard drive, and the black plastic around it began to crackle and melt.

He went to the desk where Aidan had done his homework. Aidan's schoolbooks from the night before were still stacked in the corner. He sat down and pulled a lined sheet of paper from a notebook and started writing, describing Aidan's death, and the sight of Stephen Porter's SUV, driving away.

The piece from Porter's broken taillight cover came next, a jagged shard of hard red glass that he had found in the snow beside Aidan's body and slipped into his pocket just as Caruso had arrived.

He held it in his hand, the sharp point pressing against the calloused flesh of his thumb, the pain bringing his intent into sharp focus, then slipped it into the envelope.

He wrote "John Caruso" on the front of the envelope and put it in the zippered inside pocket of his coat.

He went back to the couch and sat down; felt the weight of the gun in his pocket; thought of Sara in Aidan's bedroom, drugged and immobile.

"Shoot her dead."

"Shoot yourself."

He shut his eyes tightly to block the voices. After a few seconds of silence he took the gun from his pocket and set it on the table, next to the bong, which had half an inch of cloudy water at the bottom. He picked it up, found it still loaded. There had been times in the past when the weed had silenced the voices and calmed his nerves. He needed to be calm now.

He flicked the lighter he had left on the table the night before. The flame vibrated from the shakiness of his hand as he put it to the pot. The embers glowed as he put the bong to his mouth and sucked in, relishing the taste and feel of the harsh, sweet smoke streaming through his throat and into his lungs.

He put his legs up on the couch and leaned back, his eyelids fluttering shut as exhaustion from the long night and day pulled him into a daze. There was a vague tingling underneath the skin of his face, a feeling of weightlessness as he imagined that he was gazing down at his own body, lying still and composed.

And then the flames flared through the open door of the stove, momentarily brightening the light of the room.

"Kier…an."

He opened his eyes. Aidan was standing near the doorway that led to the original part of the house. He looked as he had at five years old, *the day after his birthday.* Kieran knew it by the sight of his brother's light blue flannel pajamas, and his high, childish voice.

"Help me."

The sound of racing car engines filled the room—a roar loud enough to hurt his ears as images of stock cars filled the screen of the television.

He became aware of another presence. He tried to move—to lift his head toward the sight at the edge of his vision—but was immobilized until the figure came into view; at first a familiar, bulky shadow, until the light from the fire fell on her face.

It was Nurlene, in the flesh-colored bra and the black jeans that she had yanked on as she had stumbled out of bed, cursing at being awakened at an early hour by the sound of the television that Aidan had turned up to ear-splitting volume and forgotten.

He watched helplessly as the dream image of Aidan shrank back, his eyes wide and terrified as she approached—

And slapped him.

Aidan's tiny knees buckled. Kieran heard the ringing in his brother's ears as if it was his own, and had a momentary vision through Aidan's eyes, looking up at her, her mouth spitting saliva through an angry rant, her words lost in the roar from the television.

And then he watched as she grabbed the back of Aidan's pajama top and carried him, wriggling and screaming, toward the closet in the front room of the trailer. He heard the *thump* of Aidan's body hitting the inside closet wall. And then he saw a teenaged vision of himself standing in the front room, next to a table he had started working on in shop class the day before, his open toolbox on the floor.

He turned back to look at Nurlene as she kicked Aidan in his stomach.

She's going to kill him, he thought.

Right here; right now.

The rest unfolded in a wavy procession of images as he saw himself moving as if he was underwater, acting on sudden impulse but swimming against the current as he grabbed the claw hammer from the toolbox, his footsteps lost in the roar of the television as he advanced, holding the hammer with two hands as he came up behind her.

His voice was a breathless scream as he brought it down, claw-first, against the back of her skull.

He heard a wet *thump* and a grunt from her mouth as blood flew up in a spray against the dirty white wall, and watched as she dropped to her knees and then fell face-down on the floor. Her hands and fingers scrabbled outward from an involuntary twitching of nerves before a last, faint gurgle came from her throat.

Fully immersed in the recollection now, he watched himself from a distance, setting the hammer down and picking Aidan up and carefully turning his head away from Nurlene's still body. Blood dripped from Aidan's nose and onto his shoulder as he took him from the closet to his bedroom and laid him down on the bed. In his memory he whispered calming words into Aidan's ear but he didn't know now or then if Aidan had heard him.

He knew she was dead when he came back in the room and prodded her shoulder with his foot. She was completely still, a massive, unmoving pile of flesh.

He leaned forward, his hands on his knees, and felt a suffocating pressure on his lungs.

The tremors came next, radiating through his entire body as he stepped forward and grabbed the back of the couch to steady himself and looked around the room—at the blood on the wall and the pool of it beside her head—as all of the colors faded into shades of pale blues and grays.

He thought of the deputies coming to the house, arresting him and sending him away. And then he thought of Aidan, abandoned and alone. A terror that quickly cleared his head and enabled him to see the only way out.

He made the 911 call two hours later. By then the room where Nurlene had died had been scrubbed clean and her body had been moved outside the side door, the back of her head placed against the edge of the concrete landing and her body sprawled face-up on the icy steps below.

John Caruso had been the first deputy to arrive. But Caruso had been to the house countless times before, taking his reports on the injuries reported by the school nurses and the social workers. Saying nothing about the impending death of his own son even though it was known to everyone on the mountain, yet conveying, with every interaction with Nurlene, a simmering rage over the abuse he and Aidan had suffered.

After pretending to believe the story about the fall, Caruso had sat with him during the questioning by a detective and yet another social worker, nodding as he repeated the story, word for word, again.

Weeks later, with help from Caruso, he was under the care of a psychiatrist and the spell of the medications that brought him balance against the two selves battling for control of his mind. The *killer* who caved in Nurlene's skull. And the *savior* of his little brother's life.

Aidan.

Gone now.

Broken neck dead and cold.

He opened his eyes, and slowly sat up, felt the weight of the gun in his pocket.

With me.

He looked around the room, feeling Nurlene's presence without seeing her there; understanding then what the voices had been telling him ever since he dropped to his knees and held Aidan's body in his arms.

"You protected him in life."

"Protect him in death."

He picked up the gun and thought of how terrified Sara would bc when she saw it. Not that it mattered. It was going to happen quickly. A retribution that would take place at the side of Rolling Road, at the exact spot where her father had run Aidan down.

❄ ❄ ❄

Sara heard the creak of the floorboard outside Aidan's room and slowly sat up. Pain speared her temples as images ran like rapid snapshots through her mind: Kieran gripping the wheel of his truck. The snowy woods rushing by. The blood on Kieran's black leather coat.

"Aidan's blood."

Kieran's voice came from the memory of him standing over her, forcing her to acknowledge what her father had done.

And then she heard the sound of the deadbolt, flicking open.

Kieran stood in the doorway, still wearing the bloody coat. He had one hand in his pocket, and she could tell by the crook in his arm that he was holding something in it.

"Kieran…" Her voice was weak. "What are you doing?"

He said nothing. The stubble on his face was darker and thicker. She tried to remember how he had looked at her in the past, the flicker of warmth in his eyes, the magnetism that had always seemed to connect them.

The feeling was gone now.

"You drugged me, locked me in here." The defiance in her own voice surprised her. "Why?"

"You know why," he said.

"Because of something my *father* did? Which was an accident and something I had nothing to do with?"

"Lie down," he said.

"No."

Another step and he was standing over her.

She glanced past him. He had left the door open. She tried to imagine herself punching him between the legs, forcing him to double over in pain, giving her time to leap from the bed and rush through the front of the house and outside—

Impossible.

She looked up and did her best to bring the defiance back.

"Are you going to hurt me?"

He put his hand on her shoulder.

"*Please just tell me what you want!*"

His grip tightened as he pushed her down on the bed. She surprised both of them with a hard kick that landed against his side. He grunted faintly from the blow and suddenly thrust one arm under her back and flipped her over. She tasted dust from the bedcover as she gasped for breath, and felt her hands being yanked together and bound. She recalled the stories about her mother and the murdered women on his computer.

He killed them.

And he's going to kill you.

He grabbed her shoulder again and tossed her off the bed as if she weighed nothing. She landed painfully on her knees. The room swayed around her as he grabbed the back of her shirt and pulled her to her feet. Then before she could react he wrapped his forearm around the front of her neck and prodded her forward.

He walked her into the front room and gave her a hard push that knocked her sideways over the arm of the couch. Both of the windows in the room were covered by blinds and the only light came from a lamp on the desk and from a low glow from the woodstove.

He left her there and went over to the desk and picked up an envelope. He held it in his hands and went still, as if he was suddenly lost in thought.

She looked around the room, searching for a way out. A memory came back to her; a glimmer of hope.

"I need to go to the bathroom."

Kieran said nothing. He looked as if he hadn't even heard her.

"Kieran—*please*?" She practically shouted.

"Then go. You know where it is."

She awkwardly stood up, her balance off-kilter with her hands behind her back. "I can't, like this."

He stared at her for a moment longer, then went into the kitchen and opened one of the upper cabinets and pulled out a metal box and set it on the counter. He pulled his keys from his pocket and inserted one into the lock. She remembered him telling her that Aidan had gone through a phase of fascination with sharp objects, an obsession that Kieran believed he had grown out of but only after he had come up with a way to keep the kitchen knives out of his reach.

He pulled a long, narrow knife from the box and held it at his side as he came back toward her. She shut her eyes as she felt his grip on her wrists and the cutting of the duct tape that he had used to bind them.

She let her hands drop to her sides, realizing only then that her fingers had begun to grow numb. She felt him watching her as she headed toward the bathroom in the original trailer section of the house, and quickly turned around and pushed it shut.

The plastic shower curtain was closed. She pinched the bottom corner and gently pulled it aside. The dismantled shower head she had seen the night before was still there, surrounded by tools on the shower floor. She started to reach for them but stopped at the creak in the floor on the other side of the door.

He's waiting, she thought. *Listening.*

She lowered the seat of the toilet so it made a noise that would be audible outside the door, slid her skirt and underwear down and sat. For a long moment she thought it would be impossible to pee but finally she managed a faint trickle that she expected he would hear.

She heard another creak of a floorboard just before she flushed, the sound of Kieran walking away. She moved quickly to take advantage of the soft roar of water refilling the toilet and stepped over to the dismantled shower nozzle. There was a Phillips head screwdriver lying on the floor. The shaft was short—no more than five inches—and the molded plastic handle fit easily in her hand, the tool small enough to have been forgotten in Kieran's efforts to keep dangerous items out of Aidan's reach.

She slipped it into the side pocket of her skirt then quickly turned back to the sink. She stared for several seconds at her reflection in the mirror. Her skin was completely drained of color and her pupils were dilated. She felt the shape of the screwdriver through the fabric of her skirt and tried to imagine herself wielding it as a weapon, *stabbing* him.

It was a horrifying thought. She leaned forward and remembered looking into the same mirror the night before. Dabbing gloss onto her lips, anticipating the touch of Kieran's hands—

Feeling love.

The toilet stopped filling. The room was silent.

She turned the doorknob and slowly opened the door, still expecting him to be standing there. But he was back in the main room, sitting on the edge of the sofa.

She glanced toward the front door, thought briefly of trying to run, but knew she wouldn't get far. Instead she reached into the pocket of her skirt and slowly walked toward him. She stared at the back of his leather coat; tried to imagine how far the short metal shaft of the tool would penetrate if she stabbed him, and watched as he brought his hands up and covered his ears and started rocking, forward and backward, a low hum coming from the base of his throat, as if he was in some kind of trance.

She took one more step, heard him whisper "No…*no*!"

And knew that what she had seen hours before was happening again; knew that he was hearing things.

The humming sound in his voice became louder, and the forward and backward motion stopped. He lowered his head and began to cry.

She felt a sudden swelling at the back of her throat, and thought of the wracking sobs that had overtaken her so often after her mother's death.

She took a step forward, her knees still weak. She took her hand out of her pocket, and gently placed it on his shoulder.

He tensed, then and stood up and turned around to face her. There were tears running down his cheeks.

He covered his face with his hands. She felt a sudden, powerful urge to hold him in her arms. She resisted, but reached up and lightly covered his hands with her own.

The touch of his skin sent a tingling sensation down her arms.

"I loved Aidan too," she said.

He slowly drew his hands away from his face. And then suddenly he was looking at her the way he always had. In the tutoring room as she worked with his brother. Behind the closed door of his office as she told him things she could tell no one else. In this same room the night before, with Aidan at her side.

In that moment he became the Kieran she knew.

There are two parts of him.

She knew it for certain as she saw the pain in his eyes.

One to love, and one to fear.

"You have to get some help."

He went completely still. She heard a faint crackling sound in the stove, and then saw a flash of flame, as if a piece of wood had reignited.

Kieran's eyes widened slightly, and she saw the motion of his Adam's apple as he swallowed, and then with a spasmodic jerk of his head as he stared into the fire. His mouth started moving, soundlessly, and his eyes opened wider, as if he had just seen something horrifying.

"Kieran—" She touched his forearm.

He jerked it back and covered his ears with his hands.

She tightened her hold, staring at the beads of perspiration on his forehead.

He shook his head back and forth, whispering, and then shouting "No no *NO!*"

"Kieran—"

He slapped the side of her face, sending an explosion of light in front of her eyes as she went down over the arm of the sofa. He grabbed the back of her shirt and yanked her back up and spun her around, his left arm flat against her stomach, his right coming around into a chokehold on her neck. Panic shot through her as the crook of his arm tightened against the soft spot below her windpipe. Her right hand brushed against the handle of the screwdriver but she had no chance to reach for it as Kieran shifted his weight and tightened his grip, applying more pressure to the side of her neck, locking her in a vise.

She shook violently in his arms, and managed to punch her elbow into his stomach. She heard a grunt and felt a rush of air on the back of her neck and broke away as he doubled over. She spun around and rushed toward the door—almost making it before he grabbed her around the waist and threw her back down.

She saw the edge of the table an instant before it struck her, dead-center at her forehead. She felt a sharp, hot pain. And then she saw nothing but the darkness, swallowing her whole.

27

Stephen made his way along the mountain road one step at a time, balancing precariously on the icy surface of the pavement as the pain pulsed through his ribs. The muscles of his face felt frozen, immobilized by the snow he had pressed against his nose to slow the bleeding. His mind fixated on the certainty that he would soon see the headlights of a car; that he would stand in the middle of the road to stop it and get the driver to call 911 while taking him back to O'Shea's house. Sara would be there, waiting for him. He would admit everything to her and admit it all again when the police arrived.

And then it would be over. He would be charged with a hit and run death. There would be headlines. And shame, he thought, for Sara and Kenneth too.

"Please...*God*." He whispered the words out loud, praying for the first time in years, and found himself back at Lori's funeral, gazing at the casket. Looking to Sara on his right and Kenneth on his left with the terrible sense that his children were likewise slipping away from him.

And now he knew it was going to happen. He was going to prison. The separation of his family would be complete.

His legs stiffened and began to shake. And then suddenly he could barely move as he shut his eyes and saw Kieran O'Shea looming over him .

He could have killed you.

The thought pushed him to keep moving, with shallow, anxious breaths amid the flashes of pain in his upper body, listening for the signs of an approaching car.

28

Joseph Niles kept a stolen Glock 17 in a locked drawer that was part of the built-in shelving in his bedroom closet. The gun was in good shape; Joseph disassembled and cleaned it once a month. The drawer also held a suppressor that fit the threaded barrel and muffled the sound when he took it out for target practice in the woods. He affixed the suppressor to the barrel and went into the master bath to get a hand towel that he wadded up and put in his pocket, which held the disposable cell phone he had just purchased at a convenience store that did not appear to have a security camera.

He looked into the mirror over the sink and stared at the dazed expression in his eyes and the blue-black bruise. The wound still hurt like Hell—a persistent reminder of the clumsy punch from Marco the day before. The punch had landed high, but with enough force to send him into an uncontrolled rage, resulting in a flurry of blows that nearly knocked his stepson unconscious.

That beating was nothing compared to what had just happened, in the family room at the back of the house. Marco hadn't fought back this time—the first sucker punch robbed him of that opportunity, and Joseph had had to force himself not to finish him off.

Would have been so easy to kill him, he thought now. *Right there. Problem solved.*

But the real problem would have still been there, tracking him for life.

He went downstairs. Marco had been lying in a fetal position on the floor an hour earlier, groaning and whining enough to make Niles wonder about internal bleeding.

The space on the floor was empty. Marco made his way over to the couch and was in a fetal position once again, but with his eyes closed.

Joseph took a few steps closer, listened to the ragged sound of his stepson's breathing. He then went out through the family room at the back of the house and into the three-car garage. The Hummer that Marco had been driving when he was arrested was still in the impound lot and wouldn't be released until after the Monday morning hearing. But the second one that he had bought ten years before was there, in perfect condition thanks to clockwork maintenance.

He stepped past it toward the Taurus that he used for work. It was gun-metal gray and unmarked, and probably less likely to be remembered by anyone in passing traffic. He slipped in, turned on the ignition and cranked up the heat before taking out the cell phone and tapping out a short text to April Devon.

And then he was moving through the suburban streets. The early afternoon temperature was well below the freezing mark, but the pavement that had been plowed and salted earlier gave him some traction as he headed out of his suburban neighborhood and the back roads that would take him up the mountain.

He checked the phone for a reply when he was within ten minutes of April's house. There wasn't one, and when he called her cell he went straight into voice mail. He hung up, sticking again to his rule to never leave a recording of his voice on her phone.

The final quarter mile to the house took him up along one of the highest ridges of Short Mountain. The house was built on the edge of the ridge overlooking the valley below, a simple brick ranch set back at least fifty yards from the road amid tall trees.

He knew the house well, because he had paid for it.

With blood money, he thought. *Draining you dry.*

29

Madison looked down at her Range Rover from the second floor dormer window of Kenneth Porter's house. The Rover was parked in Kenneth's driveway, looking beat-up from the salt that had been used on the road and the fresh sheen of ice on the windows. The last hour had a surreal quality and her mind was still trying to make sense of everything Kenneth had done for her; emerging from his garage with a shovel, working with surprising strength and stamina to free the Rover's back wheels from the snow, wrapping his arms around her trembling shoulders and asking—no, *insisting*—that she come into his house to warm up.

It was equally strange now, to be in his bedroom, sitting face to face on some very nice blue and white upholstered chairs, drinking coffee out of what looked like hand-painted mugs, and hearing Kenneth ask her, for the third time, if she was all right.

This time she answered honestly. "I'm tired I guess. Late night last night." She tried to smile. "Probably didn't help my driving much."

Kenneth glanced out the window and made a dismissive motion with his hand "The whole street's a sheet of ice, Madison. It could have happened to anyone."

He looked like he would say anything just to keep her from being uncomfortable. It was a strange feeling, to be *liked* so much, especially by someone she had been so awful to. In hindsight it was hard to imagine what had possessed her to call Marco and bait him with the idea that poor Kenneth Porter had some kind of gay infatuation with him. Hard to imagine how she could have been so cruel.

Kenneth gave her a slight, shy smile.

"What?" she asked him.

"Nothing." He blushed, as if he'd been caught admiring her.

"You're too nice, Kenneth."

He shrugged.

"No really. I don't deserve this."

"What makes you say that?"

If you only knew. She took a longer look around the room. He had insisted on bringing her up here, talking for several minutes about his favorite artists and about the college—a "design school" she had never heard of—that he hoped to attend in a few years. She had listened with interest, intrigued by his intensity and thinking—with the lingering weed and vodka buzz—how funny it was to be in the room of a teenaged boy who wanted to do nothing more than *talk* to her.

And even now—knowing how hellish it must have been to be beaten up in a high school hallway, how alienated he must have felt when no one but his sister tried to help him—she had the feeling that none of what he was going through at the moment was very important.

Like he's in his own world, she thought. *An artist in his garret, biding his time until he gets away from people like you.*

"I know about what happened," she said. "Yesterday, at school."

The light fell from his eyes. She felt a flash of guilt.

"I'm sorry Kenneth."

"Sorry?" He frowned, as if she had just given herself away.

"Yes…" She sat back slightly, searched for the right words. "I mean, I don't know why anyone would hurt you."

Her mouth hung slightly open, as it always did when she thought she might be caught in a lie. Kenneth was still staring at her, still expecting her to tell him something that would explain why he'd been beat up.

She thought of one very simple way to do that.

"Can you imagine what it would be like to go through life knowing that your own father hated you?"

He gave her a confused look. "Uh, no."

"Well that's what it's like for Marco."

She paused, suddenly conscious of a chill at the back of her neck. Marco had always been superstitious about revealing anything about what happened in his house, and she was certain that she was the only one who really knew.

"His family is nothing like yours. Your father would do anything for you."

He looked down into his cup. "I know."

"Which makes you ten times luckier than me."

"What's that supposed to mean?"

She attempted a good-natured smirk. "My family's a mess—always has been. I think they would have been just as happy if I hadn't come along."

"Madison, that can't be true."

The earnestness in his expression made her smile. "Yeah well, it is." She looked around the room again, feeling a sense of calm in the clean, peaceful blue and tan tones. She had often imagined that one day in the not-too-distant future she'd follow her mother's lead and start spending half her nights in therapy. She expected she'd feel as she did at the moment—encouraged and emboldened to speak about her worst fears: That ten years from now she'd be looking back and wondering how she had gotten through high school at the height of popularity but without any real friends. That her attraction to Marco had become an obsession that was going to break her heart. That she and Marco were both headed for some impending tragedy due as much to their completely dysfunctional families as to the horrible way they had both been behaving.

Particularly when it came to people like Kenneth and Sara Porter.

Innocents, she thought, with a fresh wave of remorse.

"We're not perfect either," Kenneth said. "Sometimes I think our problems are even worse. My mom. My dad. My sister."

"Your sister's a nice girl," she said, without thinking.

Kenneth frowned in surprise, because they both knew there was no longer any semblance of friendship.

"I'm sorry I was such a bitch to her." Her voice cracked.

"You should tell her that."

"I will," she said, knowing she would never have the courage. "Is she around?"

Kenneth shook his head and gazed past her, toward the dormered window.

"She went out a couple of hours ago. With Mr. O'Shea."

"*What*?"

Kenneth sat back slightly, looking surprised by the intensity of her reaction.

She carefully set her coffee mug down on the small table next to the chair. "Are you sure?"

"Yeah," Kenneth said. "I saw her walk out of the house and get into his truck right after I woke up."

"Do you know why?"

"No. Maybe it was because of what happened to Mr. O'Shea's little brother. She was his tutor."

She leaned forward slightly, her palms pressed between her knees. "So you heard what happened to Aidan."

Kenneth nodded. She stared at him, her heart sinking once again with the thought of Kieran and Sara at the tutoring center at school; the memory Kieran's hand on Sara's shoulder as he leaned down and said something that made her smile.

She felt her mouth going dry. "Where do you think they went?"

Kenneth stared down at his phone. "I don't know but something's wrong. I can feel it."

"Maybe they're at his house," she said. "Up on Short Mountain."

He frowned. "You know where he *lives*?"

She nodded, remembering the time she had spent online after seeing Kieran and Sara in the tutoring room, and the address she had found for Kieran online. Curiosity overwhelmed her as she thought of them, mourning the loss of Aidan together.

"Yes I think we could find it."

"Do think we should—"

"I think we *have* to," she said, cutting off any debate. "If you really want to make sure she's okay."

30

Caruso went to a conference room to make the call to April Devon. After three rings he went into her voice mail, and left a terse message: "I know about your history with Joseph Niles. Call me ASAP. We need to talk."

And then he waited, scrolling through the crime scene photographs and transcripts and reports of a six-year-old murder that he had pulled from the VICAP and NCIS databases and news media web sites and saved to his laptop. A crime of uncanny similarities to his currently active investigations.

April called him back five minutes later, sounding anxious and short of breath. Under different circumstances he would have asked her to come into headquarters to talk with him in an official setting but he wanted to ensure she wasn't spotted by Niles. Fortunately she was already downtown, and agreed to meet him in a more informal setting that was probably better suited to his purpose.

❄ ❄ ❄

He watched her enter the restaurant from a booth at the very back, seeing her differently now behind the artsy glasses and pale red hair and black, nondescript clothing. Her shoulders were slumped as she walked, conveying an obvious reluctance to be there.

She stood still for a moment when she reached the booth, and gave him a long look, as if she was trying to discern how much he knew. He gave her a half smile and a nod back. He needed her to be relaxed, her guard lowered.

"Thanks for coming," he said.

"Like I had a choice?"

He motioned toward the opposite seat at the booth. "You're here voluntarily as far as I'm concerned. Just helping me clear a couple of things up."

April gave the room around them a quick, nervous glance and sat down. The waitress came to the booth. She ordered coffee, which was delivered quickly from the nearby bus station. Caruso waited until she poured in the cream, and then got right to the point.

"I guess I can start by telling you I arrested Niles' stepson today, for DUI and possession of marijuana."

She stared down at the tabletop, both hands gripping the mug. "Is that what we're here to talk about?"

"Partly. But I'm more interested in Niles' ex-wife. Your sister, Sheila."

She shut her eyes, looking as if a long-dreaded moment had finally come.

He opened up the laptop and brought up the first file, a screen shot from an adult entertainment site showing covers of DVDs that featured the performer who went by the name of Sheila "Sexton" in hardcore S & M films. Like April, she had strawberry blonde hair and blue eyes. Unlike April, who didn't appear to wear makeup and who couldn't have weighed more than a hundred pounds, she had outsized and obviously enhanced breasts, elaborate tattoos on her arms and lower back, and a bold, come-on expression well-suited to her profession.

April glanced briefly at the screen, and shook her head.

"Sorry," he said.

"It's nothing I haven't seen before."

"You want to tell me more about her?"

Her nostrils flared as she looked back down at the tabletop. "Which part about do you want to know? The drug addict, or the mental case, or maybe just the *perverted*—"

"How did she hook up with Joseph Niles?"

He watched the rise and fall of her chest, a series of deep breaths that seemed to calm her down.

"In Nevada, from what we know. That's where she went when she ran away from home at seventeen. She'd already been doing drugs for years and had become a complete stranger to our family. We found out a few years after she left that she had a child. She wrote us a letter and said she was getting married and moving back to northern Virginia. We learned later that she'd been working as a prostitute. It's legal there. That's where she met Joseph. He got a job with the DC police and they moved to a suburb just outside the city. She kept her last name."

Caruso nodded, mentally checking off what she told him from the details he had compiled on his own.

"I think she got a weird thrill out of marrying a cop," she said. "Particularly someone like Joseph, who had all kinds of perversions, according to what she told me later. It was a scary relationship—the whole moth and flame thing. He regularly beat the Hell out of her; she allowed and probably encouraged it. But eventually they came to *hate* each other."

"So he killed her."

She stared at him across the booth, acknowledging it without saying a word.

After a moment he turned the laptop back around so she couldn't see the screen, then scrolled through shots of a crime scene. It was the first floor bedroom of a house in Fairfax County, Virginia. Sheila Devon's face was bruised and battered beyond recognition. Her nightgown had been ripped from her body, and she'd been manually strangled. The autopsy suggested the killer had put his full weight on her chest, breaking two of her ribs as he squeezed the life out of her.

Just like the death of Cherilynn Jenkins, Caruso thought. *A first floor intruder, in the middle of the night. And similar enough to the murder of Danica Morris, with the beating and strangulation.*

"It was set up to look like a break-in," he said.

"Yes, that's what I heard."

"But Joseph wasn't charged."

"No, he knew what he was doing. He came up with an alibi by booking himself into a hotel in Virginia Beach that weekend, but he could have easily driven back for a few hours in the middle of the night. There wasn't any physical evidence tying him to it. He lawyered up with someone from the police union. And since there wasn't any proof of his involvement the lawyer was able to keep the whole thing off his record."

Caruso nodded. In the absence of charges a good police union advocate would have ensured Niles' file was clean.

"I'm guessing you knew that he never would have been hired here if we knew," he said.

"Of course not."

"So you blackmailed him."

Her jaw dropped slightly, a telling sign. "That's not true."

"You moved here right after he got hired, April. And I just talked to the real estate agent who handled the purchase of your house up on the mountain. She told me it was a cash deal."

Her face reddened. "That doesn't prove anything."

"Maybe not. But it's suspicious enough since you rented your last home in Virginia and the space you used for your business. And you paid plenty for the new place—buying the view I suppose."

"None of that means anything."

"Maybe not, in the long run. And I don't really care."

"Then why did you bring it up?"

"Because it points to a pattern of deception. You told me you don't have any clue what happened to Lori Porter."

She blinked nervously; another telling sign.

He waited a moment and then, as he had planned, he extended the olive branch.

"Look, I messed up too, April."

She gave him a guarded look.

"Niles and I have been working together for almost a year. We each had different responsibilities on the murder cases. He volunteered to search the databases for any other crimes that were similar to the Danica Morris murder and told me there weren't. If I'd done that on my own I might have found your sister's murder, and seen that she was married to Niles and figured it out. But because I left it up to him the connection wasn't made."

"Poor you."

"Don't be sarcastic."

She pursed her lips, still looking anxious about what was coming.

"The point is I've got to play catch up now—have to learn everything I should have learned before and have to figure out how to put the squeeze on him. So I'm asking you to please come clean about everything you haven't told me about Lori Porter, Danica Morris and the woman who was killed yesterday."

She looked past him, toward the swinging door that led to the kitchen.

"Please," he said. "Just tell me what you know."

She sighed, and met his eyes. "I already told you I don't believe Lori killed herself. I knew her well enough to know she wouldn't have done that."

"Prove it," he said.

She pursed her lips again, showing her anger at being pushed.

He tilted his head slightly, waiting for her to finish.

"We confided in each other after we got to be friends. She had a troubled marriage. Felt a lot of guilt about an affair she had, and how much it hurt her husband. I told her about my screwed up sister—told her everything in all of its horrible detail. She was the only person I was ever able to talk to about it. The best friend I had."

"You told me before you were barely acquainted. Why?"

"Because I didn't want to talk with you about any of this anymore. I was just as worried as you were about the connection between Lori's death and that woman—Danica's—murder. I knew that you'd have a lot more questions if you knew Lori and I were close."

And that I'd keep looking at your past, and Joseph's past, he thought. *And that secret deal you worked out—*

"But that's not the only reason," she said, as if she'd read his mind.

"Then why else?"

Her eyes welled with tears.

"Shame."

"What do you mean?"

"Exactly what I said. I was ashamed, embarrassed about my sister...and what kind of person she was. And I sure as Hell didn't want to believe Joseph had any connection to the murder of that girl."

"Even though it happened shortly after he moved here and took this job."

"Yes. I wanted to believe it was just a coincidence."

"But now you think otherwise?"

She nodded.

"So you know Niles killed Danica Morris...and Cherilynn Jenkins." He made a point to use their names. "In the same way he killed Sheila—"

She shook her head. "No."

"You just said you do."

"No, I said I don't believe it's a coincidence."

He frowned, as if she had to be kidding.

"I always had an ulterior motive for moving here after Joseph got the job. I *wanted* to be close to him, so he would always know I was watching him, after what he did to Sheila. I confronted him the day after I heard about the death of that woman, which happened close to my house. He swore he didn't have anything to do with it—even made a big deal out of the fact that her brother, who also lives up on the mountain, has been arrested for dealing drugs a couple of times, and that her killer was probably one of the low-lifes he dealt with. And then he proved he couldn't have been there when it happened—showed me a receipt from Billiards and Brews out on the highway…I didn't want to believe him, but it was time-stamped so I took it for what it was, as physical proof that he was there the night of that murder. But even so I knew he was telling the truth. I hate Joseph but I also understand him. I know what makes him tick. And I knew from his reaction that he didn't kill that woman, and he didn't have anything to do with Lori's death."

"You really believe that."

"It's not a matter of belief. It's about what I know, and about the other woman who was killed yesterday."

He watched as she took another long, deep breath.

"What are you saying?"

She met his eyes with a look of sad resignation. "I saw the story on the noontime news, so I knew about the similarities to my sister's murder, and the murder of that woman the night Lori died. And then I saw the follow-up stories this morning, and called Joseph right away. I asked him again—*did you do it?* He denied it but I said if you didn't, then who did? And that's when he told me I should know.

"I didn't say anything—I was confused. But then he said 'It all goes back to Sheila, who she was and what she did.' And then I remembered the victim was a teacher at Langford Secondary. And then it all made sense. Sheila and Joseph. The way he killed her. And the reason."

She paused, looking past him once again, as if her mind was drifting.

"My sister molested her own son. Sexually and repeatedly during the last year of their marriage. She even videotaped some of it, and showed it to Niles."

Caruso felt a chill between his shoulder blades. It crept down into his stomach and settled there as the photos of Sheila Devon's body flickered back through his mind.

"That's probably the worst part—that she *wanted* Joseph to know about it. In her sick and twisted way, it was her way of making him jealous. Pitting the two of them—her husband and her *son*—against each other. In the end *that's* why Joseph did it. That's why he killed her."

31

Marco Niles gripped the banister with both hands as he climbed the stairs. The vision in his right eye was blurred and the whole right side of his face felt as if it was on fire. Minutes earlier, when he had come-to on the basement floor, he had reached up and felt a knot rising on the right side of his forehead, just above his eye. He remembered his stepfather jerking him around and wrenching his arms around his back and slamming him into the concrete wall. The inside of his cheek was bleeding and he felt a loosened tooth with the tip of his tongue as he reached the top of the stairs…and made the mistake of turning around, and looking down.

The foyer below him rolled unevenly in his vision. He grabbed the handrail again and just barely stopped himself from falling backwards as he regained his balance and made his way to his bedroom and then into his own bathroom and saw his face in the mirror. His right eye was nearly swollen shut and the skin around the knot on his forehead was mottled and purplish-black. He opened his mouth and saw blood between his teeth, then leaned over and retched. A string of reddened saliva dropped into the sink. He stared dazedly at it for a long moment before stepping back into the bedroom.

The cracked full-length mirror rested against the wall. There were spots of blood on the light blue flannel shirt that he had put on just after the text message from Madison. He gazed at the blood stains, remembering…then felt for his cell phone in the pocket of his jeans.

The text was there, and the photo. Madison's nipples were erect and her hand was inside her underwear. He remembered taking the photo and then handing the phone back to her and fucking her with her arms pinned to the wall behind her.

His cock responded to the memory, becoming rock-hard and constricted in his jeans. His head grew light and he had to put his hand on the wall for balance as he made his way over to his desk.

His computer was as he had left it, with all of the windows closed and the history of Web sites deleted. He unzipped the fly of his jeans and sat down and opened the browser. He sucked lightly on the loosened tooth, and felt a fresh pulse of pain as he typed in the address of the Web site and watched as the screen came to life. Time stopped as he stared at the images of the women, the curves and the flesh, the wares on display. There was no end to the photos and videos; there were thousands, beckoning, pulling him along. He watched for several minutes before going to the "search" box and entering his terms and then waiting for the mix of responses that came back to him, then typed in a few more terms and saw the options narrowing. Most of the profiles were familiar, the photos embedded in his mind to be called up at will, but three new ones had been added within the last day. He saw the flashing green lights that indicated which women were online at that same moment—gazing at his own profile, the descriptions of what he liked.

A live chat box floated onto the page.

He squinted and looked closer at the profile photo and read through the things she had written about herself—

And started typing into the box.

She responded almost immediately and he responded back, just as he had to the teacher, Cherilynn Jenkins, who he had also connected with through the site. She had been cautious at first, believing from the bogus profile that he had created that he was a guy who worked construction, and had insisted on meeting him in person. She had arrived, as promised, at the Starbucks at Patriot Mall, and had waited an hour for her mystery man to show, unaware that he was watching her from a distance, an inconspicuous teenager who bore no resemblance to the thirty-year-old she had expected.

Eventually she had driven home, unaware that he had followed, in preparation for the surprise visit with the stun gun two nights ago.

It hadn't worked that way with Danica Morris, the sister of the guy who sold weed up on the mountain where April lived. Her car had broken down in the rainstorm. She had recognized him as one of her brother's customers as he had pulled over, her hair plastered to her face from the rain, smiling with relief, as if she had no doubt that he was going to help her. He had returned the smile, keeping her completely at ease. It had already been dark but she had not noticed when he turned off his headlights and emerged without a flashlight; had simply said *hello* and made a joke about knowing she should have known a little more about cars as she handed him the tire iron.

He swung it fast and hard just as she turned to get out of his way, shattering the left side of her face and knocking her sideways into the underbrush, out of sight of the road. She swatted clumsily at the air, blinded by the blood in her eyes as he dragged her ten feet into the woods. He hit her once more—a hard punch against her sternum that shocked her into silence—and then held her down with the tire iron against her throat while he fucked and choked the life out of her just seconds before the Lexus came around the bend in the road.

The driver had slowed down at the sight of the disabled car, and then she had stopped and stepped out, her umbrella turning inside out with a gust of wind as she stooped down to pick up the flashlight that had rolled into the center of the road, and seen him, at the edge of the woods.

She had reacted quickly—dropping the flashlight and running back to the idling car and speeding away. It had taken only a minute to catch up to her. The hairpin curve had taken her completely by surprise.

He learned it was Sara and Kenneth Porter's mother the next day, first through hallway rumors and later through the stories on the news.

And now the game was starting again. He watched as words appeared in the chat box at a rapid, uninhibited pace; *tell me what you like; imagine I'm fucking you, right now—*

The words blurred in his vision. He realized he had typed them subconsciously.

He pulled his hands away and dropped them to his sides.

You can't.

He knows.

The two thoughts melded in his mind as he thought about yesterday's text message—get home now—from his stepfather. And the sight of Joseph standing at the foot of the stairs as he walked through the door, holding the wallet that had fallen out of his pocket outside the teacher's apartment the night before.

The violence that followed had been the worst of his life, but it was nothing compared to the beating that came this morning, after Caruso arrested him for the DUI.

His phone chirped. He absently reached for it, intending to ignore it until he saw it was from April, the aunt who treated him like a stranger. He let the call go into voice mail, then listened to the message; his rage surging back as she told him she knew about the dead women, and telling him she had to see him, *now*, at her house on the mountain.

32

Madison was still grappling with the idea of Sara Porter comforting Kieran and the ironic fact that she and Kenneth were checking on Sara together as she turned off the interstate and onto Route 15. Aidan's death felt like a justifiable reason to try and patch things up, despite the text message Sara had sent her the previous morning: You really are a whore Madison. I never even wanted to be your friend.

Like she knew exactly how to get under your skin, she thought.

A *ding* came from the dashboard. She looked down, saw the gas gauge hovering near empty.

"Goddamn it," she muttered.

"What's wrong?" Kenneth asked.

She felt embarrassed. She had known yesterday that she needed to buy gas but the drama with Marco had superseded everything else.

She remembered a mini-mart at the base of the mountain, with two self-serve pumps and a small store, which might have been closed because of the storm. She had to make a decision. Playing it safe meant turning around to avoid the chance of being stranded on the mountain, in the snow.

But it also meant going home without knowing what had drawn Sara up there, with Kieran.

Finally, the neon antique Exxon logo appeared in the near distance. She tapped the brakes and heard the warning sound again. She was practically coasting by the time she reached the station.

She sighed with relief and pulled in.

Kenneth got out as soon as she stopped. “I’ll pump it for you.”

“Okay but—take this.” She pulled one of her mother’s credit cards from her wallet and handed it to him and watched him as he got out and came around the front of the Rover. His coat was too light for the freezing air and she could tell he was shivering as he reached for the hose.

His hands dropped to his sides as he turned and glanced toward the store.

She opened the driver’s side door. “Everything okay?”

“The credit card thing on the pump isn’t working,” he said. “I have to pay inside.”

He moved quickly toward the store, his ruddy hair blowing wildly across his forehead in the cold wind, looking so *earnest* in his concern that something bad was going to happen to his sister. The thought gave her a twinge of melancholy as she gazed out at the empty road that lay in front of them, and then into the side mirror as she heard the sound of an approaching car. It was a small white SUV. She turned her head as it passed, noting the slogan—A STITCH IN TIME—on the side and the driver, a slim, blonde woman with both hands gripping the top of the wheel, leaning forward in an anxious posture as the vehicle sped past and disappeared over the cresting rise in the road ahead.

33

Joseph Niles slowed as he neared April Dyson's house at the top of the mountain, watching the road ahead and the rearview mirror for any other vehicles.

He then looked toward the driveway. April's Sorrento wasn't there.

Not good, he thought, but made a quick decision to proceed. He shifted into reverse and went back a few hundred yards and pulled onto a shoulder that formed the entrance to one of the few logging roads that had been cut through the forest the summer before. The Taurus was partially visible to passing traffic but the need to keep her driveway free of tire tracks gave him no choice but to leave it. He then slipped deeper into the woods so he would stay concealed as he approached the house, and made his way through the knee-high snow between the trees.

He knocked twice at the side door that led to the kitchen, and after half a minute with no response he slipped on a pair of latex gloves and turned the knob. As expected, it was locked. April had added deadbolts to every exterior door shortly after moving into the place, telling him, "I have to protect myself from you." She had her gun pointed at him as she said it, adding to his humiliation after being *summoned* up to the mountain so she could dictate, in person, her terms for what she called a "truce."

He stepped away from the door, hoping that she hadn't yet added the electronic alarm system that he knew was coming, and then moved swiftly down to the back of the house. There was another door that led to the basement, concealed from view by a row of tall pine trees on the sloping back yard that overlooked the valley.

He punched out the glass directly over the knob, then reached in and unlocked it, then stood for a long moment at the threshold, holding his breath as he waited for the sound of a siren.

When it didn't happen he stepped inside. The light in the basement was faint but significant enough for him to make his way past the shelves of paints and the stacks of canvasses and bolts of fabric April stocked there. He mounted the stairs slowly, keeping his footsteps at the edges of the treads to minimize the noise on the off-chance that she was inside despite the absence of her car.

He took the gun from his pocket and stepped through the next door and into the kitchen.

The house was silent but for the sound of the mantel clock ticking in the back room that overlooked the valley. On a normal day there would have been a panoramic view, but with the heavily falling snow his sight was limited to a short stretch of road around the sharp bend that killed Lori Porter, visible through a clearing of trees at the edge of the gorge.

He watched as April's Sorrento rounded the bend, then turned away from the window, knowing he had no more than three minutes before she pulled into the driveway.

He stepped toward the door that led from the driveway to the kitchen, listening for the sound of her footsteps on the side landing and the twist of her key in the lock, then stood as still as a statue as she stepped in and stooped down to untie her snow-covered boots.

"Hey," he said.

She gasped and turned and looked up into the barrel of the gun, her eyes widening for an instant before he shot her in the face.

She fell backwards, her skull hitting the hardwood floor with a *thump*. He stared down at her as the blood spread out from beneath her head, and then lightly kicked the side door shut.

He left her there, on the kitchen floor, then reached into her purse and took her wallet and pulled the diamond ring given to her by her mother from her right hand. He took the jewelry from the box on top of her dresser next, and then did a quick sweep of the second bedroom used as an office, shuffling the contents of drawers and file cabinets in what approximated a rushed effort to find more valuables.

Satisfied that he had set the scene to look like a random break-in, he slipped back into the main room, intent on slipping out the side door. And then he glanced at the floor-to- ceiling window that offered the view of the valley, and saw the rise of inky black smoke rising from the road below.

34

Sara opened her eyes to darkness, and slowly began to make out the blurred, vibrating shapes above her. She blinked—thought *where?*—and then recognized the frames of car windows high above the cramped, dark space where she was lying. She breathed in musty smells—motor oil and dirt—and realized then that she was on the narrow floor of the back seat in Kieran's truck and the truck was moving fast.

She swallowed, felt a raw pain in her windpipe, and brought her hands to her throat as she remembered the chokehold and the blow to the side of her face that had knocked her out.

And then she remembered the weapon in the pocket of her skirt.

She shifted her weight and felt the hard molded plastic of the handle through the fabric as a sudden centrifugal force bumped her head against the door. She brought her hands up and pushed against it, managed to sit partially up on the floor and got a view of the truck rounding a curve. The front end of the truck was lower than the back.

Driving down the mountain, she thought. *Too fast—*

She saw the way it would happen: Kieran smashing the gas pedal to the floor, the truck going airborne, shooting over the cliff and into creek at the bottom of the gorge; imagined that she screamed *"NO!"* as she gripped the top of the front seat and abruptly pulled herself all the way up and raised the weapon.

Kieran met her eyes in the rearview mirror and hit the brake, throwing her forward as she brought it down. She felt the puncture of the metal point in his leather coat and heard him grunt as the rear of the truck began to slide sideways; glimpsed the wide view of the gorge and then the woods rushing by as he yanked the wheel to the right—an overcorrection that sent them into a full spin. The left rear tire slipped over the edge of the roadway as his arm flew up and knocked her backward.

There was a long moment of weightlessness as the truck left the pavement and the trees rushed at the windows, and then a crash of metal and glass that slammed her back against the floor.

❄ ❄ ❄

For several seconds she could barely move. Her right shoulder ached from the collision and there was a sharp pain at the base of her neck as she turned her head. The air in the truck felt colder and she heard the moan of the wind as she gripped the top of the front seat and slowly pulled herself up again.

The windshield was cracked and the front passenger side window had been shattered. Kieran was motionless, his head against the window frame, his shoulder against the door.

She looked out the windows to her left. The truck had hit a tree head-on and come to rest half on and half off the road. At the moment of impact she had been below the windows and had been slammed into the door. Kieran had been fully upright and had been thrown headlong into the windshield.

She took the first wavering step out of the truck, felt the slickness of the pavement, and steadied herself with a grip on the door. The top of Kieran's face was covered in blood, bright red against his pale skin.

She looked down at the pockets of his coat, thinking of his phone. She reached forward and touched his chest and felt a tingling surge of energy that swept up her arm and shot like a pinball into her heart as she stared down at him.

Have to help him.

But he was going to kill you.

Her feelings clashed as she felt the bulge in his coat and traced the shape of a gun and looked at Kieran's wrist. He was still wearing his braided bracelet, identical to Aidan's. The thought sent a shaky wave of emotion through her as she imagined Aidan, lying bloodied in Kieran's arms.

Both of them dying.

Because of you.

Tears sprang to her eyes as she leaned back down, her thoughts and her emotions clashing again as she listened for the sound of breathing. Hearing nothing, she pressed her fingers to Kieran's neck, felt a faint pulse, then put her palm against the side of his head and wrapped her right arm around his upper body.

She lifted his head carefully, and pulled him gently away from the jagged glass. There were tiny shards embedded in the wound, and his blood covered her hands and ran in rivulets down her arms as she shifted him onto his back on the front seat. She checked his pulse again and then opened his mouth. There was a moment of indecision—a memory of her volunteer training at the nursing home—and then she had her mouth over his, the tip of their tongues briefly touching before her first forceful exhalation. Then after two more she checked his pulse again, feeling nothing now, her own heart pounding as she scooted back and positioned herself over his chest, the heel of her left hand pressing against his breastbone, her right hand pressing down on the left, her jaw clenched and her own breathing halted as she began the compressions, mentally counting to ten and then losing count as her mind told her *you're losing him...*

She heard her own soft, plaintive moan.

And her pleading voice "Please...*Kieran...*"

And then she heard a *pop* from the front of the truck, and saw the spike of flame rising from the crumpled hood.

❄ ❄ ❄

Kieran was weightless, suspended amid flickering light and looking down at his body lying across the seat of the truck. Pain pierced his forehead, sharp as a spike in his skull.

He watched as the light began to fade, and as random thoughts swirled through his mind.

You're dying.

Like you wanted.

Aidan…

Suddenly he was blind, eyes wide in search of his brother but seeing nothing in the pitch darkness. He imagined that he called out:

I'M HERE. TO SAVE YOU.

He heard nothing, but felt a shrinking sensation in his arms and a bending in his knees, and the sudden presence of solid walls around him.

The closet.

A flash of bright white light and a blast of cold air and the sight of Nurlene towering over him came next. Her body was solid this time, without the translucent glow. And she was holding a claw hammer at her side.

He screamed. His voice had a strange sound—and a high-pitched, childish tone. He looked down and saw himself as a young boy, wearing nothing but loose, white underwear, and watched as blue-black bruises appeared on his tiny legs, and as a shard of broken bone poked through the skin of his right arm.

You, then.

You, now.

Broken, beaten.

The thoughts rushed through his consciousness as the walls closed in, pining his arms to his sides, crushing his lungs, tight as a vise.

He managed to look up once more as the hammer came down, the claw cleaving his skull, splitting it like the rind of a melon as Nurlene stood over him, her grim triumphant, telling him—

This is death.

Only this.

He imagined that he screamed again as the light began to flash like a strobe, and then suddenly he was staring up at Sara instead of Nurlene. He felt her tongue and a forceful breath into his mouth and a hard pressure against his heart.

And then he heard her voice: real, alive:

Please...Kieran.

Glimmers of a calmer light brought him tactile sensations: the tip of his tongue between Sara's lips, a memory of her breasts in his hands, and then a hard, rhythmic pressure on his chest, a motion that began to push the darkness farther away as her face took on a clearer shape above him, her long black hair falling forward, a feathery tingle against his neck, her hands over his heart, bringing him back.

❄ ❄ ❄

The flames under the hood were spreading amid billowing clouds of gray smoke. Sara felt the heat on the side of her face and coughed as the smell of burning rubber filled her lungs. She envisioned the gas tank exploding an instant before she felt the sudden movement in Kieran's chest. She looked down at his face and started to say his name again as his eyelids fluttered and stilled, and then caught sight of a vague light in her peripheral vision.

Help, she thought, as the sound of an approaching car drew her attention to the road.

❄ ❄ ❄

Marco saw the glow on the roadway the moment he started around the curve. The Hummer had wide Pirelli tires but there was a sudden absence of traction on the slick surface when he hit the brake. The Hummer spun in a 180-degree arc toward the burning pickup truck that blocked the road and cleared it by inches as it came to a stop.

He sat still for several seconds, feeling stunned by the shock of the near-collision with the burning truck in front of him. He had started to regain the rest of his sight in the eye that had been blackened by his father's beating, but there was a halo around everything in his vision as he looked into the rearview mirror. A girl was running from the burning truck, her gait awkward and rushed, long black hair blowing across her pale face.

Sara Porter.

She slid on the ice but kept her footing as she reached the driver's side window. Her mouth was moving, mouthing his name. There was blood on her face—covering her cheeks, mouth, and chin, and it stuck to the glass when she touched the window.

He dazedly reached down and opened the door.

She stepped back. Wet snow clung to her black hair and her teeth were chattering from the cold.

"Marco, you have to *hhh-help* me…That's Kieran O'Shea's truck. He's hurt."

He slowly swung his legs around and stepped out of the Hummer and looked at the truck again. The front end was completely engulfed, and there were popping and pinging sounds coming from underneath the crumpled hood.

"He's lying on the front seat." Sara grabbed his forearm. "I tried to pull him out but he's too heavy."

He looked past her, toward the road that would take him the rest of the way to April's house, where April was waiting after telling him she wanted to go with him to give himself up for the dead women.

He had had a different idea, which was why he had brought the Taser with him.

Sara tightened her grip on his arm. He shook her off, but his mind flashed on a memory of her on a warm day in the fall; the shape of her long, smooth legs and the curve of her ass.

And knew what was going to happen.

He touched his forehead, gave her a blank look, as if he was searching for his bearings. The inside of the Hummer was still warm from the drive. *Do her here*, he thought as he stepped out onto the icy road and reached into his right hand pocket and grasped the Taser.

Still dazed by the collision, he pulled it out a bit slower than he intended and held it down at his side.

Sara's eyes widened as she caught sight of it. "What…?"

He brought it up and pointed it at her chest, but with a sudden swift move she swatted his hand and knocked it to the ground.

She froze and stared down at the weapon as if she was stunned by what she had done.

And then she ran—with flailing arms and unsteady legs, going no more than ten feet before she lost her footing and fell on the icy roadway. He caught up to her just as she stood up; got his arm around her neck and threw her to the ground again as headlights appeared from the upward slant of the road.

Sara scrabbled backwards away from him as the gunmetal gray car came to a stop.

The driver's side door opened and his stepfather got out. Joseph looked past him, toward the burning truck in the distance and the Hummer across the road and the Taser on the roadway, and at Sara as she slowly stood up and started backing away, her hands outstretched.

And then Joseph looked at him, his expression radiating disgust as he took a step forward, his hands and fingers flexing, his legs set slightly apart in the fighter's stance.

Marco stared back at him, knowing he wouldn't throw a punch in front of Sara Porter but suddenly wishing that he would.

"Go ahead." His voice was a taunting whisper. "Show her."

Joseph shook his head, too smart to strike him then and there. Marco stared back at him, the pain pulsing through his wounded eye as he thought of the beating an hour before; the battered furniture in his bedroom and the jagged crack in his mirror and the drying blood on the basement floor.

And then without another thought he ducked his shoulder and slammed it into Joseph's gut.

They crashed to the pavement together; Joseph grunting as the breath was knocked from his lungs. Marco landed the first punch against the bridge of Joseph's nose. Joseph landed the second at the base of his throat—a hard blow that knocked him backwards. He gasped and grabbed at the front of Joseph's coat, then felt the butt of a gun in an inside pocket and went for it. There was a long silencer attached to the pistol that caught on the canvas fabric as he tried to yank it out. His hand wrapped around the grip an instant before Joseph landed another punch at his gut.

The blow knocked all the strength from his upper body as he fell back, gasping and coughing as Joseph bucked his legs upward and slid out from under him. The motion freed the gun from the pocket but weakened his hold and with after another short sideways kick from Joseph it fell to the pavement.

Marco rolled sideways and tried to reach for the gun again but Joseph got to it first. And then there was nothing but the flash of the muzzle and the force of the bullet that shattered his forehead and blew out the back of his skull.

35

Stephen had seen the smoke rising over the treetops in the distance, a thin, gray stream that made him think it came from a chimney marking a house where he could call the police. But seconds later the smoke had thickened and turned black, and then he heard the whirring sound of heavy tires on the ice.

He ran toward it, his heart pounding as he thought of the impact of his car on the boy's body the night before.

❄ ❄ ❄

Niles stood over Marco's body, momentarily transfixed by the boy's shattered face and the brain matter blown backward from the top of his head into the snow. His mind raced to the possibility of self-defense or even a rescue, an attempt to protect Sara Porter, an accidental shooting.

But he knew it wouldn't work. Because the bullet that killed his stepson had come from the same gun he had used to kill April.

He looked toward Kieran O'Shea's burning truck, and saw the jagged remnants of the passenger side window and the open driver's side door and Kieran lying motionless in the front seat. He then turned around and saw Sara Porter crouching behind the open door of the Hummer, cowering like a frightened child. A *witness*. He kept the gun down at his side as he took a step toward her. He had to silence her quickly. Shoot her and get the hell out of there.

Think—make it work.

He clenched his jaw as he stepped toward her. He knew she recognized him—he had stood next to Caruso at the funeral of their mother.

"Move away from the car."

His tone of voice was a misstep. She crouched lower, mewling like a frightened cat. He took a step closer, and tried to bring a concerned look to his face, a disarming *everything's all right* now expression.

"It's okay," he said. "You can come out now."

She shook her head back and forth in a frantic motion—and leapt into the Hummer and slammed the door.

He advanced without thinking, his breath shortened by anger at her defiance. The inside of the Hummer was dark but he saw the motion of her arm as she tossed something on to the seat.

He banged on the window with his left fist, yelled "Open up!" as she jerkily scooted away, slinking low in the seat and making the shot even more difficult.

He grabbed the handle to the door.

Locked.

"Fucking bitch!" he yelled as he stepped back, knowing he had lost control completely as he brought the gun up and aimed through the windshield. His finger twitched against the trigger. He was an instant away from pulling it when he heard the sound of another approaching car.

❄ ❄ ❄

Stephen kept his eyes on the smoke on the road ahead of him and just barely managed to keep his footing as he reached the top of an incline. And then he stopped, transfixed by the sight of a black pick-up truck smashed against a tree, its front end engulfed in flames. And the Range Rover approaching from the opposite direction. And the white Hummer sitting crosswise on the road.

Joseph Niles was pointing a gun at the window of the Hummer. He was wearing dark clothes—a heavy parka and jeans and a baseball cap with a wide brim. At the sound of the approaching Range Rover he spun around and reached into the pocket of his coat and pulled out his wallet. He held the wallet in one hand and the gun in the other, both arms outstretched in front of him as he approached the Rover and yelled:

"Out of the car!"

Niles then shoved his wallet back into the side pocket of his coat and gripped the gun in a shooting stance and pointed it at the driver of the Rover, as if the occupants of the car posed some kind of threat. The driver's side door opened and a teenaged girl stepped out. She wore a white ski jacket with a fur collar and had long, blonde hair, whipped sideways by a gust of wind as she raised her hands.

Madison, he thought. *Sara's friend.*

Niles grabbed her forearm and pulled her away from the car and continued holding the gun out in front of him as he walked quickly around the front.

The passenger side door opened.

His son stepped out.

"Ken!" he called out without thinking. Niles jerkily looked his way, his eyes widening for an instant before he wrapped his arm around Kenny's narrow chest and held the gun to his head.

Stephen stayed silent, terrified of any sudden sound or motion that would make Niles pull the trigger, and heard a faint, high-pitched sound and looked toward Madison, then followed her line of sight.

There was a body on the road, lying in a pool of blood.

Madison shook her head…and tried to scream, her voice stunted even before Niles swung his gun arm around and slammed his elbow into the side of her face, knocking her to the ground.

Kenneth met Stephen's eyes, his feet frozen in place as Niles jammed the barrel of the gun into Kenneth's ear. Kenneth was wearing the North Face coat Lori had bought him in the fall but no hat or gloves, and was visibly shivering in the cold, his eyes hollowed by fear.

Stephen tried to fathom the words that would stop Niles from pulling the trigger.

Calm him down. Reason with him.

"Detective Niles—"

"Shut the fuck up!" Spit flew from Niles' mouth as he whipped Kenny around as if he weighed nothing; Kenny's feet moving in frantic steps to make contact with the ground as Niles headed toward the white Hummer. A gust of wind lifted the cap from Niles' head and sent it flying. The gust was followed by another, the sound like a roar sweeping down from the top of the mountain, nearly drowning Niles' voice—

"I'll shoot him!"

Niles was directing the threat toward someone inside the Hummer. Stephen squinted, his eyes stinging from the frigid air.

And watched as the passenger side door opened.

Sara.

She was crouched very low in the seat, her head just barely rising above the dashboard, as if she had taken cover. Her face was emaciated by terror, her mouth open and moving, as if she was struggling to breathe.

Niles took a step toward her.

"Get the fuck OUT!"

Stephen saw a change in Sara's expression. Her eyes were sharper, *calculating*, he thought, as Niles took another step toward the Hummer. It looked as if Niles' attention was focused solely on Sara as she slowly opened the door, her head still low and her body level with the dashboard. Stephen silently prayed, *don't get out* and tried to imagine that the tight space in the car would protect her as she slid sideways in the front seat, her boots planted on the ground beneath the open door.

Niles took no notice of the sudden change in Kenneth's posture—the drop of his shoulders and the forward roll of his head. But then from twenty feet away Stephen heard him grunt with exertion as Kenneth's whole body went limp in Niles' arms, his weight no longer supported at all by his own legs. There was another sound—a weary exhalation as Niles gave up trying to hold Kenneth's dead weight and shoved him away.

Kenneth fell clumsily down on his knees. The sight took Stephen back to the night before; the tears streaming down Kenneth's cheeks after the beating at school. He felt a tightening in his chest…and watched as Kenneth stood back up and ducked his head and charged back at Niles, with two running steps and a leap that rammed his shoulder into the small of the big man's back.

The sight was surreal—Kenneth's 130-pound body knocking Niles into a forward fall, Niles' arms flying outward to keep his balance as Kenneth toppled to the ground behind him. Niles landed on his knees but quickly got back up, still unsteady and surprised, his attention diverted to Kenneth as Sara stepped out from behind the door of the car, awkwardly holding something in both of her hands that looked like a gun.

A *clack-clack-clack* sound filled the air.

Niles screamed, his lips rolling back from his teeth as he dropped to his knees again. Sara was holding a stun gun with both hands, her face reddened by the sudden exertion. Niles fired his gun wildly into the air and flailed toward Sara, his arm knocking the weapon from her hand.

And that was when Stephen charged forward, ignoring the ripping pain in his rib cage as he rammed his shoulder into Niles' gut.

Niles doubled over as the air rushed out of his lungs, then landed a hard punch against Stephen's chest, knocking him to the ground.

He rolled sideways as Niles aimed a kick at his head, felt a rush of air at the side of his face and frantically scrabbled back, conscious of nothing else but the gun in Niles' hand and the sudden steadiness of his posture as he raised it.

He stared up into the barrel of the gun and then looked into Niles' eyes, searching for the slightest inkling of compassion, or reason, or anything to stop him from pulling the trigger.

Niles stared back. A bubble of blood popped from his left nostril and trickled toward his mouth. He squinted, pressed his lips together.

"DADDY!" Sara screamed, and ran out from behind the open door of the Hummer.

A clear shot, Stephen saw what was about to happen. *Sara and then Kenneth and then you—*

The sudden blare of a horn filled the air, seizing Niles' attention toward the burning truck, sitting crosswise on the road, the driver's side door wide open. But then the flash of a gunshot from behind the door sent Niles into a rolling dive behind the Hummer. Niles came up and fired back, shattering the truck's intact window as Kieran O'Shea came out from behind it, his face masked by blood, staggering as he stood up and looking as if he was about to topple back down as he held his gun in a trembling, two-handed grip—slow, unbalanced and no match for Niles as he brought his own gun up into a concentrated aim. But then three more shots in rapid succession came from O'Shea's gun, two pinging against the Hummer's metal hood, the third striking Niles with a muffled, wet sound against his thigh, *not enough to hurt him*, Stephen thought, an instant before a stream of blood shot out from Niles' leg—a bright red geyser that arced upward in rhythmic spurts as Niles fell back against the car. Stephen heard a guttural sound and watched as Niles dropped the gun. The blood streamed up in a low loop that ended five feet from his body. Niles gasped as he clamped both hands against the wound, the blood shooting between his fingers and becoming a diffuse, wide sweeping spray. Stephen felt the wet mist of it on his face and stumbled backwards, his eyes spotting the discarded gun in the snow, his mind telling him to grab it but his legs immobilized as he watched Niles pull one hand away from the wound and yank at the zipper of his coat and then frantically jerk it down.

He realized the bullet had hit Niles' femoral artery. Niles was struggling to unbuckle his belt, *to tie off the wound*, Stephen thought as their eyes met and Niles silently implored him—*help me*. He took a step forward and Niles fell to the ground, the blood shooting off to the side but arcing out at a shorter angle. Stephen felt his own balance tilting, a buzzing dizziness in his head as he stooped down and caught the stench of feces as Niles lost control of his bowels. He gagged, his gut clenching as he loosened Niles' belt buckle and pulled. The leather stretched slightly but it was pinned between Niles' heavy weight and the ground. Stephen grabbed it with both hands and pulled harder. Niles' face was wrenched in agony, his breath coming in short audible gasps, both of them realizing the belt wasn't going to come off as Niles jerked violently, the pressure sending waves of pain through his leg, his skin graying with the onset of shock.

He pressed both of his hands against the open wound and turned around and searched for Sara and Kenneth, to tell them to call for help. The motion pulled his hands away from the wound. The blood shot upward and struck the underside of his chin. He heard Sara scream for the first time as he reflexively leaned back.

His next thought—*You can't stop*—came to him as Niles' eyes widened and then rolled backwards. He looked down. Blood covered his arms and neck and chest. The stench of it and the stench of waste filled his throat and coated his tongue but he managed to suppress the urge to gag as he pressed down again, realizing then that the pace of the bleeding had slackened.

He kept his hands in place but knew there was nothing else he could do as he turned and caught the sight of movement near the

Hummer. Sara's friend Madison was back on her feet and staring down at the body in the road, a large red welt blooming on her cheek. In the distance Kieran O'Shea collapsed against a tree just a few feet from the back of the burning truck. To his left Kenneth and Sara were holding each other in a tight embrace, both of them staring fearfully at Niles, as if he might somehow rise back up.

Stephen stayed in place, still conscious of the phone in his pocket and the need to call 911 and the forlorn sound of the wind.

"It's okay, you're safe," he told them, as they watched Joseph Niles bleed out into the snow.

SATURDAY

ONE WEEK LATER

36

Sara slipped into her new coat and wrapped a soft flannel scarf around her neck and took a moment to compose herself before stepping into the first floor study and lying to her father for what she hoped would be the last time.

The door to the study was almost completely closed, but through the two inches of space she saw him behind the desk. He was gazing straight ahead, the tip of a pen resting on his chin, *concentrating on something*, she thought.

She hoped his preoccupation would work in her favor.

"Daddy?"

He smiled. His eyes were less bloodshot than they had been for the past week, as if he had somehow finally managed to sleep, but his skin was still pale and she knew he had lost weight.

"Yeah honey, come in."

She stepped up behind him, and gave him a brief hug. The desk's file drawer was open and the desktop was covered with bank statements and financial forms.

"I'm heading out," she said.

She felt a tensing in his shoulders. He placed his hand over hers with a gentle pressure, as if he wanted to hold her back.

"Where to?"

"I need to check on Madison."

Her voice wavered. She was glad he wasn't looking at her face.

"I told her I'd spend a little time with her. She hasn't been doing too well."

He turned around and gave her a long look, as if he was worrying as much about Madison as herself. "Is she going back to school on Monday?"

"I don't know," she said. "It's only been a week. There are all kinds of rumors flying around and I don't think she's up to reliving any of it."

She gave the papers on the desk another glance, saw an open tablet of lined paper next to them. Her father had written "Monthly Expenses" and the top and had drawn two columns, "Fixed" and "Optional" underneath. She wanted to believe he was doing nothing more than routine budget balancing but felt a pressure around her heart as she spied the smaller scribbles at the right of the page.

6 MONTHS

1 YEAR

3 YEARS

5 YEARS

She stared at the numbers for several seconds, until the feeling of regret became too much.

She kissed the top of his head and turned toward the door.

"Sara."

There was a rasp in his voice.

"Be careful."

He looked as if she had just given him a fresh reason to worry, as if he somehow knew what she was about to do. She started to remind him that Madison's house was only a few blocks away but didn't want to repeat the lie she had told the week before.

She glanced down at the table beside the door. There were three NetFlix envelopes there, a reminder of the evening he had planned. Next to them was another stack of DVDs they owned—movies that she and Kenneth loved and viewed over and over. She knew that he had retrieved all of them just to be assured there would be something they would all want to watch.

Anything to keep us home, she thought, *with him*.

"I'll be back by 8 o'clock," she said. "Any movie you want is fine with me."

He looked both grateful and relieved. "Good. We'll have dinner first. Kenny's finally got an appetite so we need to make the most of it."

She smiled back, thinking of the three of them in front of the fire and the television, a Saturday night at home with her father and her brother and no one else. The last thing she would have wanted a week ago; the thing she wanted most right now.

"I'll be here," she told him, doing her best to ignore the flurry of nerves that stayed with her as she turned away.

37

John Caruso sat behind his desk and read through the *Frederick News Post* articles that chronicled the most intense week of his professional life, an experience that would have been rewarding if not for his nagging dread of what was to come.

The stories began with a Sunday morning story about the crime scene on the mountain, with a description of the deaths of Joseph and Marco Niles and the injuries to Kieran O'Shea—an initial just-the-facts rendition written under a reporter's deadline that promised more details in the coming hours.

As chronicled by the stories that appeared at the middle of the week, bullet casings from the April Devon crime scene matched those fired by Joseph in his attempt to take out Stephen Porter and his family. An inspection of Marco Niles' computer showed he visited the sex site where Cherilynn Jenkins had posted her online profile, and his DNA was a match to the semen taken from her bed sheets and that left on Danica Morris' body as well.

And then there were the emails, between April Devon and Lori Porter, a written record that chronicled April's shame in knowing about her sister's sexual abuse of her own son, her sister's murder by Joseph Niles, and her belief that Marco Niles had seen it happen.

The arrest warrant for Stephen Porter was ready. He had delayed serving it after the violence on the mountain, giving Porter and his family some space to recover. The evidence against Porter now included a DVD of video footage that had been taken at the Advance Auto store in Rockville, Maryland. The store was brightly lit against the pitch darkness outside the windows, and the security camera video of the checkout line was shot from a distance of about eight feet. Unfortunately the picture was grainy, the images equally indistinct on the original and the copy.

He had tracked down the video after learning from the inspection of Porter's vehicle that that the cover to the rear taillight had very recently replaced. There were only a handful of places where Porter could have purchased a cover in the brief period of time before the vehicle had been seized and he only had to hunt a short while to find the store and the video, which was time-stamped at 6:13 a.m. on the morning of Aidan O'Shea's death.

The man in the video was approximately Porter's height but he seemed much heavier in his nondescript dark coat. He wore a knit cap that was pulled halfway down his forehead, which would have looked awkward if not for the frigid temperatures outside. The glasses were a brilliant touch. Close up they had altered the man's appearance just enough to make it impossible for the clerk to positively identify him in the driver's license photo of Stephen Porter that Caruso had presented to him. The thick lenses in the glasses also reflected the overhead lights in the grainy footage from the security cameras, and almost completely obscured the man's eyes.

Which meant that the video would ultimately fall short of proof, without positive identification from the clerk and with the difference in the way Porter would look in a courtroom. Porter had made things both worse and better for himself by paying cash and rushing away without waiting for change. The behavior was erratic enough to embed the interaction in the clerk's memory, but because of it there was no electronic record of what Porter had purchased. Caruso had only been able to suggest, "Could it have been a tail light cover?"

The clerk had nodded, but with a shrug and then told him he really had no idea.

Caruso put the DVD into the player at the side of his computer one more time, mentally chastising himself once again for the vague hope that Porter would somehow avoid the trouble that was coming to him. The feeling would have been complicated enough without the haunting memory of Kieran O'Shea holding Aidan in his arms. O'Shea had been held in the hospital for two days after the accident and shootings on the mountain—spending half of the time in the Intensive Care Unit as the doctors monitored the swelling and damage to his brain. Caruso had questioned him twice in the days since. O'Shea was now claiming that he had almost no memory of the accident that killed Aidan. Caruso would have known he was lying even if O'Shea hadn't pointedly mentioned that the doctors had told him that his head injury would affect his memory for awhile, but "there's a good chance it'll come back."

As if the only question is when, Caruso turned back to the computer screen, his instincts telling him once again that O'Shea was holding back for a reason, biding his time. Eyewitness testimony was the most important factor in a successful hit-and-run prosecution. If O'Shea did indeed *remember*, then Stephen's fate would be sealed. But without an eyewitness the case was limited to circumstantial evidence compromised by the weather and conditions at the scene.

Certainly not a slam-dunk, he thought.

Especially with a good defense team.

And the inevitable sympathies of a jury.

An electronic chirp from his computer signaled an incoming message from the civilian consultant who had been tasked to find anything that might be useful on Joseph Niles' home computer. Caruso had made a special request based on the emails between Lori Porter and April Devon. His hopes were unrealistically high given the low likelihood of success.

He took a deep breath, and clicked it open.

Found it. Let's talk.

❄ ❄ ❄

Sara was surprised by the damp warmth in the air as she walked to the rendezvous point—a cul-de-sac that the developer had cut out of the woods and paved the previous fall. Within a few months another group of big houses would rise up from the empty lots but for now the area felt a little spooky in the early dark.

Madison Reidy was waiting for her in the Range Rover. She slipped out of the driver's seat and left the door open as Sara approached. They spoke in near-whispers in the conversation that followed even though they were 200 yards away from anyone who might have heard them.

The conversation ended with one final, anxious question—*"Are you sure about this?"*—from Madison.

Sara nodded, feeling surprisingly touched by the girl's genuine sense of worry for her safety, and impulsively stepped forward and gave her a hug.

"I'm not scared," she said, "and you shouldn't be either."

She slipped her hand into the pocket of her coat, grasped her new phone, and got behind the wheel.

"I'll call you when I get there," she said. "And again when I'm ready to come home."

38

Kieran stood next to the window in the front section of the house and held the curtain a few inches aside and watched Sara Porter step out of Madison Reidy's Range Rover. She had told him about the turnabout in their "friendship" in one of the long, rambling voice mails she had left him. He was still confused about how it had happened, and the sight of Sara in the girl's car felt like yet another aftershock to the events of the week and the terrors that surrounded Aidan's death.

Sara was talking on the phone, her expression impossible to read in the darkness of the overcast night. She had begged him to allow her to come see him—telling him through three calls and at least as many texts that she was "worried" about him. He had delayed his response as he tried to sort through his feelings, to see how things with Caruso evolved, and had waited a whole week before deciding what would happen next.

He watched as she hung up the phone, and felt an anxious shortening of his breath as she stepped onto the front stoop of his house. Her long black hair hung loose and swayed back from her face in the light wind, stirring his memory of her hands against his heart, coaxing his body back to life and saving him from the nightmare of his death. The concussion had led to two days in the hospital and the sensation that his brain had somehow been reset with a new round of medications. The voices and the visions of Nurlene were gone, the memory of the accident like the scene of a bad dream.

He wanted to believe it would be this way from now on; his mind clear and steady. But he knew the grief would stay with him, a leaden weight to carry forever.

He opened the front door before she could knock. She anxiously met his eyes. He had no doubt about why she had insisted on seeing him, and he was prepared to do as she was about to ask.

For a price.

There was a determined set in her shoulders as she crossed the threshold, *steeling herself*, he thought, as she entered his house for the last time.

39

Sara had envisioned the reunion often during the week since Kieran had saved her and it felt like a dream as it was happening, a shifting collection of images that would become forever ingrained in her mind.

He was standing with the door open as she approached. He shut it quickly as she stepped inside. She thought she heard the *thunk* of the deadbolt being thrown but surmised that it had been her imagination as she turned to look at him in the dark entryway. He was barefoot, wearing faded jeans and a dark, loosely fitting sweatshirt. She tried not to stare at his half-shaven head with its criss-crossing stitches. After all that had happened she had expected to feel terrified and even repulsed by his presence.

She had been wrong. Her heart felt like a hummingbird trapped in her chest as she stood on unsteady legs and thanked him for agreeing to see her.

He said nothing, and the slight shrug of his shoulders made her feel as if he would have been fine leaving things the way they had been a week before, as if he had no curiosity or concern for how she or her family were faring.

The thought worried her as he turned and led her back into the main room that Kieran had built. She gave it a quick glance—saw dishes scattered across the table and the couch pillows flattened and disarrayed, as if Kieran had been sleeping on them.

And then she glanced toward the hallway that led to the bedroom and remembered the horrible moment she had looked at his computer and seen the links to stories about the killing of Ms. Jenkins, the death of her mother, and the other woman who had died on the same night.

A misunderstanding. Her mind skipped through the simple explanation she had put together for all of it. Kieran had been thinking about her mother's car accident and the murder on the mountain because they had happened within a couple miles of his house. And like everyone else at Langford he'd paid special attention to the death of Ms. Jenkins because she was a teacher he saw every day.

She told herself once again that it all made sense, despite the phantom pain in her wrists; the memory of Kieran holding her against the floor; and the memory of the anger in his eyes, which had made her feel as if he truly wanted to hurt her.

Your imagination, she thought.

Your fears.

She stood still as Kieran sat down on the coach, then sat on the upholstered chair across from him.

She nervously felt the worn nubs of the fabric underneath her fingertips and crossed her legs at the ankles and thought of the words she had arranged and rearranged in her mind, telling him that she knew her father was about to be arrested and going as far as asking him if Detective Caruso had come to his house during the past week before the narrowing of his eyes and the rush of color in his face stopped her.

"So that's what this is about."

The tone of his voice hit her like a warning. Her breath faltered. She shook her head and told him, "No."

"Then what do you want Sara? Why are you here?"

He got up and stood over her. He was staring at her as if she had betrayed him—as if the attempt to protect her father had been the only reason for her need to see him again.

She scrunched her shoulders close to her neck, a self-protective reflex.

"I'm here because you saved me," she said.

She thought of the strangling force of his arm around her neck on the night of the accident; and the slickness of his blood on her face as she blew air into his lungs.

"And because I saved you too."

The words hung in the air. After several seconds she saw a slight tensing in Kieran's shoulders. His face seemed to narrow in front of her eyes, his cheekbones taking on sharper angles, his eyes glazing. He looked wounded—as if she was forcing him to relive what had happened. She dreaded the thought of leaving him there, alone in his dimly lit house; tried to imagine him calling someone who would comfort him. She had always known that he had no real friends; that his devotion to Aidan left no time for them, and that her own affection for his brother had been the lifeblood of the bond between them. A bond she desperately wanted to feel again as she stood up, feeling the magnetic force that drew her to him, even now. He stayed still when she stepped toward him, his legs slightly apart, looking as if he was daring her and willing her to come closer, until suddenly he was only inches away. She tilted her head upwards, the room blurring around her as she imagined him months into the future, his hair thick and flowing, hiding the scars, his face and body no longer weakened by his injuries.

She placed her palm against his chest and felt the rapid beat of his heart for one long wonderful moment before he reached up and grabbed her wrist.

His grip was tight and almost painful as he leaned down and kissed her, faintly at first, their lips just barely touching before she felt the tip of his tongue. She responded as she always had, overcome with desire as he held her, and allowed herself one long moment of imagining the two of them together before she opened her eyes and gently stepped back.

"I..." Her breath faltered. "Need to go."

He moved her hands down to the backs of her thighs and pulled her against him. The walls of the room seemed to fall away, the desire nearly overpowering her before she broke away again.

"I'm seventeen," she said.

A shadow crossed his face.

"You could get into trouble."

It sounded like a threat, the opposite of what she had intended. His jawline hardened as she looked toward the front door, gauging how long it would take to get there. To turn and walk calmly away, as if she had nothing to fear.

Instead she stayed where she was, and reached up and touched his cheek again, and told him:

"I love you Kieran. I always will."

He drew slightly back, as if she had somehow managed to give him the same off-balance feeling he had always given her. The shift in power was subtle but certain and transpired in the span of a few seconds as she stepped away and moved toward the front of the house and methodically reached for her scarf and coat.

She imagined herself using the power, asking him once again about the possibility of saying nothing about what he had seen on the night Aidan died. The words—*please don't let this happen to us*—almost came to her as she turned around to find him standing next to the desk, a white envelope in his hand.

He stepped forward before she could think of what to say, then pressed the envelope against her chest and held it there until she took it from him.

The envelope was worn, as if it had been folded and unfolded, and discolored. The words JOHN CARUSO were written on the front.

"You're right," Kieran said. "You *saved* me."

His voice was hoarse, and weak.

"This is what you get in return."

She looked at the envelope again. There was a hard triangular shape inside. Kieran had made it sound as if giving it to her was a sign of gratitude, but she saw a mix of pain and anger in his eyes.

"I don't understand," she told him.

"I had it in my coat pocket last Saturday. So it would be found… after."

His voice faded. He held her eyes as a resolute look came to his face.

"Give it to your father. But read it first."

She turned the envelope over, looking for some additional clue as to what it contained. Despite the look in Kieran's eyes she tried to imagine that this night wasn't the end, that he could somehow see her as someone he could love.

But how do you love someone you tried to kill?

She slipped the envelope into her coat pocket and then wrapped her knit scarf around her neck and walked to the front door. Madison Reidy's Range Rover was parked where the Jeep had been a week earlier, and covered with a fine mist that caught the glow from the light over the concrete stoop.

She headed toward it, feeling certain that she had failed as she turned to see Kieran watching her from the front window, waiting for her to go.

40

Stephen was in the kitchen and thinking about dinner when his cell phone rang. He pulled it from his shirt pocket, saw John Caruso on the caller ID, and reflexively put it back. He wondered if Caruso was calling to tell him that Frederick County deputies were on the way to arrest him, but he knew the time for gestures of consideration was over. The arrest, when it happened, would come without any warning.

But please, not tonight, he thought. *I'm not ready.*

He looked out at the family room, taking in the burning fire, the quilts atop the sectional couch, the picture of at-home serenity, and thought back to his ruminations in the study. A conviction and prison time for manslaughter would mean the loss of the house, because without an insurance settlement for Lori's death he could only keep up the payments with savings for a matter of months. Sara and Kenneth would be uprooted once again, to guardianship by his brother's family, in upstate New York.

Upsetting but not terrible, he thought. Frank and his wife and kids had always adored Kenneth and Sara, and he had no doubt his kids would manage to find the emotional equilibrium they needed to survive if he was indeed sentenced to prison.

Unfortunately that certainty did nothing to stop the stinging sensation in his eyes and the tightness in his chest as he thought of being separated from them, in a cell hundreds of miles away.

The phone stopped ringing but he continued staring at it for nearly a minute before he heard the beep indicating he had a voice mail.

He paced across the kitchen as he listened to the message. Caruso's voice was matter-of-fact but without the official edge. He had "new information about Lori" that he considered "extremely important." He wanted to pay a visit within the next half hour.

He put the phone down on the counter, telling himself to think it through. Caruso wanted to charge him in the death of Aidan O'Shea and by now he would have gathered all of the physical and circumstantial evidence he needed. But none of that had anything to do with Lori. As of a week ago Caruso had still refused to believe she had killed herself and from the beginning he had been intent on proving it.

He picked the phone back up, opened it to the dial pad. Electronic music pulsed from Kenneth's room upstairs. Within the hour he and his sister would be sitting across from him at the counter, eating dinner and making conversation, talking about anything but Lori's death. He was still wary of facing Caruso and getting more questions, but if there truly was important news about their mother they deserved to hear it.

He took a long, deep breath, willing himself to stay calm as he called him back. Caruso answered on the first ring and Stephen heard the sound of traffic in the background, as if he was already on his way.

❄ ❄ ❄

The conversation was awkward from the beginning, with terse hellos and uncomfortable eye contact as he led Caruso into the den off the foyer and quietly closed the door. He thought of offering coffee but held back as he considered the stiffness of Caruso's posture and the probability that he would be even more uncomfortable with the pretense that it was a social visit.

The right decision, he guessed, as Caruso told him:

"I'm not going to talk about Aidan O'Shea, Stephen. It wouldn't be appropriate without your lawyer present at this stage in the process."

Caruso's tone brought a sinking feeling to his chest. "All right," he said, and sat down on the edge of the couch.

Caruso took a chair and sat slightly forward, his hands clasped together, forearms on his knees.

"You've watched the news this week, so you already know a lot of what we know about Joseph Niles."

He nodded. The coverage had been voluminous and had gone into great detail about the shooting death of April Devon and Niles' attempt to kill Sara and Kenneth.

"On the phone you said you wanted to talk about what happened to Lori."

"Yes," Caruso said.

He sat very still. "Then…I'm all ears."

"You know about the woman was killed at the side of the road the night Lori died."

He nodded.

"I've always believed Lori either saw it happen or drove past right afterward. I thought the killer knew she could identify him. I think he chased her and that she was trying to get away from him when she came to the curve. She wouldn't have had a lot of time to react if she hadn't been expecting it."

He stared back at Caruso, remembering the high bluff and the gorge below, imagining the sight of headlights in Lori's rearview mirror as she pressed the gas pedal to the floor.

"So you're saying it wasn't suicide. And that all along you thought she was *chased*."

"That's been my theory."

He felt strangely alienated. Regardless of everything else that had happened he had always believed that Caruso would have kept him informed about every aspect of his investigation into Lori's death; facts and theories alike.

"You never told me."

"I didn't really know how," Caruso said. "It was a terrible thing for you to have to imagine. But you've known all along that I didn't believe she killed herself, Stephen. And now we have proof."

He felt a sudden shortness of breath. "What kind of *proof*?"

"Five years ago Joseph Niles murdered his wife. But because there wasn't any physical evidence tying him to the crime he was never charged. We didn't know about this when he was hired here in Frederick County last year, but April Devon did."

Caruso paused and held his eyes, watching him carefully.

"How?"

"April was his wife's sister. She knew his job would be in jeopardy if we became aware of his past. I believe she blackmailed him—forcing him to stake her in the business she opened. I can't prove it, but there are financial transactions that make me pretty sure I'm right."

"Okay." He looked past Caruso, toward the window and the darkness outside, thinking of the few times Lori had mentioned April, usually in the context of the decorating but at least once in a conversation about her kindness toward Kenneth.

"I never met April," he said. "But I know Lori liked her. So I'm guessing there's more to this story."

Caruso nodded. "At first I assumed April's motives were financial—she had something on Niles and used it to her advantage. But shortly before she was killed she told me she had more personal reasons for being here. She wanted to keep an eye on him, to make sure he knew she was watching him. And she felt a lot of anxiety over what was going to happen to his son, Marco. She knew that he was already a seriously messed up kid because of things that happened to him as he grew up."

Stephen stared down at the floor as he remembered the conversation with Kenneth about being beaten up by Marco Niles, and the deaths on the mountain.

"Niles shot his own son too," he said.

"Yes, right before you got there," Caruso said. "They had been at each other's throats ever since the death of Niles' wife. Niles hated Marco. And I think he lived in a constant state of threat, knowing April could expose his past at any time. I don't believe Niles knew his son murdered Danica Morris at the time it happened, but I know for a fact that he was worried about any connection between that investigation and your wife's death. He knew that if I continued to view it as a homicide I'd keep the pressure on April, since Lori was on her way to see her when she died. He knew they were friends and worried April would eventually crack and say something about his past. And then it would only be a matter of time before he was implicated. So he came up with a way to halt the speculation for good."

The note, Stephen thought. *Under the mirror, inside our house.*

Caruso gave him a slight nod, looking as if he had read his mind.

"We seized Niles' home computer and combed through his hard drive and found a copy of that bogus suicide letter on it. Niles obviously hoped it would end our speculation that Lori had been murdered. He deleted it—or thought he had—but a digital imprint is impossible to eradicate. Nothing ever disappears from a computer completely."

Stephen felt dazed as he tried to understand the significance of what Caruso was telling him, his mind telling him he needed to hear it again.

"So what are you saying?"

"I'm saying I was right. Your wife didn't commit suicide. We can prove it now, so you don't ever have to worry about it again."

He leaned forward, subconsciously reflecting Caruso's posture, his forearms on his knees, hands clasped together, a lump at the back of his throat.

"There's more," Caruso said.

He sat back, still acutely conscious of being observed, as if more bad news was coming.

"We confiscated April Devon's computer. We know from the emails that Lori looked at April as someone who needed *rescuing*, for lack of a better word, because she had confided a lot of terrible things about her sister. And about things her sister did to her own son in the year before Niles killed her. Terrible things that April couldn't get beyond. April told all of it to Lori, and made her promise to keep it between them."

"What do you mean—what kinds of things?"

"Imagine the worst."

Caruso crossed his arms over his chest. In the silence that followed Stephen saw himself standing over Lori's laptop, staring down at the history on her browser, struggling to comprehend the *terrible things* she had been reading about.

Sadomasochism. Incest. Pedophilia.

"I can't give you any more details," Caruso said. "But I know from the emails between them that Lori really wanted to help April deal with the shame and guilt she felt over what her sister had done. The ironic thing is...April sent her an email saying she felt like she was about to have a breakdown shortly before Lori went to see her."

Stephen looked at the smiling photos of Lori on his desk, thought once again of her demeanor the last night of her life.

Rushing out into the rain.

To help a friend.

"That was Lori," he said.

"What do you mean?"

"Someone who would do anything for the people she cared about."

Caruso nodded. "I think the relationship was important to both of them. April needed a friend who wouldn't judge her. And Lori never did. She also confided a few of her own regrets."

Stephen anxiously met his eyes. "What kind of *regrets*?"

"I…can't say."

But you know, Stephen thought. *About the affair. And the guilt she lived with. And how I couldn't forgive her.*

He imagined Caruso reading through all of the emails between the two women, learning more about Lori's mindset than he could ever understand.

"She was lonely," he said. "Out here in a new place, Away from the friends she used to have."

Caruso nodded, and looked toward the family photos on the desk.

"I know all about loneliness. I lost my wife to it, too."

It was the first time Caruso had mentioned any family, or anything about his personal life.

"What do you mean, John?"

Caruso sighed. "Her name was Cassie. We married young—too young. A decision we made because she was pregnant. A good decision at the time because our whole life became about our son, Elliott. But then he…died."

Stephen waited for him to continue, thinking after a moment that he would say nothing more. But then Caruso reached into his inside coat pocket and pulled out his wallet and showed him the photo of a little boy who looked to be about four years old. He was sitting in a hospital bed under a HAPPY BIRTHDAY ELLIOTT banner, surrounded by stuffed animals and nurses and smiling broadly and bravely despite his tiny, hairless head.

Stephen's throat swelled shut as Caruso ran his thumb gently across the photo.

"Childhood leukemia," Caruso said. "Diagnosed when he was four."

Caruso flipped to the next plastic-wrapped photo, a studio shot of himself at a much younger age, alongside a petite and very pretty, dark-haired woman and Elliott as a chubby, smiling toddler.

"Nothing was the same after that. We didn't know how to be together without him. We were living in my family's cabin on the mountain. Cassie was there alone way too often while I threw myself into my job and just *worked* all the time. She left me about six months after Elliott died. Went to a new state. A new life. A place where she could have some real distance from the pain. Away from me and all of the memories of us together, as a family."

Caruso's eyes were glazed, and his voice had gone hoarse with emotion. But then he cleared his throat and looked at Stephen again.

"The point is, I know what you did, Stephen, and why you did it, because I would have done the same thing. But I can't protect you from the consequences. You need to own up to it. Admit the truth."

"I *can't*."

Stephen felt the rush of breath from his lungs as he spoke those words. Caruso stared back at him, clearly anticipating he'd say something more. Instead Stephen pressed his lips into a tight line, recognizing the near certainty of prison time and the final disintegration of the frail bonds that held his family together.

The silence lengthened between them, until Stephen cleared his throat and said:

"Thank you, John... for finding the letter. Proving what happened."

Caruso gave him a slight, sad smile. "You're welcome Stephen."

He smiled back, feeling grateful for the momentary expression of kindness as he gazed around the room. The sparse furnishings. The paintings still stacked in corners, still waiting to be hung on the walls. The room, like his life, suspended by the sadness of Lori's absence and the speculation of how she had died.

Speculation that would now end.

"Your mother didn't leave us."

He heard himself telling Sara and Kenneth that their worst fears were unfounded. Their mother's death was beyond her control.

"She loved us. All of us."

"Stephen?"

Caruso's voice sounded as if it came from an echo chamber.

"Are you all right?"

Caruso was staring at him. Stephen saw him through a glaze of tears, felt his mouth working, struggling to speak.

"I know what's coming," he said.

Caruso sighed, looking weary and sad. "It's going to be a tough fight for you."

"I know."

"I can't wish you luck," Caruso said.

"I *know*..." His voice faltered.

Caruso raised his arm, his hand hovering inches above Stephen's shoulder.

"It's okay," Stephen said, and walked him to the door.

❄ ❄ ❄

Sara drove as far as the gas station near the foot of the mountain before pulling off the road. The station was closed, the parking lot empty. She was worried that she was going to get a call from her father and didn't want to be there for very long.

The envelope was in the passenger seat. She picked it up and held it in her hands. She felt as if she was still awakening from a dream as Kieran's words lingered in her mind. He had implied that the contents of the envelope were a reward for saving his life even though he made her feel as if there was something terrible yet to come.

Acting like it wasn't really over, she thought, as she slipped her index finger under the seal and tore it open and then switched on the overhead light to make it easier to read.

The words swam in her vision, blurring and then coming into focus and then blurring again. The paragraphs were short and were written in Kieran's tight script and in a strangely factual tone. The details were specific—Kieran describing how Aidan had slipped out the window of his house and the sound of a car skidding on the ice and the precise description of "a silver Ford Explorer driven by Stephen Porter." The piece of ribbed glass had come from the taillight of her father's car. "Physical evidence," Kieran wrote. "If you need it."

"I had it in my coat pocket last Saturday. So it would be found... after."

Kieran's voice came back to her, telling her what she had suspected, that he had planned to kill himself, because the grief from Aidan's death was too much for him to bear. She knew that it still was—knew it from the memory of him standing alone in the dim and disheveled room at the back of his house, looking completely *lost* as he watched her go.

A wave of shame swept through her as she recounted what she had done to prepare for this night: the mascara she had stroked onto her lashes, the careful selection of clothes, her carefully thought-out description of her father's fragile state of mind; all driven by willingness to do anything to keep Kieran from telling the police what he knew.

She knew that she had succeeded. The envelope was resting in her lap, the piece of hard red plastic in the palm of her hand. It would be easy to get rid of it now, to toss it and the note into a random trash can.

Just forget you ever saw it.

But she knew that she never would; and knew the crime her father had committed would stay with her, for the rest of her life.

Just as Kieran wanted.

She gazed at her reflection in the window. A mind's eye image of Kieran gazed back. She flinched and looked straight ahead, toward the dark and empty road that would take her home.

41

Here it is, Stephen thought. *The last normal night of your life.*

The kitchen island had three place settings, with sisal mats that Lori had bought specifically for the room and blue and white plaid napkins threaded through red ceramic rings that had been a wedding present twenty years before. In the middle was a tray of snacks Stephen had laid out for Sara and Kenneth to nibble on before a dinner of lasagna and crescent rolls; the best kind of comfort food for a winter night.

He looked at the clock. He was still worried that Sara might call and ask to spend the evening with friends—and felt a sense of relief when he heard footsteps coming down the stairs and saw Kenneth, in sweatpants and a T-shirt, his hair still damp from the shower. Kenneth had spent most of the afternoon utilizing the World Gym membership that Lori had bought for the family the previous fall. It was his fourth workout in one week. The first one had occurred two days after the nightmare on the mountain. Kenneth had come home straight from school, biked there in thirty-degree temperatures, and worked out for over two hours.

Stephen had asked him about the sudden interest in physical activity.

Kenneth had answered him with a shrug and turned toward the stairs, making it clear he didn't want to discuss it. Each workout that followed had been longer than the last. Stephen noticed a subtle but definite change in the way his son carried himself now. His shoulders seemed higher, his gait more assured. And when Stephen had broached the subject of returning to school Kenneth had answered, "Sure, why not?"

Conquering his fear, Stephen thought now. So far his discussions with Sara and Kenneth about what had happened had been brief—sparked by his invitations "to talk about it whenever you're ready." But Stephen knew that his son's heroism would take center stage when the conversations finally did happen because Kenneth had fought back against Joseph Niles. He had shown astounding bravery. He had saved his sister's life.

He thought about the other conversation that he would have with both of his kids at some point during the night, when he would be able to tell them with certainty that Lori had not taken her own life. The knowledge felt promising, a first step toward rebuilding the sense of family stability that he had once taken for granted.

He tried to ignore the feeling that it wouldn't be enough; tried to believe that the hours that Kenneth and Sara spent behind the closed doors of their bedrooms and the long periods of heavy silence that descended whenever the three of them were together were transitory, a mere symptom of a phase of grief and uncertainty that would fade away.

"You okay, Dad?"

Kenneth's concerned expression only made him feel worse.

"Yeah." He turned toward the refrigerator and took out two red peppers and set them on the wooden chopping block. "We'll eat as soon as your sister gets home."

"What did Mr. Caruso want?"

He froze, conscious of Kenneth behind him, staring at his back. The music had continued to drift down from his son's room throughout the short meeting with Caruso and he had hoped that

Kenneth had somehow not noticed the sight of the Frederick County Sheriff's Car in the driveway.

"He was just checking in, making sure we're okay."

Kenneth frowned, as if he wasn't sure he had heard him right.

"He's a good man," Stephen said, for lack of anything better. "A friend."

"Did he tell you what he's going to do?"

"What do you mean?"

Kenneth stared down at the counter. His lips were pressed tightly together, as if he was determined to hold his tongue. Stephen remembered him sitting at the same place the morning after the accident, asking him about the police car in the driveway. Remembered the first wave of lies he had told, preparing his family even then for the alternate version of the night's events, the fictional scenario that he hoped would protect him.

The sound of footsteps on the front porch saved him from answering. He looked toward the foyer and saw Sara in the narrow window alongside the door and started to call out to her as she entered.

A glance at her face as she headed toward the stairs stopped him.

"Hey, Daddy." Her voice was strained. She went upstairs without taking off her coat, moving quickly as if to ensure she wouldn't be stopped.

He looked at Kenneth, and knew that he had likewise gotten a glimpse of her teary eyes and the narrow streaks of ruined makeup on her cheeks.

A crying jag, he thought.

It was a reasonable assumption. His own nightmares had jolted him awake at several points in the nights after the shooting. An Ambien prescription now enabled him to sleep for several hours at a time but hadn't succeeded in shutting down the mental snapshots of the violence that came back to him without warning during the day.

Give her some time alone, he thought, and turned back to the chopping block.

Kenneth was still looking toward the foyer, his expression still troubled.

"You think she's all right?" Stephen asked.

Kenneth let several seconds slip by before he answered. "I don't know."

He glanced at the clock above the stove; realized Sara had been gone for over two hours, and remembered that she had been noticeably jittery when she left.

"Maybe I should check on her," he said.

"Okay."

Stephen looked at him, surprised that he was so quick to agree, then went to the stairs, stepping lightly, worried about intruding even before he saw that her bedroom door was shut. The floors were solid and his feet were bare. He doubted she heard him as he approached and stood a few inches away.

He heard sobbing—with short, gasping breaths. He started to knock but stayed still, vacillating between his desire to comfort her and his certainty that she wanted to be left alone. He knew how the evening would go—in half an hour she would come downstairs, quiet and composed. She and Kenneth would spend the evening quietly with him, without fighting.

Acting brave for you.

Knowing what's coming.

Sara's crying had stopped. He wasn't sure when—his mind had wandered as he stood outside her doorway and he felt lightheaded and conscious of the need to retreat as the door suddenly opened.

She stepped back in surprise, as if she had caught him, spying.

He pressed his palm against the wall. His mind blanked as he tried to think of what to say to her.

"You okay honey?"

She nodded. She had dabbed a bit of color on her cheeks and pulled her hair back from her face. She looked as he had expected, as if she had worked through what was troubling her, gotten herself together.

Or at least tried. She met his eyes for an instant and then looked down at the floor. Her posture was unnaturally erect, her hand still grasping the doorknob, making him wonder if she was going to retreat back into her room.

"I'm fine," she said, and tried to meet his eyes again, determined this time, *struggling*, Stephen thought.

He wanted to pull her into a hug, but knew that she would be stiff in his arms.

"I'll go downstairs now." She angled her body to slip past him, her smile self-consciously brightening. "Almost movie time right?"

"Yeah," Stephen said, and let her pass.

She went down to the family room without looking back. Stephen felt a heaviness in his chest as he watched her hastily moving away. The light in the hallway seemed to dim as he looked toward his bedroom at the end of it. The lightheaded feeling worsened, and made him feel as if he had no choice but to lie down.

His legs were unsteady as he stepped into the room.

This is the way it's going to be now.

He sat on the edge of the bed and looked toward Lori's dresser, and saw himself in the wavy glass of the antique mirror as he sat back against the upright pillows, still feeling the nervous, uncomfortable energy that had passed between himself and Sara in the hallway. He tried to imagine some point when they would get beyond it—a time when his kids could look at him without thinking about what he had done.

You need to tell them why you're doing this, he thought. *Why it's all right.*

But when he looked in the mirror again he was not sure that he could. He tried to envision sitting them down, explaining his reasoning. The certainty that drunk driving and manslaughter would land him in prison. His belief that the willingness to swear under oath that he was innocent was morally acceptable given the tragedy that they faced as a family.

Justifying the lies

Again and again

His stomach tightened, triggering a shot of heat that ricocheted through his rib cage, inflaming the pain of the injuries he had suffered a week before. He felt an uneasy sense of motion and had to lean forward; his hands covering his face, shutting out the overhead light that suddenly seemed painfully bright.

It wasn't enough to stop the wave of nausea that swept up the back of his throat. He stood up and stumbled into the bathroom. He hit the light switch with his forearm and found his way to the toilet and leaned over it. He gagged violently, in spasms that made the room spin around him, powerless to resist and losing all track of time until the sensation ran its course and he was able to step back, one hand gripping the side of the marble vanity and the other pressed against the wall.

He turned the light off and went back to his bedroom, and sat on the edge of the bed.

It's the lying that will make you lose them.

He knew it for certain as he gazed out the window and thought of how Sara had been barely able to look him in the eye.

The knowledge—like a curse.

He pressed his palm against the mattress on Lori's side of the bed, feeling suddenly and strangely serene, knowing what he had to do.

"I'm sorry honey," he whispered.

He felt a faint, calming pressure on his shoulders, a warmth that enveloped his chest and held him in an embrace. He reached for the pillow and wrapped his arms around it and stifled a sob.

You're going to change this.

Show them what you taught them.

A cool sweat brought beads of moisture to his forehead. The sensation was oddly pleasant and peaceful, like the breaking of a fever.

He heard a slight crack in his backbone as he sat up and went back to the list of recent calls, then dialed John Caruso back and listened to what seemed like an endless number of rings before he heard Caruso's voice mail greeting.

He waited for the prompt, then said:

"Let's meet tomorrow John. I'll tell you the truth."

He paused, conscious of the stillness in the room, the certainty and finality of his decision.

"Just name the time and the place, and I promise I'll be there. Just please make it then and not tonight. I *need* tonight, with my kids."

He put the phone down as he stood up and opened the bedroom door. The sound of the television drifted up from downstairs. He went down to find Sara and Kenneth standing side by side at the kitchen island, nibbling on the cheese and crackers and dip he had laid out before going upstairs; their attention drawn immediately to him as he stepped into the room, watching him carefully, as if they knew that something had changed.

His eyes stung as he looked at them, standing shoulder-to-shoulder, close enough for him to know they had been talking quietly, sharing confidences or secrets or fears. *Because they had each other*, Stephen thought, taking solace in the knowledge that their closeness had as much to do with the childhood that he and Lori had created for them as the natural affinity that had always been there. A closeness that had ultimately saved their lives.

He thought of all of the things he needed to tell them. *"I'm so sorry, but I made a terrible mistake and then made it worse. You know what I did. Know I've been lying. And now it has to stop."*

He thrust in the pockets of his jeans and scrunched his shoulders against his neck and felt a raw, scraping sensation at the back of his throat as they stared back at him, waiting.

He allowed himself a long moment of sadness, knowing that they were strong enough to withstand what was coming, yet wishing, once again that Lori was standing with them; that they were all together.

We're going to get through this, he thought. *As a family. No matter what.*

"Who loves you?" he asked.

They shared a look and then a smile as he reached out and wrapped them in his arms, and pulled them close.

ACKNOWLEDGMENTS

By now, if you read this story from start to finish, you know it's about people who aren't quite as good or bad as they seem to be. Fortunately in my own life I'm surrounded by people who only become more wonderful day by day. Thanks to Brian Sharp, Jiles Shipp and John Shanks, law enforcement professionals who offered expert advice on crime scene investigations and procedures. And to many fellow writers, who helped me work my way through so many different drafts. And also to my "work family" at Council for a Strong America, an organization of "unexpected messengers" who truly are building a better world.

But mostly to the two best editors I know, Jeffrey S. Stephens and Kevin Smith, and to Anthony Ziccardi and the entire team at Post Hill Press, who worked so well to bring this story to life.

ABOUT THE AUTHOR

Chris Beakey tells stories of good people caught in bad places. He writes fiction from his homes in Washington, D.C. and Lewes, Delaware, and nonfiction as a ghostwriter for an organization that promotes bipartisan policies that strengthen the nation through smart investments in youth. His first, novel, *Double Abduction*, was a finalist for the Lambda Literary Award.